SENSING TROUBLE

SUSAN C. DAFFRON

A JENNINGS & O'SHEA NOVEL

BOOK 1

Published by Magic Fur Press
An imprint of Logical Expressions, Inc.
P.O. Box 383
Ponderay, ID 83852

This is a work of fiction. All names, characters, places, and events are either the product of the author's imagination or are used fictitiously. Any resemblance to actual persons, living or dead, business organizations, events, or locales is purely coincidental.

Sensing Trouble

Copyright © 2017 by Susan C. Daffron
All rights reserved.

No part of this book may be reproduced, transmitted, or distributed in any printed or electronic form without the prior written permission of both the copyright owner and the publisher.

ISBN: 978-1-61038-048-5 (paperback)
       978-1-61038-049-2 (EPUB)

Like all of my books, *Sensing Trouble* is dedicated to
my husband James Byrd,
my best friend and biggest supporter.
Thanks for everything!

Books by Susan C. Daffron
The Alpine Grove Romantic Comedies
Chez Stinky
Fuzzy Logic
The Art of Wag
Snow Furries
Bark to the Future
Howl at the Loon
The Good, the Bad, and the Pugly
The Treasure of the Hairy Cadre
The Luck of the Paw
Daydream Retriever
The Hound of Music

The Jennings & O'Shea Mysteries
Sensing Trouble
Sensing Secrets
Sensing Truth

Chapter 1

Lost But Not Forgotten

I sat on the front steps of my mother's cottage in the small town of Alpine Grove, trying to avoid facing an inescapable conclusion: I lost Mom.

By lost, I don't mean she died or we had a rift in our relationship. I mean she was gone. Missing. MIA. Disappeared. And I had absolutely no idea where she went.

So there I was staring blankly at the dreary late-March sky in this tiny town in the middle of nowhere, trying to decide what do next. The house was vacant, as if it had never been lived in by anyone, much less my mother. I walked around and peeked in the windows, but not a trace of evidence indicated that she'd ever lived there. I expected that her rental house would be jammed full of knickknacks and old furniture from my childhood home. But the place was completely empty.

It was strange because a mere two days ago Mom called and demanded that I get on a plane to come out and visit her. She kept repeating that it was "important." So I called the travel agent, booked the next flight, and went to Alpine Grove.

I've had some health problems that forced me to give up driving a car, so the trip involved a complicated negotiation with some third-rate shuttle company that was willing to drive me from LAX all the way to the small mountain community.

Both the last-minute plane tickets and the shuttle ride cost a small fortune, but I'm not the kind of person who is going to say no to the woman who raised me from birth.

When the shuttle dropped me off at Mom's house, I thanked the driver and waved as he drove off. I quickly discovered no one was home, and it occurred to me that transportation might be a bit more of an issue than I was expecting. Not sure what else to do, I dragged the strap of my tweedy Hartmann suitcase onto my shoulder and turned to walk down the wet sidewalk toward the main street of town. At least it wasn't pouring rain. The sky was oppressively overcast, but so far no raindrops had fallen.

A Mustang convertible roared up to the curb in front of Mom's house. The cherry-red classic had the top down, so I could tell that the skinny man driving it was in a rush. Even though the weather didn't warrant them, the guy was wearing dark sunglasses, and his long, dark wavy hair looked as if it were tangled into a gigantic knot. How could anyone with hair down to his shoulders not understand the importance of ponytails when driving a convertible? More striking than his bad hair day was the fluffy white dog riding shotgun. The canine copilot in the passenger seat looked significantly more composed than the driver.

As if on command, both man and dog jumped out of the car simultaneously and ran past me up the walk and the short steps to the house. I turned to follow, readjusting my heavy bag on my shoulder. If this guy knew where Mom had gone, I wanted some answers.

The man pounded on the door and the dog turned away from him to bark at me. I tried to smile, but it was a feeble effort. "Nice doggie."

Glancing down at the dog, the man said in a low, almost raspy voice, "Zelda, that's enough." He pulled off his sunglasses and looked down at me with deep brown eyes that were so dark they were almost black, like a cup of bitter espresso. "Who are you?"

I straightened my shoulders and tried to look businesslike. Because he was so tall and thin, he seemed to tower over me, and I felt like a midget next to him on the small doorstep. "Meg…Margaret Jennings, and this is my mother's house. Who are you?"

"I'm Riley O'Shea. My father and your mother are friends…or involved…or something. Dad mentioned you, I think."

"Is your father here?" I did that thing where you pretend that the top of your head has a helium balloon strapped to it, in an effort to seem taller than my five-foot-five inches, but it wasn't working. How tall was this guy? Definitely way over six feet, that was for sure.

"I haven't seen anyone. I think my father wanted me to meet your mother, but the place is empty. I thought they were living here together." He tucked the sunglasses into his shirt pocket and scratched at the scruffy stubble on his chin. "I'm trying not to think too much about the whole parental romance thing."

I pushed my long auburn hair behind my shoulder. After an interminable day of travel, the curls from the hot rollers were a distant memory and the limp tresses flopped over my hand. I tilted my head back to look up at Riley, and squinted in the afternoon sunlight that flared through a break in the clouds.

As I studied him more closely, my first inclination was to blurt out, "What happened to you?" but that probably wouldn't be polite. Instead, I said evenly, "I've seen photographs of you, I think." Taken back at a time when he looked a whole lot better and less like a skeletal vampire. He had dark circles under his eyes and it looked like he hadn't slept in a year. Maybe he had some type of disease. I took a step backward, away from him, and my heart lurched at the unmistakable sensation of falling. I whirled my arms, attempting to retain my balance as I teetered on the edge of the step.

Riley grabbed my arm and yanked me toward him to keep me from doing a header into the hedge. He released me quickly, as if I had a raging case of cooties, but tempered it with a polite smile that didn't quite reach his dark eyes. "Oopsie."

"Thank you." I put down my suitcase, which wasn't helping my balance one bit.

He leaned back against the front door, slid his hands into the pockets of his jeans, and gazed down at the dog. "I'm not sure what to do. Dad got in touch with me and acted like it was some kind of emergency and he absolutely had to talk to me in person. So I jumped in the car and drove all the way up here."

"I did too," I said. "My mother called me and demanded I fly out because she had to tell me something important. I was thinking maybe they got married."

"Oh jeez, I hope not." Riley glanced at me. "Nothing personal against your mom or anything, but…"

"I know. It all seems really sudden. They only met a little while ago, and then last month she told me they were engaged. I couldn't believe it."

"Do you suppose they did it? I didn't think Dad would ever be willing to tie the knot again. If they did, that would make you my stepsister, wouldn't it?"

"I guess so." I turned and leaned back against the door next to Riley, joining him in canine observation. Zelda was staring up at us, wagging and panting, so it looked like she was smiling. Odds were good that the dog was the only one who was pleased about our parents' possible nuptials.

Riley pulled a hand out of his pocket and gestured toward the car. "I waited around for a while, then when the shuttle came up, I figured it had to be Dad. But it was you. Where *are* they?"

"I have no idea." My stomach growled loudly, which was more than a little embarrassing. "The only thing I've had to eat today is one of those tiny bags of peanuts on the plane."

Riley wrinkled his nose. "Yuck."

"I don't suppose you could drop me somewhere, could you? I can't stay here and I don't have a car." My stomach growled again. "I need to get something to eat."

Apparently tired of sitting around waiting for the humans to make a move or a decision, Zelda launched down the steps and jumped into the passenger seat of the Mustang, claiming her shotgun position.

Riley chuckled and put his sunglasses back on. "I can drop you at the Enchanted Moose. I have to stay there because it's the only place around that takes dogs. But you'll have to sit in the back."

"Fine." I walked down the steps toward the car, trying not to panic about Mom. Where *was* she?

Riley followed me, stowed my suitcase in the trunk, and shoved the dog aside so I could tilt the seat forward and crawl into the backseat of the car. He went around to the driver's side and stopped. "I just thought of something. I'll be right back. Zelda, *stay*."

With a baleful expression and small snort of impatience, Zelda rested her muzzle on the back of the passenger seat. We both watched as Riley ran toward the house and around the side to the backyard. I reached over to run my hand across the soft white fur on the dog's head. "Don't ask me. I have no idea what he's doing either."

Zelda thumped her feathery tail a few times and we both continued to stare at the little cottage, curious as to what Riley might be up to.

~

A few minutes later, Riley reappeared from the backyard. He walked around the car to the driver's side, got in, and handed a piece of paper to me.

The note used some type of strange language or letters, and I held it up. "What is this? Hieroglyphics?"

"No, it's a code my father invented when I was little. He put notes into my lunch box when I was a kid. I didn't want other kids to know what they said, so he made up a language."

"Can you read it?"

"It says 'talk to Dean Wolfe.'" He took the paper back from me, crumpled it, and threw on the floor of the passenger side.

"That's it? Who is Dean Wolfe?"

"I have no idea." He started the car, which seemed even noisier now that I was inside.

I rummaged around in my bag for an elastic to pull back my hair. Once my tresses were safely confined, I leaned forward and yelled at Riley, "Is something wrong with the car?"

"I customized it a little." Riley flipped a switch under the dash, and the engine noise went from angry mountain lion to grumpy house cat.

We exited the residential neighborhood toward the main street of town, then out to the highway. According to the sign, the Enchanted Moose was a convention center, motel, and RV park. From the looks of it, the place had been around since dinosaurs roamed the earth. One end of the parking lot had a chain-link fence enclosure filled with construction equipment, but it appeared that the restoration work had been suspended for the winter. The half-done remodeling project hadn't done much to improve the tired, worn look of the facility.

Riley parked in front of a sign that said "Office" and turned to look back at me. "Are you planning to stay here too?"

"I'm not sure. Right now I want something to eat. Are there any other motels nearby?"

"There's the H12 in town, but from the outside it doesn't appear to be any nicer than this place."

"Great." I looked around the parking lot, and wistfully recalled the high-end hotels I'd stayed at back in DC.

He pulled the keys out of the ignition. "I'm going to go check in. Zelda, stay."

I looked at Zelda, who seemed content to remain in the Mustang. She was a remarkably obedient dog and obviously an experienced traveler. The dog I had when I was growing up was named Buster. We didn't take him on vacations because his carsickness was legendary. Spending approximately thirty seconds in a vehicle inevitably caused him to lose the contents of his stomach in projectile form. Trips to the veterinarian were inevitably messy, and my mother used to sigh audibly when we received vaccination reminder cards from the vet.

The Enchanted Moose's restaurant was on the other side of the parking lot and I leaned forward to reach the seat lever, so I could get out of the car. Zelda stood up, glared at me, and made an indignant snorting noise. I'd never met a dog that snorted before. What did it mean? Was a snort aggressive like a growl? Maybe it would be a good idea to wait for Riley to come back. He'd been nice enough to drive me, so I should at least say good-bye.

Riley returned and raised his eyebrows at me in query. "Something wrong?"

"What does it mean when a dog snorts at you? Is it threatening?"

"If you mean Zelda, she was expressing her opinion. What did you do?"

"Nothing! I was going to get out, but she snorted at me."

Zelda wagged her tail and Riley patted her head. "I'll drop you at the restaurant. I need to go to our room and unload everything. We've had a long day and Zelda wants her dinner."

My heavy suitcase was still in the trunk, and I'd have to drag it with me into the restaurant. What a pain. "Wait. Could you put my suitcase in your room for the time being?

I'm hungry, and If I don't eat, I get a headache." I didn't want to go into detail about my recent bizarre medical maladies with this guy, but the bottom line was that I needed food *right now*.

"I suppose." He started the car again and drove around the building to a room in the back that was across from a few rustic wooden picnic tables. They sat in a muddy area that might have been filled with grass before the construction work began.

We got out of the car and Riley opened the door to room 142. Zelda rushed inside and began sniffing the floor of her new digs while Riley dragged in luggage. I pulled my Hartmann out of the trunk. It wasn't a huge space, but the trunk was crammed full of stuff. Riley and Zelda sure weren't traveling light.

As I walked toward the room and passed Riley, I gestured toward the car. "That's a lot of camping gear. Are you on a vacation or road trip or something?"

"I, yeah, well, I decided to take a little time off from work."

I put the suitcase down on the bed and waited for Riley to return with another load of stuff. Coincidentally, I also was taking a break from my job. My boss and I had agreed to call it medical leave, but I wasn't sure if I'd ever be able to go back to work. So far, 1997 had been a spectacularly bad year for me, and it was only March. On the other hand, it had been great for DC-area health-care providers, which were making a mint off all my medical tests.

Riley walked into the room and threw more stuff on the bed. "That's the last of it. I didn't know what to tell the people at the front desk about how long we're staying. I thought we'd crash with Dad, but now I'm not sure what we're going to do."

"Are you hungry? Maybe you could tell me more about your father and this Dean Wolfe person over dinner."

"There's not much to tell. Let me feed Zelda and then I can watch you eat, I guess."

"Aren't you hungry? I'm starving."

He shook his head. "I don't eat much."

That was obvious. I had an unexpected flash of a memory of my grandmother's voice saying, "We need to fatten you up!" I'd never thought of myself as maternal, but I understood the sentiment. Riley was so thin that his legs and arms seemed elongated, like spindly spider legs. Although he was wearing a long-sleeved shirt, it was baggy and I could see his knobby wrist bones poking out from under the cuffs.

I sat on the end of the bed while he fed Zelda, who clearly had no appetite problems at all. The dog wolfed down her food, strolled over to a corner, belched loudly, and curled up for a nap.

Riley gestured toward the door. "She's happy, so we can go."

We walked across the parking lot to a small restaurant that didn't appear any newer than the rest of the Enchanted Moose. The decor reminded me of a fifties diner like you'd see in a movie, complete with red vinyl booths and shiny chrome napkin holders on the tables. Riley sat across from me with a pained expression on his face.

"Is something wrong?"

"It's nothing." He pulled a menu out from behind the napkins, opened it, and put it back. Then he grabbed it again. "I feel better than I thought I might. Maybe I'll see what they have."

Something was off about Riley and I hoped again that whatever was wrong wasn't contagious. He had the exhausted, drawn look of someone dealing with a serious disease like cancer or AIDS. Maybe he was on medication or getting treatments that caused nausea or digestive trouble.

I had my own problems, but they didn't have anything to do with food, and when I scanned the menu all the options looked fantastic. I narrowed my options down from everything, settling on the biggest sandwich they had.

After we ordered, I didn't know what to say to Riley. My thoughts turned to Mom again, so I pulled a red crayon out of the mug on the table and doodled on the paper placemat to distract myself.

Riley leaned forward and said, "Tell me again. What exactly did your mom say to you before you came out here?"

"Nothing more than what I already told you. She kept telling me she had to talk to me and that it was important."

"Right." He rested his elbow on the table and placed his chin on his palm, looking thoughtful. His thick black eyelashes were so long they practically cast shadows on his gaunt cheeks. I would kill for those eyelashes. It wasn't fair. Why did men always end up with fantastic lashes? Even with thirty pounds of mascara on them, my eyelashes couldn't compare.

We sat in silence for a few moments, and finally I said, "You honestly don't know who this Dean guy is? I'm trying not to worry, but I'm terrified that something might have happened to my mother. It's not like her to run off without saying anything. Is your father like that? Spontaneous, impulsive?"

"Dad was an engineer for thirty years. The quintessential geek, complete with pocket protector. Spontaneous is not a word anyone would ever use to describe him."

I drew a heart with little curlicues on the placemat. "I'm hoping they're just on some last-minute romantic getaway. But it doesn't feel like that."

"No, it doesn't. It feels like something bad."

The knot in my stomach tightened and it wasn't from hunger. I was afraid Riley was right.

~

The waitress delivered my gigantic Dagwood-esque sandwich and I dug in. I was so focused on eating that it was a few moments before I took a breath and looked up at Riley again. He was picking at a bowl of cottage cheese with his fork, like a little kid forced to eat soggy overcooked brussels sprouts.

I put down my sandwich and pointed an accusing finger at the bowl. "Is there something wrong with it?"

"It's fine." He took a sip of his ginger ale and grimaced.

"Are you sure?"

"Yeah." He took a saltine off the plate and nibbled at a corner.

"I notice you seem to have a fondness for bland, pale food." Who orders cottage cheese, rice, and crackers? Was he on some type of strange fad diet?

"I'm not fond of any food. But if you don't eat, getting sick and dying are unfortunate side effects."

"You don't like food? Why not?" I was starting to feel a little self-conscious about the massive pig-out I had going on my side of the booth. But not so much that I wasn't going to scarf down the rest of my French fries.

"It's kind of weird."

I flapped a greasy fry to direct his attention back to the plate. "More weird than eating that?"

He set down his fork and leaned back, away from the table. "I don't like talking about this, but basically everything smells."

"You mean it smells bad?"

"Not exactly. More like it smells too much. Those fries, for example, are over-the-top revolting. The oil they were cooked in was starting to go rancid and the fries themselves had a massive case of freezer burn. I'm guessing they were past their expiration date."

I looked down at my plate. "That's appetizing. Thanks for sharing. They taste great to me."

"You probably don't want me to go into detail about what's in that sandwich."

"I'm thinking I could do without that information."

"You don't want to know. I wish I didn't know. This rice was made with water that doesn't have chlorine or fluoride in it, which is a nice change. Maybe it was well water." He took another sip of ginger ale. "I feel better since I got here. I haven't been out to any type of restaurant in months. It's a miracle I can sit here and watch you eat rancid fries without having to leave the room."

"I feel special. Maybe it's all the fresh air out here in the sticks."

"I don't know what it is and I don't care. I need to look for my father."

"I've been thinking about that too. I'll get a room here and then start making some calls. Maybe one of my mom's friends knows where she went."

We both turned at the sound of a man loudly saying, "Yo, Dean-o!" as he clapped his hand against the back of another guy.

"Dean-o? Like Dean Wolfe, maybe?" I said.

Riley frowned. "Maybe. Turn around, dude, so I can see you."

The two men parted. One left the restaurant, but Mr. Dean-o Dude walked toward the counter. Like almost every other man in the place, he was wearing a flannel shirt, but his was snug in all the right places, the red fabric stretching across his muscular arms and chest. He had thick, slightly curly light brown hair and a swoonworthy smile. Suffice it to say, Dean-o was a mighty fine-looking fellow. With an effort, I returned my focus to the problem at hand and leaned forward toward Riley. "I thought you didn't know who this Dean person was."

"I didn't think so, but that guy looks familiar. I'll be right back." Riley slid out of the booth and walked over to the man. He said something and gestured toward me. Then the two turned and walked back toward our booth.

Dean sat across from me and introduced himself. Trying not to drool over his gorgeous hazel eyes, I shook his hand. "I'm Meg. Do you know anything about where our parents have gone?"

"I'm glad I ran into you two," Dean said. "I know your parents. Ellen and Tim are great people and we ended up spending quite a bit of time together. I need to tell you a few things."

As he slid into the booth next to me, Riley said, "We're listening."

"Have either of you been having any odd experiences lately? Feeling strange?" Dean asked.

I glanced at Riley and he met my gaze. I knew about his odd food issues, but he didn't know about my little problem. I said, "Maybe. I'm not sure what you mean."

Dean said, "Strange sensations. Things that are hard to explain."

"I guess so." Riley said.

"Yes," I said.

"Interesting. Tim thought that might be the case." Dean glanced up at the counter. "Oops, I need to go grab my pie and coffee. Sheila didn't realize I'm over here. Be right back."

Dean got up and stood at the counter, trying to flag down Sheila so he could pay.

Riley turned to me. "You have strange sensations? What do you mean? You can obviously eat with no problem."

"It's different."

"Different how?"

I glanced over at the counter, but Dean wasn't there. "Where'd he go?"

"Maybe the men's room? His coffee and pie are still sitting there."

"No one would ever leave pie. Except maybe you."

Riley picked up the red crayon and tilted the tip toward me. "Did you know that they put lard in pie crust? Do you know how incredibly disgusting lard is?"

"New topic: do you suppose Dean knows whether or not our parents are married? Because I want an answer."

"Are you worried that you might technically be related to me?"

"I didn't say that. Where did he go? I'm tired of people disappearing. What is it with this town?" I waved a soggy French fry toward the restrooms. "It's been long enough. You need to go find him and drag him back out here. We've got all these questions and no answers."

"All right." Riley slid out of the booth and strolled toward the back of the restaurant.

I gobbled down the rest of my sandwich. At least I was starting to feel human again. I'd become anxious about eating because over the last few months, when I skipped a meal, I paid for it.

Although I'd hoped to forget about my recent medical issues on this trip to see Mom, Riley wasn't the only one who was having a few new strange experiences. I felt like I was walking on eggshells half the time or simply losing my mind.

I popped another French fry into my mouth. What was even more strange was the fact that Dean already seemed to know that something was wrong with me, even though I'd never told Mom.

Riley hustled back to the table and slid into the booth across from me. "Dean isn't in the men's room. Did you see him out here?"

"I've just been sitting here eating, along with everyone else. No one has moved that I saw."

"He's gone."

I looked into Riley's dark eyes. "Are you telling me we lost another person?"

"I'm afraid so."

~

A crash came from outside the restaurant and I got up so I could see out the window. Riley stood next to me. Something was going on in the parking lot.

A dark blue van with two occupants was parked in front of the restaurant. The two men were in suits and wearing dark glasses. Charcoal-gray suits were an uncommon sight in this area where jeans and flannel shirts were the norm.

My jaw dropped when I saw another man dragging Dean toward the van. Riley and I slid out of the booth and ran toward the exit. As we approached the door, one of the men slid open the van door, forcibly shoved Dean into the van, and got in after him. The door slammed shut and the van pulled out of the parking space, careened out of the parking lot, and turned onto the highway.

Riley and I stood in the space where the van had been, staring in stunned silence trying to assimilate what had happened.

The door of the restaurant slammed as few other people came out to see what the commotion was about. From behind us, an angry voice barked, "Hey, you! I need you to get back inside and pay for all that food you ate."

I turned to look at our waitress. "I think that man was kidnapped. Didn't you see?"

"I didn't see anything. If there's a problem, call the sheriff. In the meantime, we need to be paid or I'll be calling the sheriff myself."

Riley said, "Calm down. We're not going to stiff you." He took my arm and moved me toward the entrance.

"But we need to follow them!" I said.

"My car is over by the room, and they're already gone. Let's just pay, get Zelda, and go. We know they're heading south and if we speed, we might be able to catch up to them."

I stopped at the counter and waited for the waitress to total our bill. I turned to Riley, "I don't suppose you noticed the license plate number, did you?"

"No."

"Me neither."

Riley pulled out his wallet, paid the cashier, and we left the restaurant as quickly as possible.

"Thanks for dinner," I said as we crossed the parking lot.

"You can repay me by helping me find my father." He unlocked the door of the room and Zelda rushed toward us, wagging happily. "C'mon Zee, let's go."

The dog ran out the door and gracefully hopped into the front seat of the Mustang.

Riley grinned and the sudden flash of his straight white teeth was a startling change from his typical somber expression. "Looks like you're riding in the back again."

I tried not to roll my eyes. Zelda had the whole "calling shotgun" thing figured out better than your average ten-year-old.

The sun was starting to set and the sky had mostly cleared, except for one huge looming dark cloud. We got in the car and roared out of the parking lot. Apparently Riley had flipped the switch on the dash that made the Mustang louder again. It also seemed to make the car go faster. A *lot* faster. Riley hadn't been kidding about speeding. With the wind whipping through the back of the car, I felt like I was in the middle of a tornado going a zillion miles an hour.

When we reached Alpine Grove, Riley slowed down, but once we were past the residential areas and cutesy shops, he floored it and we were jetting down the highway again. I was rapidly getting cold, and I wrapped my arms around my torso, trying to stop the shivering. The telephone poles, electric lines, and radio towers zipped by in a blur of wood and metal.

Zelda turned around in the front seat, looked back at me and made an *rrr*-ing noise. She was wearing a doggie seat belt that was attached to the car's shoulder harness, but I had the feeling that if she could have jumped into the back with me, she would have.

A massive bolt of lightning cracked across the sky, followed by a boom of thunder. Zelda barked at me as Riley swerved and pulled the car over to the shoulder. He jumped out and ran to the back, unsnapping the convertible cover and throwing it into the trunk. A few fat raindrops landed on my face before he got back in and flipped a switch on the dash. The convertible top whirred and rose above my head. After he clipped the latches above the windshield, he started the car and pulled back onto the highway.

Lightning flashed around us and the crashes of thunder were even more deafening than the car. Zelda made another odd low grumbly growly sound and then what I'd been dreading finally happened. Wild Technicolor fireworks flashed in front of me and I blinked a few times, trying to make it stop.

I glanced at Riley, who had a strange blue glow around him. Were we driving past a neon sign or was it me? I hunched over and put my palms over my eyes, mumbling "Oh no, not again." The lights and fireworks became more intense and

I squeezed my eyes shut, trying not to give in to it and lose consciousness.

I thought I heard a scream and then there was nothing, except blackness.

When I opened my eyes, Zelda was in the backseat with me and Riley was leaning around the front seats, resting his palm on my cheek, staring intently at me with a terrified expression.

Riley jerked his hand away and let out a long sigh. "Thank God. Are you all right?"

"I'm fine." I sat up straight again and pushed the dog's muzzle away from me. "It's okay, Zelda."

"I know I don't know you very well, but most people don't scream like that when they're fine," Riley said.

"I suppose not."

"What happened?"

I let out a deep breath. Although I didn't want to get into it, Riley deserved an explanation. "You might have noticed I was concerned about getting something to eat earlier."

"I noticed."

"In the last few months, I've had a little problem."

"It doesn't seem particularly little."

"Different things set it off. I'm not sure what causes it, but sometimes if I don't eat for hours, like today, I can end up with a migraine. Well, that's what the doctors call it anyway. It's like a migraine, but I don't get a debilitating severe headache. It starts with colors, then sometimes there are lights in front of my eyes, sometimes with hallucinations or unconsciousness thrown in. Imagine a freaky light-infused nightmare without the sleep part and that's more or less what happens."

"So it's like a really bad acid trip."

"I wouldn't know, but you were blue."

"Blue?"

"In my hallucination, I mean. Never mind. Anyway, this is why I can't drive anymore."

"You scared the crap out of me." Riley scrubbed his face with his palms. "I think you even freaked out my dog, and it's hard to rattle Zelda."

"I'm sorry. Believe me, I wish there was something I could do about this. I've had every test imaginable and the doctors have no idea what's going on. I was sure I had a brain tumor and was dying, but as far as anyone can tell, I'm perfectly healthy."

"Healthy except for the hallucinations and screaming, you mean."

"Well, yes, except for that. The other possibility is that I'm going insane. But wouldn't I know that? I don't feel crazy."

"Do crazy people know they're crazy?"

"I don't know. Maybe not."

Riley sat up straight in the seat again and ran his fingers through his long hair, yanking at a few knots. "It's pouring and I can barely see the road. Dean is gone, I'm exhausted, and my nerves are shot. Nothing's going to happen tonight. Let's go back to the motel."

Zelda returned to her post in the front seat and Riley turned the car around. He wasn't the only one who was tired. What a bizarre day. I wanted to curl up and sleep for a week.

Now that Riley knew I might be losing my mind, he also might be regretting that he'd ever met me.

Chapter 2

Half-Baked

After we returned to the Enchanted Moose, Riley called the sheriff's office and we spent what seemed like an excruciatingly long time explaining to a deputy what had happened to Dean Wolfe. I also volunteered that our parents were missing, but we weren't sure how long they'd been gone.

Although the young man dutifully scrawled notes on a little notepad, it didn't seem like he was taking our report terribly seriously. Maybe he was simply inexperienced. With his close-cropped hair and baby face, he looked about twelve years old. I'm thirty-two, but I felt like I was this guy's grandma. The fact that he kept calling me ma'am didn't help.

Once Baby Face finally left the room, I flopped down on one of the beds. Zelda leaped up and laid down alongside me, making a few contented snorfly noises. I ran my hand across the long silky fur on her back and looked up at Riley. "I think your dog likes me."

"You should feel special. Zelda is the greatest dog in the entire world and she's rather selective."

Riley was unpacking some of suitcases he'd brought in earlier. I needed to go over to the office and get my own room, but Zelda seemed so happy being petted that I didn't want to move. She was such a sweet dog, and I figured Riley wouldn't mind if I hung out for a few more minutes petting her. I closed my eyes, trying to focus on Zelda's soft fur and not think about my mother. What if something had happened to Mom? What would I do? A tear slid from my eye. I couldn't go down that line of thinking. I just couldn't.

I opened my eyes and jerked upright. Where was I? I looked around the cluttered room and realized that I hadn't moved. Someone, presumably Riley, had placed a blanket over me. Sunlight was peeking around the curtains and Zelda had relocated to the foot of Riley's bed. Curled up into a tight ball, she thumped her tail a few times to acknowledge that I was awake. Riley rolled over, yanked the covers over his head, and mumbled something about Zelda.

I was self-conscious about being in a room with a guy I barely knew. This was like a one-night stand without the good part. I was still wearing my shoes, my clothes were wrinkled, and I badly needed to brush my teeth. Sleeping in yesterday's clothes was so *not* sexy. Yuck.

I crawled out from under my blanket and looked around the room for my suitcase. While I was asleep, Riley had taken his unpacking to a messy extreme and paraphernalia was strewn everywhere. What a slob.

I grabbed my toiletry bag and clean clothes from my suitcase and retreated to the bathroom. The warm water of the shower was welcome after so many hours in airports and automobiles. Washing off the day of travel felt fantastic and by the time I'd scrubbed myself clean, I was ready to face the reality of searching for my mother again.

Putting on my favorite kelly-green blouse buoyed my confidence level. The color looked great with my current shade of auburn hair and something about the soft weave of the stretchy fabric gave me the fortitude to take on the world.

Maybe Dean was a part of what was going on and maybe he wasn't. The main thing I cared about was finding Mom.

Steam rushed out as I opened the bathroom door. Riley was sitting on the end of his bed petting Zelda's head. He was wearing a t-shirt and shorts, which exposed the bony joints on his long limbs. Even his fingers were long and thin. I was getting a better understanding of the term "painfully skinny." It hurt to look at him.

I yanked a comb through my wet hair. "Thanks for letting me stay here. I guess I was tired."

"It didn't make sense to wake you up. Do you want coffee?"

"I can make it, if you want to take a shower." I pointed my comb toward the fog-filled little room. How awkward was this? "Or um, you know, use the facilities or something."

He rubbed the scruffy stubble on his chin and moved to gather some clothes. "Might be nice."

While Riley showered, I made coffee with Zelda closely supervising my activities. I also fumed about the disappearing people in my life, so by the time Riley emerged from the bathroom, I was downright agitated. I handed him a mug of coffee. "Have you thought about what you're going to do about finding your father?"

"To find him, it might be necessary to track down Dean first."

"I don't care about Dean. I care about Mom." I slammed the mug down on the dresser. "And it's driving me crazy that I can't drive. I'm so frustrated, I want to scream."

"Please, no more screaming. Dean made it sound like our parents are together and he knows where they are."

"I suppose. But how are we supposed to find Dean?"

"First, we can ask the people at the restaurant if anyone knows him. If he lives in Alpine Grove, someone there might be his best friend for all we know. It's a small town."

I began pacing in front of the desk, stepping over Zelda's prone form. "But what if he doesn't live in Alpine Grove? People at motels are usually traveling."

"I have another idea, but it might sound sort of strange." Riley took a sip of coffee. "It sounds strange to me and it's my idea."

"Okay, spill it." That didn't seem promising, but I paused in my pacing.

"Dean smelled like a bakery."

"That's your idea? He was eating pie. What do you expect?"

"But it wasn't only pie. It was bread and scones, muffins, and a bunch of other baked goods. I didn't see a bakery in Alpine Grove, but maybe there's one nearby."

"Why would kidnappers take a guy who smells like a bakery?"

"That's not the point. Maybe the people at the bakery know who Dean is. What if he works there?"

"You've got to be kidding. This is pathetic." I flopped my arms against my sides in exasperation. "You want to hunt for Dean at local bakeries?"

"Sorry. It's all I've got." Riley moved his shoulders halfheartedly. "What are you going to do?"

"I can't think of anything beyond calling Mom's friends. Most of them live in Washington, D.C., which is where I was yesterday morning. What are the odds that they'd know anything about any of this? My mom has been with your father for the last few months."

"True."

"That reminds me. How did you find the note at Mom's house? How did you know where it was?"

"I was a latchkey kid. Dad always put notes under a flowerpot in our back yard. I figured there had to be a flowerpot somewhere. And there was."

I sat down on the end of the bed. "That's kind of brilliant. I guess you and your dad are pretty close?"

"We were. It was just us after my brother left home. He's a lot older than I am."

"Does your brother also have an overdeveloped sense of smell?"

"Not as far as I know and I hope not. I didn't have this problem until about six months ago." Riley set down his mug and leaned forward, resting his elbows on his knees. "And to tell you the truth, it's pretty much ruined my life."

The similarity in our experiences was going beyond coincidence. "I started having my problem about six months ago too. I had to take medical leave from my job."

"I imagine screaming might have stressed out your colleagues as much as it did me. If it makes you feel any better, I had to quit working too." His eyes widened. "Hey, you know what? Last night was the first time I've gotten a good night's sleep in...well, since this problem started. All the awful smells usually keep me awake."

I looked down at Zelda. "Dogs have an amazing sense of smell and they don't have insomnia. How come they can sleep and you can't?"

"I've spent a lot of time lying awake thinking about that very question. Zelda isn't sharing her secrets, but my hypothesis is that dogs don't consider smells good or bad like people do. Everything is just *interesting*. I wish I could smell without judgment, but I can't."

"I guess being human has some down sides."

"I don't think people are built to deal with so much olfactory information."

"Maybe that's what happens to me too. My brain overloads with the fireworks and I scream."

"I may be bizarre, but at least I'm quiet about it."

I laughed. "Okay, yeah, I'll give you that."

~

Riley began picking up the detritus strewn all over the room, and I got out my little address book, so I could call the friends of my mother that I knew. It wasn't a long list and I felt a little silly asking if they knew where she was. Each person said that at last report, Mom was "out West somewhere" with some man she met. That was pretty much all she'd told me too.

I set down the telephone receiver in disgust. Calling people had been as big a waste of time as I expected it would be.

Riley threw a shirt in a suitcase. "Are you done? I need to make a call."

I gestured at the phone. "All yours."

I tucked my address book back in my suitcase. What should I do next? I needed to find Mom, but I also needed transportation. I had no plan and sitting around doing nothing would drive me nuts. I sat down on the bed and stared at Riley, who sat on the other bed with the phone pressed to his ear.

Zelda sat in front of Riley, who stroked her head and said, "I know. Just a few minutes. I'll feed you soon. Be patient, I…Hi, it's me. I'm in Alpine Grove."

Riley paused and even from where I was sitting across from him I could hear the muffled tones of irate female through the handset. Hmm. I stood up and pretended to rearrange the stuff in my suitcase in an effort to hide how curious I was about who he was talking to. Being confined in a tiny motel room didn't lend itself well to keeping secrets.

Riley said, "I know, but…"

After a few more aborted attempts to speak, Riley said, "Listen, I have to go. Yeah, you too."

He hung up the phone, got out the dog food, and fed Zelda without comment. I desperately wanted to ask who the woman was who had been yelling at him from the other end of the line. Was I really that nosy? And why should I care anyway? I barely knew Riley. Finally, I couldn't stand it anymore and nosiness won out. I cleared my throat, "So, um, who were you talking to?"

"My girlfriend. Or maybe ex-girlfriend. It's complicated."

I didn't know how to respond to that comment, so I decided to drop the subject. Although Riley had been pleasant enough, he was way too odd for my taste. He also knew I was nuts, which was embarrassing. I was looking forward to being on my own again. I spent a few moments trying to envision the woman who would be attracted to Riley and couldn't come up with an image in my mind.

I sat down on the bed, then stood up again and started pacing. "As you could tell, my calls were a bust."

"You said you didn't think it would do any good."

"I know. I'm so unbelievably frustrated by this whole thing. We have nothing to go on. *Nothing*! If this were a movie of the week, we'd have Angela Lansbury stopping by to help. I need to do something. I'm going crazy just sitting here."

"I'm sure there are some little old ladies you can talk to in Alpine Grove if you want."

"That's not funny." I stomped across the room followed by Zelda, who snorted a few times. I turned to Riley, "What is wrong with your dog?"

"I told you, she's talking to you. Once she's comfortable with people, Zelda likes to join in the conversation."

"Does she chat with your girlfriend too?"

"Erin and Zelda don't see eye-to-eye on certain matters. I told you, Zelda is discriminating in her affection."

"But she's so sweet to me." I bent to stroke the soft fur on the dog's ears. "I've always worked such long and erratic hours, I never felt like I could have a dog."

Riley rested his elbows on his knees and clasped his hands in front of him. "I miss having a job. It's not about the money either. I felt useful."

"I was a reporter. Even though there were things I didn't like about it sometimes, I was out there always in the middle of things asking questions, getting answers. I loved ferreting out the truth and every day was different." I gestured toward the room. "This...whatever it is...affliction I have has changed so many things. It's like my world is shrinking. Not being able to drive isn't so bad in the city, where everything is close together and you can walk or take a cab. But in a place like this, I feel trapped."

"You mean trapped in a tiny motel room with some guy who may or may not be your stepbrother?"

I giggled. "Yeah, pretty much. And the person I would most like to talk to about this is missing."

Riley stood up. "I don't suppose your Mom or anyone in your family had migraines or visions, did they?"

"If they did, no one ever told me."

He grabbed the room key from the desk. "I'm hungry, and you need to know that lately that *never* happens. Let's go have breakfast and talk about this some more."

I got my bag and we walked across the parking lot to the restaurant. We settled into the same booth we'd sat in the night before and I pulled out a menu.

After studying my options, I folded it and looked across the table at Riley. "Doesn't this seem strange to you?"

"What?"

"Everything. We both have problems that turned our lives upside down at around the same time and our parents both are missing. Doesn't that strike you as odd?"

"It does. There's something else I should tell you that's probably going to sound creepy, but I promise I'm not a stalker."

"Uh-oh."

"You smell good."

"Thank you. I'm fond of the new shampoo I bought for this trip."

He shook his head. "No, I mean you smell *really* good. I think it's why I managed to sleep and feel like eating again."

"I'm guessing this is the part where it becomes creepy."

"A little. I feel better being away from LA, but like I said, I think I slept better because you were there, which is like a miracle for me. Do you know how awful it is to not sleep? It messes you up."

"I suppose it does." He did look somewhat better this morning. The dark circles under his eyes seemed a little less pronounced.

"Maybe the fact that we met is fate or kismet intervening."

I picked at a laminated corner of the menu that was starting to tear. "That's ridiculous. I don't believe in that type of thing."

"Maybe not, but you never know. I think it would be a good idea for us to stay together for a little while and see what happens. It's a little self-serving because it helps me, but at this point, I'm desperate. You aren't the only one who has spent a lot of time at the doctor's office."

"I thought you might be sick. Do you have cancer?"

"There's nothing wrong with me except that because of my whacked-out sense of smell, I can't eat or sleep."

"That's it?"

"Believe me, it's enough. The last doctor was starting to talk about hospitalization and feeding tubes. There's no way I'm going there. I know you can't drive and you don't need to get back to work. I have a car and a whole lot of free time, so I think it would make sense if we look for our parents together."

"I'm used to operating alone and we barely know each other. Is this some type of come-on? What about your girlfriend?"

Riley curled his long fingers around his napkin and crumpled it. "Definitely not. As for Erin, if I start eating and sleeping like a normal human being, maybe she'll be willing to talk to me again."

"I suppose I do need a ride." I mustered a halfhearted smile. "You're absolutely sure you're not a stalker, right?"

"Would your mom marry or even associate with a man with a son who is a stalker?"

"I hope not. There are worse things than letting you drive me around, I suppose. And it's not like I have any other ideas."

"So after breakfast, do you want to hit the road?"

"All right. But I'm calling shotgun this time."

Riley flattened out the crumpled napkin in front of him. "I'm afraid you'll have to work that out with Zelda."

~

After watching Riley eat another eclectic assortment of pale food at breakfast, I cornered the waitress and asked her if she knew someone named Dean Wolfe. The gruff woman wasn't particularly enthusiastic about sharing, but I've been a reporter for way too long to let that stop me. I can be extremely persistent. Some people have called me annoying and obnoxious, but I prefer to think of it as being tenacious.

Unable to dodge my unrelenting questions, the waitress finally revealed that Dean delivered baked goods all over the region from a bakery based in a town south of Alpine Grove.

After I'd finished extracting this information, Riley and I walked across the parking lot back to the room. He said, "You're pretty good at interrogating people."

"That was nothing." I stopped and waited for him to open the door. "I'm going to call that bakery in Gleasonville and see what I can find out. I feel like we finally have something to go on. It may not be much, but it's something."

"I'll pack up the car."

I pulled the thin Cedar County phone book out of the drawer in the nightstand, grabbed the phone, and called the bakery while Riley carted his mountains of luggage out to the Mustang. Zelda ran back and forth with him, obviously enjoying all the activity after a slow morning of napping.

Talking to people and finding out what they knew was satisfying after so much travel and sitting around. I finally felt like I was *doing* something again. I dug a pen and envelope out of my purse as if I were going to take notes for an article. I missed being a reporter and burrowing deep into the details of a story so I could see it from every angle.

I'd had dreams of working at the *Washington Post*, but after graduating from journalism school, my shiny new master's degree only helped me get a job writing for a small regional rag that mostly covered happenings in the Maryland suburbs where I lived. I'd done a few investigative pieces, but it wasn't like Woodward and Bernstein were knocking on my door demanding to see my resume. I spent a lot of time covering tedious city council meetings and standing around at press conferences watching the mayor blather on about thrilling topics like road maintenance.

At this point, even covering obscure high school sporting events like Region 37 basket weaving would cheer me up. Life as a journalist was never dull, which had been great, but it wasn't like my medical leave was unwarranted. Screaming at a city council meeting would cause a serious PR incident, and the newspaper wasn't willing to risk it. To be fair, I couldn't blame them. After my humiliating meltdown at the office, they'd been justified in their concern.

I kept thinking I should be able to get control over my problem, but I didn't know what caused it. Sometimes it was stress or lack of food , but other times the episodes were random. If I were somehow able to control it enough so that it was just a few flashes of light every once in a while without the acting out, loss of consciousness, or screaming, I might be able to go back to work. That glimmer of hope kept me going. In the meantime, traveling with Riley might not be so bad if he could help me find Mom. And he did have a cool dog.

I found the listing for the bakery and dialed. A man with an extremely deep voice answered and I explained that I was looking for Dean Wolfe. Like the waitress, he wasn't receptive to my request. I said, "I saw Dean in Alpine Grove and I need to speak to him."

"Well, so do I, lady. He didn't show up for work, and I got pies that need to be delivered."

"Does he have friends or family there that I might be able to talk to? It's extremely important that I find him."

"I asked around. No one's seen him."

"Could I speak to them?"

"They're working. Like Dean should be. If you find him, tell him that if he doesn't show up or call me with a mighty good explanation real soon, he'd better start looking for a new job."

"When do your employees take their lunch break?"

"It depends."

"I assume they get a lunch break, since it's required by law. I'd like to stop by and talk to them then."

"Yeah, whatever. Unless you want to buy a pie or something, I gotta go."

"Thank you for your help." I hung up the phone and walked to the doorway to meet Riley.

He stopped and leaned against the door jamb. "What? Something wrong?"

"We need to go to that bakery in Gleasonville."

"Did you find Dean?" Riley navigated around me and grabbed a suitcase off the bed.

"No, but we need to get there when the employees take lunch. I want to talk to them."

"That was the last load of stuff. You can negotiate with Zelda about where you're sitting while I go check out of this place."

Riley turned to lock the door and I walked over to the Mustang. The weather was nice and Riley had put the top down again. Zelda had hopped in and was proudly sitting in the front seat. I leaned against the car and stroked the fur on Zelda's head. "Okay, here's the thing. I want to sit in front this time."

Zelda wagged her tail and her doggie smile was so smug that I was sure she understood exactly what I was saying, but was ignoring the request. I shook my finger at her like a school marm. "Listen, you need to get into the back. I want to ride in the passenger seat, and I'm a human, so I outrank you."

Zelda sat motionless except for her tail, which continued to wag. I gave up on the strict taskmaster idea and started petting her again. My doggie diplomacy skills weren't up to the challenge, and I clearly wasn't going to get anywhere with her.

Riley walked toward us, carrying a piece of paper, which was undoubtedly the invoice for the motel room. It occurred to me that the guy didn't have a job, and I'd crashed in his space without even asking. I should at least offer to pay for the room.

Riley patted Zelda's head as he walked by. "I see your negotiations failed."

"I think I need luscious dog treats or something. She isn't buying my argument."

He walked around the car, opened the driver's side door, and waved toward the rear of the car. "Zelda, get in back."

The dog hopped between the seats and Riley leaned around to fasten her seat belt. He turned back to me. "Ready?"

I got into the Mustang and discovered it was a lot more comfortable to sit in the front. No wonder Zelda didn't want to give it up. "You mentioned that you lost your job. I can pay for the room, since we ended up sharing."

"Don't worry about it. I didn't say I lost my job. I said I had to quit working, which isn't the same thing."

"So you do have a job?"

"Nope. I sold my company and retired."

"You're *retired*? How is that possible?" I gave him an appraising glance. Even given how tired and sick he looked, he had to be closer to twenty-five than sixty-five. "If you don't mind me asking, how old are you?"

"Thirty-four."

"You retired at *thirty-four*? From what? What did you do? I must be in the wrong field."

"I followed in Dad's footsteps and got an engineering degree, although he's an electrical engineer and I got a degree in mechanical engineering. Mostly I invented things. I have a hundred twenty-three patents. The intellectual property was the main thing they wanted when they bought the company."

I was stunned. "I never would have guessed that."

"Hey, you aren't the only one who used to have a life, you know. A lot can change in a short time."

He wasn't wrong about that. I settled back into the seat with a sigh. "That's for sure."

~

Riley drove out of the Enchanted Moose parking lot and turned toward the town of Alpine Grove and points south. After we exited the residential area and were back on the open rural highway toward Gleasonville, I discovered that it hadn't been my imagination the night before; Riley drove fast. *Really* fast. The car was hauling down the highway so fast that I felt like we'd made the jump to hyperspace. I leaned over, peeked at the speedometer, and tried not to cringe. If we got stopped, it was going to be an unbelievably expensive speeding ticket.

Fortunately, the wind wasn't as bad in the front seat as it had been when I'd been riding in back. I leaned over toward Riley. "So what year is this Mustang?"

"It's a 1968 Shelby GT500KR convertible Mustang with a 428 V-8 Cobra Jet engine. It has a Paxton supercharger, dual exhaust, power steering, power disc brakes, an upgraded five-speed transmission, Procar sport bucket seats, Grab Trak suspension, Global West subframe, KYB shocks, Magnaflow exhaust and a roll bar."

"Oh."

"Plus a lot more customizations that you wouldn't care about."

"It seems to go fast."

Riley glanced over at me and raised his eyebrows. "Well, I didn't exactly restore Shelby to original factory specifications."

"You named your car Shelby?"

"Of course. It's a Shelby Mustang. What do you expect? Only three hundred and eighteen of these were made and with all the modifications I've done, Shelby is one of a kind. All my tools are in storage, so I'll be in trouble if something major goes wrong with her."

"I'm sure the car will be fine." I hoped so. Riley seemed almost as attached to his car as he was to his dog.

"Since my health started falling apart, I haven't been able to do much beyond changing Shelby's oil."

"You're kind of a car guy, aren't you?"

"I was. Oh, I also upgraded the audio." He turned on the stereo and the Rolling Stones blasted out.

Zelda started howling along in harmony with the London Bach Choir singing, "You can't always get what you want."

Riley turned down the volume and said, "This has been my theme song lately."

"I can relate. I'm hoping that if I keep trying, Mick is right and I'll get what I need."

Riley laughed and turned the music up loud again. As we rolled on down the highway, I was starting to understand why he liked the Mustang so much. It was hard to think or fret about my troubles with rock and roll blaring and the crisp spring breeze whipping through my hair.

By the time we pulled into the bakery parking lot, it was lunchtime and around seventy-five employees were standing in line in front of food trucks that were parked along the perimeter of the asphalt. This wasn't some small hometown bakery. It was a huge operation and the entire area smelled like the inside of a giant Wonder Bread bag. Once again, I was hungry, but I was on a mission to talk to people, so I needed to do my interviews before I could focus on food.

Riley parked at the far side of the lot, away from all the activity. I turned to him. "You can't get a little closer?"

"I think it might be better if I stayed here with Zelda."

He was looking a little green around the gills and I asked, "Are you feeling okay?"

"I don't think they're making health food in that building. More like Ho Hos and Ding Dongs rotting in slime. The smell is sickening."

"Well, we know there are pies. They must have fruit. Fruit is healthy."

"And lard. I'll just be over here trying not to think about what's in their products."

"Fine. I'll go talk to them myself."

I got out and walked across the lot to the throngs of people milling about in front of the food vendors. The employees who had gotten their tacos or gyros were settled into seats at the picnic tables nearby. The scent of greasy food mingled with the sweet bakery smells made my stomach grumble. I got in line at a sandwich vendor and smiled at the woman in front of me. She had gray hair snuggled up in a hairnet and was clutching bills in her hands as she studied the menu on the side of the truck.

She glanced at me and when her eyes met mine, I took the window of opportunity to introduce myself. "I'm looking for someone who works here. Do you know Dean Wolfe?"

"Yes, of course, everyone does. Do you know where he is? I think he's in big trouble," she replied. "Do you work here?"

"No, I'm trying to find Dean. He's uh, a friend of a friend and he said he needed to talk to me. It's important. Do you think you could help me ask around while you're eating lunch?"

"I suppose. I'm a little worried about him. Up until recently, you could set your clock by him. He showed up every day to collect the deliveries at nine a.m. sharp. My name is Greta, by the way. "

"I'm Meg. Then what happened?"

"I think he started having some health problems." Greta put her hand to her chest. "Not that I would gossip or anything."

"I'm sure you wouldn't. Did these health problems begin about six months ago?"

She raised her eyebrows, which caused the hairnet to wiggle her gray curls. "Why yes. How did you know?"

"He might have mentioned something related to it to my friend. I put two and two together."

Greta ordered her food and I followed her to the picnic tables. I sat down and Greta introduced me to the others and explained that I was looking for Dean.

An older man with spiky hair raised his hand toward the sky. "I bet the radiation from the meteor got him."

A collective groan arose from the others around the table and Greta said, "Harry, would you please be quiet about the stupid meteor? Ever since you watched that conspiracy show, you've been insufferable."

"Hey, the meteors are going to kill everybody. We're all gonna die." Harry crossed his arms. "We need to watch out. Dean is the first one. You all saw how he was sick with those headaches. I bet his brain is melting from the inside."

"Dean has headaches?" I asked. That hit a little close to home. I didn't have headaches per se, but the doctors did say my problem was similar to what happened to migraine sufferers.

A young woman with purple hair that was tucked into a color-coordinated lavender hairnet piped up, "Well, that's what Dean said, but I think he had a new girlfriend so he was skipping out to be with her. I mean, Dean is a hottie. If it was me, I'd never let him out of my sight. They were probably having sex like bunnies. It beats working."

I couldn't argue with that assessment, but it didn't get me closer to finding Dean. "Have you seen him in the last day or so?"

Harry said, "He picked up the pies to take up north yesterday. Today he didn't show and the boss is pissed."

"Do any of you know his family? Anyone who might know where he is?" I asked.

There was a lot of head shaking and shrugging. Dean was apparently "not from around here," which meant he hadn't grown up in Gleasonville. I wasn't getting far with my questions and people were starting to look at their watches. The lunch break was going to be over soon, and I mentally flailed around for some more questions to ask. "So what's Dean like? What does he like to do? Does he have hobbies?"

Greta said, "I thought you knew him."

"No, he's a friend of my parents."

"This feels like gossip. I'm not going to gossip about my co-worker to you when I don't even know you," Greta said.

Ms. Purple Hair said, "I agree. Who *are* you?"

Dancing around the truth wasn't going to work, and the group was starting to look cranky. I was going to have to tell them what happened before they turned on me. "Okay, here's the deal. My mother is missing and I'm terribly worried. Yesterday in Alpine Grove I met Dean, who said he had talked to her. Then I saw him get shoved into a blue van and it didn't look voluntary. Now I'm worried about him too."

"Did you call the police?" Greta asked.

"I did, but they weren't optimistic. Anything you can tell me about Dean might help me find him and my mother. Even little things. Please."

Slowly, a few tidbits emerged about the life and times of Dean Wolfe and I scribbled them down in my notebook. Finally a loud buzzer rang and everyone got up, gathered their trash, and filed back into the building.

I looked over my notes and glanced across the parking lot at Riley and Zelda, who both appeared to be asleep in the Mustang. I needed to go over this with him. Maybe he'd see something I didn't. To me, the notes seemed to be a mishmash of unrelated random facts that didn't mean anything.

The worst part was that I had been so busy trying to extract information from Greta and the others that I missed lunch. I'd blown a lot of time in this vain attempt at an interrogation and the roach coaches were pulling out of the lot. I didn't get any food and I was still hungry.

So far, this was not shaping up to be a fantastic day.

Chapter 3

Family Jewels

I walked over to the Mustang and Zelda stood up and *rrr*-ed a greeting at me. Riley sat up, yanked some fabric off his face, and set it aside. "Are you ready to go?"

"Yes. This was a waste of time and I'm starving. I want to stop somewhere for lunch."

"I vote for somewhere that doesn't smell like the inside of a garbage disposal."

"You're tough to please, you know that?" I got into the car and picked up the fabric. "This is the blouse I wore yesterday. Did you go through my suitcase? And, by the way, *yuck*. That's gross."

"Sorry."

"I hesitate to ask, but how much of my laundry do you have? This counts as going way, *way* over the creepy line."

"Just the shirt. It was either that or leave, and I figured you wouldn't appreciate being ditched at this bakery." He started the car. "On that note, I'm ready to get out of here."

"Fine." I held up my list. "I can tell you all the exciting things I learned about Dean, like his favorite color."

"How is that helpful?"

"It's not. But in case you're wondering, it's red. Apparently he wears a red hoodie sometimes."

"That's fascinating."

"But wait, there's more! He went to UCLA for a year, but dropped out. He knows enough about computers to help Greta make her word processor work. Or at least, most of the time."

"That's nice."

"He has a great garden and loves to talk about growing vegetables. The woman with the purple hair thinks he's hot, but she saw a picture of his brother, who is allegedly 'to die for,' so Dean isn't even the cute one in the family. Ms. Purple Hair also thinks he might have a girlfriend, which she's not very pleased about."

Riley glanced at me. "So do you think Dean is hot?"

"Of course." I raised my eyebrows. "I mean, hello? I'm not blind. Returning to the point, Dean's family doesn't live around here and he's been getting headaches so he's missed some work lately."

"Wait. Stop. That one might be useful. Did they say when he started getting headaches?"

"Six months ago." I waved the paper in front of me. "I know! It's weird."

"I agree. Talk about creepy. I'd like to know what happened six months ago that affected our health."

"Well, a guy named Harry thinks there's a meteor that's going to kill us all."

"Bummer."

"I also learned that Dean sometimes works weekends at a bar about fifty miles south of here, down past Gleasonville."

Riley turned onto the highway. "I'm guessing that's where you want to go next."

"Do you have any other ideas?"

"Not really, and we might want to get away from here, since it's in the meteor's path."

"According to Harry we're doomed from the radioactive fallout, so there's no escape. I'm getting the impression that you're not taking this investigation seriously. I'm worried about my mom and we're getting nowhere."

"That's not true. I *am* taking it seriously. While you were chatting up the bakery people, I was thinking."

"It looked more like you were sleeping."

"Thank your shirt for that. Being able to take a nap at that revolting bakery was great. Anyway, like I said, I was thinking. What if our parents went back to Alpine Grove?"

"So while we're driving away from there, what if they're sitting at home wondering where we are?" I flopped my hands in my lap in exasperation. "But the house was empty. I doubt they're sitting around in a house with no furniture. Where did it all go?"

"Is there anyone we can call in Alpine Grove who could check and see if Mom, Dad, or the furniture have returned to the house?"

"We called the police. They'll check, right?"

"They should, but if they don't, we could ask them to."

"I wish I still had my cell phone. When I was a reporter, it was great to be able to call anyone any time."

"I'll take your word for it. I hate talking on the phone. We're on a highway in the middle of nowhere and you'd never get a signal anyway."

"The bakery had all kinds of cool satellite dishes on the roof. I bet I could have gotten a signal there."

"Or ordered lots of pies made from decomposing fruit."

"You're being a grump about that bakery."

Riley turned his attention from the road to give me a quick scowl. "That's because it was gross."

"Says the guy who likes dirty laundry. The bakery smelled great to me. Isn't there any place along here where we can eat? I'm starving."

"Calm down. We're almost to Gleasonville."

"When I had a cell phone, I could call for take-out orders or pizza, no matter where I was. I miss that."

"You have a major fixation on food."

"So do you, but in a very different way."

"Touché."

The town of Gleasonville was significantly larger than Alpine Grove. Because it was more of a sprawling metropolitan area, it didn't have quaint small-town charm going for it. Big box stores and fast-food outlets lined the highway and there was a mall with the typical complement of department stores and clothing outlets. The area didn't feel terribly dissimilar from suburban Maryland where I lived, chock full of the same chain stores and franchises I knew well. Except for the occasional Western wear or hunting and fishing store to add a bit of rural flavor, Gleasonville could be any small city almost anywhere in the United States.

My stomach growled and behind me Zelda barked. I turned in my seat to look at the dog and heard her make some grumbly noises, and then a few lights began to glimmer in front of my eyes. My heart pounded in my chest and I looked over at Riley, who had a blue haze around him again. That wasn't a good sign. Crap. Not again. Not *now*.

I squeezed my eyes shut and leaned forward, trying to will the lights to go away for once. I didn't want to deal with this right now. I could feel the car slow and stop, and then the warmth of Riley's hand on mine.

He clasped my palm hard. Having something to hold onto helped, but the lights continued to swirl and gain intensity. I saw the blue van that had taken Dean as if it were coming out of a fog. Then there was an image of Mom walking away from a tent. The vision was like watching a movie in super-slow motion.

I gasped, opened my eyes, and sat up again. Zelda's muzzle was right next me, her nose snuffling my ear. Riley was leaned over, practically in my lap, looking into my face. One of his hands was next to my head on the headrest, and he pulled both hands away from me as if I were on fire and mumbled, "Sorry."

I smiled faintly. "That was weird."

Riley leaned back in his seat, closed his eyes, and let out a long breath. "Jeez, you have *got* to stop doing that. My nerves can't take this. What happened?"

"I saw Mom and the blue van."

He turned his head to look at me. "What do you mean *saw*?"

"Instead of passing out, I had a hallucination. First, I saw the blue van that took Dean. Then Mom walking next to a tent. It's all kind of disjointed, but I'm sure it was Mom."

Riley closed his eyes again and said more softly, "At least you didn't scream this time."

Zelda put her chin on the seat back next to Riley's face and poked at his ear a couple of times with her nose until he reached around to pet her. "It's all right, Zee."

I continued, "I'm thrilled I didn't pass out. You grabbed my hand, and it was like I knew you were there, so I didn't fall down the black hole."

"What black hole?"

I tugged at the seat belt, moving it away from my body. "That's how I think of it. When this happens, sometimes it's like there's a black hole trying to suck me into it. I scream because I get scared. The first time this happened to me, I thought I was dying. It was the most terrifying experience I've ever had. But somehow I wasn't scared this time. It was more like watching a movie."

Riley didn't say anything, but he still looked extremely upset.

I volunteered, "I feel okay now. When it started, you were blue again."

"I guess it's fair to say I've been happier. Being around you has some real down sides."

"No, I mean you were literally blue. You had a blue aura around you. It was a gorgeous color. Kind of a sparkly teal or cyan, like a mountain lake."

A corner of his lips turned up in a half smile. "Gosh, I feel pretty."

I jerked on the seat belt again, readjusting it away from my neck. "Well, it's a lot better than the black hole, believe me."

"I'll take your word for it. Was your mom in the van?"

"No, she was next to the tent." I unfastened the seat belt and held the strap away from my body as it retracted.

"Do you mean she was at a campground or something?"

"It wasn't that kind of tent. Mom hates camping. It was a big white tent like you'd see at a wedding or party."

Riley paused in petting Zelda, letting his palm rest on her head. "Interesting. What if what you saw was like a prophesy? Maybe you saw your mom because you're some type of mystic or a saint."

"Give me a break. I am definitely not a saint."

"That does seem unlikely, but you never know. I've read about this type of thing. In medieval times, there were people who claimed they had religious visions. They thought all the auras and lights were a manifestation of God. All the flashing lights were filled with cool hallucinations too. Maybe you should join a convent or go to the Himalayas."

"I don't think so." I grabbed the seat belt again and yanked the strap out in front of me, pointing the metal fitting at him as if I were a flight attendant going through pre-flight procedures. "As a career choice, nun doesn't work for me. It has a few requirements I'm not too excited about."

"I suppose. But isn't it possible your visions could mean something?"

"I doubt it. Mostly, I'm glad I didn't scream or do something embarrassing. Maybe it means I could go back to work. I hate not working. What am I going to do with the rest of my life?"

"I ask myself that question regularly." Riley pointed at my seat belt. "How about you put that back on and let's get something to eat. I'm starting to see the wisdom in keeping you fed."

I clicked the seat belt in place. "A little food might do *you* some good too. You need to put a little meat on those bones, as my grandma would say."

Riley gave me an icy glare as he put the car in gear. "Gee, thanks for that little pearl of wisdom. No one's ever mentioned that before."

~

Riley and I stopped for lunch at a tiny cafe with outdoor seating. It didn't have many menu options and had only a single table outside. While Riley managed to slowly choke down some toast, I inhaled a bagel and felt a thousand times better afterward. The cafe was located near a park and Riley went for a walk with Zelda while I reviewed the notes I'd taken. There wasn't much to go on. So far, the Find Dean project wasn't going too well.

Riley and Zelda were gone for an extremely long time and I was starting to wonder if they were okay. Maybe Riley had collapsed somewhere out there in the trees. The guy couldn't live on toast forever. However, he'd left me with the Mustang, and I was sure he'd never willingly abandon that car. Finally, they emerged from the forest, and we continued south. My stomach started growling again, which made me nervous. I didn't want to have another 'episode,' particularly since the last one seemed to have left Riley a little frayed around the edges.

As we zoomed down the highway, we spent a lot of time debating possible places to stop for an early dinner. I wanted to stop everywhere, and Riley wanted to stop nowhere. He vetoed all my favorite chain restaurants, shooting down all my suggestions for trivial reasons. What a pain. He was blurring the line between picky and curmudgeonly.

On the one hand, I understood his situation. On the other hand, by the time we ended up at the bar where Dean worked south of Gleasonville, we'd run out of restaurant options. I was so hungry and irritated I wanted to throttle Riley, jump over his body, and snarf down as much greasy bar food as I could stuff into my face.

Riley wasn't the first to point out that I get a little cranky when I'm hungry. I used to chalk it up to low blood sugar, but now it was worse because I could end up screaming or passed out on the floor. And he *knew* that, for heaven's sake. The last thing I wanted was to create a bizarre spectacle in a public place again.

I got out of the Mustang and slammed the door. Zelda yanked on her seat belt harness, wanting to be released.

Riley leaned around his seat, unhooked Zelda, and turned to look at me. "Why don't you go eat something? I'll feed her and join you in a few minutes."

I spun around and charged toward the entrance. They'd better have French fries at this place. I needed an infusion of fries ASAP.

The bar was going for a honky-tonk motif, with sawdust on the wooden floor and an elevated stage where a band was sitting around on stools getting ready for the evening. Several grizzled-looking middle-aged men were picking at their guitars, halfheartedly tuning them.

I ordered a burger and fries and was digging in when the door opened, letting a stream of late afternoon sunlight into the dark area. The place had no windows and dim lighting, which undoubtedly helped encourage people to drink more as they lost any sense of time. Riley entered the bar and scanned the room.

In the low lighting, I had a flashback of what he looked like in the photographs my mother had shown me during her last visit. Riley was tall and lanky, and if he ever gained back some of the weight he'd lost, he might be attractive in a dark, Irish kind of way. Certainly not my type, but if you went in for the whole broody element, he could be kind of sexy. Maybe. At a minimum, getting a decent haircut and shaving every once in a while wouldn't hurt either.

He sat down across from me at the wooden table. "Nice place."

"At least they have something to eat. I was dying."

"Well, if you keep eating like that, you're going to end up having a heart attack."

"Says the guy who doesn't eat." I held up the burger. "Pardon me if I don't take nutritional advice from you terribly seriously."

"I'm sure I've read more about nutrition than you have, or you wouldn't be gorging yourself on that plate full of grease. It has zero heath benefits and is garnished with rancid oil. Doesn't anyone clean their kitchens around here?"

"It tastes good."

"I don't understand why you don't weigh four hundred pounds, given the garbage you eat."

"I'm blessed with a speedy metabolism." I stopped chewing. "Well, I was. It might have slowed down a little since I stopped working." I didn't want to think about the fact that for the trip to Alpine Grove I'd packed mostly stretchy clothes, and even now I was wearing my "fat jeans." They had been an emergency purchase after I couldn't wedge my butt into my old jeans anymore. That had been a demoralizing discovery.

"I'm going to see if I can find anything I can stand to eat here." He stood up and went over to the bar.

I yelled after him, "Could you get me a beer?"

He nodded and entered into negotiations with the bartender. The odds of Riley finding something acceptable to eat at this place were next to zero. I returned to my burger and finally began to relax.

If I were being honest with myself, I'd have to admit I'd been drowning my anxieties in food. There was no rhyme or reason for when my episodes happened. Yes, some had occurred when I was hungry, but a few had not. I was using eating as a way to feel better. Food had become my best friend. Whenever I was angry, afraid, or stressed about the strange things that kept happening to me, I turned to my friend for comfort.

Riley returned with a plate filled with an odd collection of items. There were orange and grapefruit sections, pretzels, nuts, carrots, celery, and artichoke dip. He handed me my beer and set the plate on the table.

I thanked him and eyed his meal, which looked healthy, and dare I say it? Good. "See! All that whining was for nothing. You were able to find something, after all."

"It turns out the guy in the kitchen is a closet health nut and makes meals for himself all the time. They have to have citrus for drinks, and he whipped up the artichoke dip."

"It looks tasty. Maybe I should think about ordering off the menu more often."

Riley set down his tonic water and leaned forward. "So about that. If we're going to be on the road together, maybe we should think about how we're going to keep you from getting too hungry."

"I'm all for eating more regularly."

Riley ignored my comment and continued, "When I left LA, I was in such a rush to see my dad, I didn't bring a cooler, but it might be a good idea to have one. Keeping us fed is important, if not for the same reasons."

I sighed and looked down at my empty plate. "That makes sense. I should eat better. Right now, I feel a little ill. I've been pigging out on a lot of junk, even for me."

"Maybe we can find a grocery store once we're done here."

Our conversation was interrupted by a blast of screechy noise from one of the speakers. The dudes in the band stood up and were looking more alert as they fired up their amplifiers. I made a wry face at Riley. If that sound was any indication, this evening's performance could be unpleasant. Maybe Dean's headaches were from the music.

A man with a long gray beard stepped up to the microphone in the center of the stage and strummed his guitar a few times. A steel guitar whined from behind him and the man's gravelly voice began crooning a dreary country tune about a woman named Doris who made blueberry pies.

Riley leaned over and said in my ear, "What is it with baked goods around here?"

I laughed and gave him a mute shrug as the singer droned on. As the song progressed, I realized I'd heard some of the lyrics before.

The singer crooned, "Have you had some strange sensations? Yeah, sensations. I'm talking about odd experiences, you know."

I shoved Riley's shoulder to get his attention. "That's what Dean said. Almost exactly word for word."

"What?"

"Dean! Remember when we were at the restaurant? He asked us if we'd had strange sensations or odd experiences."

I motioned toward the man on the stage. "That's what the song says too."

Riley jerked his attention back to the performance, then turned to me. "That can't be a coincidence, can it?"

"I don't think so."

~

We suffered through a few more mournful country songs and after the set was over, Riley and I hustled up to the stage to talk to the members of the band. The lead singer had a long gray beard and looked like he could be a member of the ZZ Top Facial Hair Club.

Riley said, "We wanted to ask you about the first song you performed this evening."

I added, "Do you know Dean Wolfe? We're looking for him and it's extremely important that we find him."

The man looked startled by our intensity and tugged at his beard. "Well, sure I know Dean. Everybody around here does."

"I noticed in the song you sang that the lyrics mentioned strange sensations. Is that something Dean said?" Riley asked.

"Well yeah, I guess you must know him pretty well then." The man put out his hand. "My name is Ernest, but you can call me Ernie."

Riley shook his hand. "That was something he said to us. He used the term odd experiences too, which was also in your song."

"Yeah, it's about his headaches." Ernie shrugged. "Poor guy hasn't been feeling that great lately."

"Someone else I talked to mentioned his headaches. Do you know what's wrong?" I asked.

"Well, he said it was like everything was too loud all the time and it gave him a headache that wouldn't go away." Ernie shrugged. "When it was real bad, I guess he had to take off work. We missed him 'round here too. He's a great bartender 'cuz he's an incredible listener. When I was having troubles with the wife, he was right there for me while I was cryin' in my beer."

I said, "Do you know where he is? We asked at his other job and they said he didn't show up for work. I think people are worried."

"Nope. He doesn't work here 'cept on the weekends. Maybe he got sick."

"When was the last time you saw him?" Riley asked.

"Hmm, mighta been a couple weeks now. He missed last weekend. He said he mighta found a doctor who could help." Ernie shook his head. "I didn't get the details or nothing."

"Is there anything else you can tell us about where he might be?" I asked, starting to get desperate for even a tiny tidbit of information we might be able to use. At this rate, we were never going to find Dean, much less my mother.

"Nope. I oughta play some songs now I suppose. Crowd's starting to form." Ernie said.

I looked over my shoulder. The "crowd" was a couple who had sat down at one of the wooden tables. "Are any of your other songs related to Dean in any way?"

Ernie shook his head and picked up his guitar. "Nope. I wrote that one after I spent so much time talking to him."

Riley and I thanked Ernie, wished him a good evening, and walked back to our table. I grabbed Riley's arm. "I guess we can get out of here now. Maybe find a place to stay?"

"All right. And find out where the nearest grocery store is too." He moved away from me and pointed at the sign for the restrooms. "I'll be right back. Meet you outside."

"I'll go keep Zelda company. Maybe she'll have some ideas about where Dean went."

Riley flashed a grin as he turned toward the back of the bar. "She *is* very smart, you know."

I stopped at the table and sat down for a moment to finish the last of my beer as the band began playing another dirge about lost love and despair. Some country music had a way of making you want to crawl into a hole and die.

Once I'd drained the ale, I set down the glass, got up, and headed for the door. I had no idea what to do next. It was easy to imagine driving around for days or weeks with Riley and never finding our parents. They could be anywhere. Eventually, Riley and I would give up and we'd part ways. And I'd have to accept the fact that I might never see my mother again. I pressed my hand to my stomach. It hurt to even think about that possibility.

I pushed open the heavy wooden door and the cool evening air hit my face. It was a relief to be out of the bar. Even though smoking wasn't allowed in California bars anymore, the place was still stuffy and the fresh air felt good. I looked across the parking lot at the Mustang. Zelda was standing up and looking remarkably attentive. She barked at me and launched out of the car, growling and barking furiously.

I looked behind me. A man in a dark gray suit was reaching to grab for me. I had a flash of disbelief combined with terror as my stomach clenched and my throat closed up. My scream was muffled by a meaty hand clawing against my mouth.

I flailed against the man, who grabbed my arms and moved me toward a dark blue van. Zelda's loud growling intensified and another man said, "Get away from me, you mangy mutt."

The man dragging me toward the van kicked at Zelda, then with a shriek, he loosened his hold on me. I bit one of his fat fingers and he jerked his hand away. I moved away from him, and it was as if time fell apart, so everything was happening in slow motion. I took a long look at the man's face, analyzing it as if I were writing a description for an article. Heavy brows, dark brown hair, brown eyes, low forehead, buck teeth, broken nose.

Zelda lunged at the other man and sank her teeth into his hefty butt, slamming him to the ground. The man I felt like I'd been staring at for hours moved toward me again and I kicked out with my foot, neatly landing a power shot directly into his nuts with the pointy end of my shoe. He grabbed his crotch, bent over, and crumpled to the ground.

I stood for a second in stunned silence, then turned at the sound of Riley's footsteps as he ran toward me. He reached for my arm and looked into my face, "Are you all right?"

I nodded and pointed at the man Zelda had attacked, who was upright again. Riley let go of my arm, grabbed the guy, and slammed his fist into his face. He waved a hand in the direction of the Mustang. "Go, *now*! Zelda, you too."

Zelda pivoted on her rear legs and galloped back to the car, followed by me. She jumped into the back as I got into the front. Riley was right behind us and got in, slamming the door behind him. He fired up the Mustang and we hauled out of the parking lot. I wrapped my arms around myself and began shaking. My pulse was pounding in my ears and

I tried not to cry, but the shock of what had happened was overwhelming.

Once we were on the highway, cruising at some extremely high speed I didn't want to think about, Riley took his eyes off the road to glance at me quickly. "Are you hurt? You don't look hurt. You're not hurt are you, right? Tell me they didn't hurt you."

"Yes…I'm fine. But…" I put my hands over my eyes. "That was like my worst nightmare come true. Thank God Zelda was there."

Riley reached over and pulled one of my hands down from my face and squeezed it. "It wasn't just Zelda. I'm pretty sure that guy is going to remain in a fetal position for quite some time."

"I took self-defense classes because I had to walk around so much at night covering events for the paper. I was getting scared of the dark and I didn't want to feel that way."

"Your instructor would be proud."

I thought about the woman who had taught the classes. With her Marilyn Monroe bleached platinum hair, you wouldn't have guessed her occupation, but she didn't take any crap from anyone. "Yeah, Diane would love that I nailed him right in the family jewels."

Riley squeezed my hand again. "It's over. You're all right."

"Those were the people who took Dean."

"I know."

"Now, they're after *us* too. What if those guys took our parents? I'm scared. What are we going to do?"

"I have no idea."

Chapter 4

Sniff the Breeze

When I woke up, it was pitch dark, except for the shine of the headlights on the highway. At some point, the draining of the adrenaline out of my system, combined with the hum of the car, had lulled me to sleep. I readjusted my position in the seat and looked around at Zelda, who was curled up in a tight ball in the backseat. Riley was staring at the road ahead with a thoughtful expression on his face.

I cleared my throat. "Where are we?"

"On the high road to Nevada."

"*Nevada*? How did we get here?"

Riley glanced at me. "Don't get agitated. We're not in Nevada yet. How do you *think* we got here? We drove, or more accurately, I drove."

"How long was I asleep?" I looked at the dashboard. "You have every possible dial and gauge in this car, but no clock?"

"I wear a watch." He pressed a button on the stereo and immediately turned down the volume. "And if I'm listening to a CD, the stereo displays the time."

"I thought we were going south? We weren't headed to Nevada when we stopped at the store."

"I know, but now we're going east."

"Shouldn't we keep going the same direction? Why did you turn?"

"I wanted to get away from the people who attacked us. At the store, I saw a flyer advertising a circus hanging on the door. I was going to talk to you about it, but you fell asleep."

"You want to go to a circus?"

"In your vision, your mom was near a big white tent. It sounded like a circus tent."

"But that doesn't mean anything!" I crossed my arms across my chest. "I can't believe you didn't talk to me about this first. I think we should keep going south. That's probably where they were going—maybe to LA or San Diego."

"I don't want to see those people again or end up in Mexico." Riley nodded at a sign whizzing by. "According to the signs, there's a motel up ahead that's supposed to be family friendly, which I'm hoping includes pets. I vote we stop for the night."

"We're in the middle of nowhere."

"Exactly." He slowed the car and turned into a somewhat seedy-looking motel with a sign that proclaimed "Vacancy" in huge red neon letters.

"This place makes the Enchanted Moose seem more enchanting," I said. "And look, there seems to be plenty of room at the inn. What a shock."

Riley laughed and got out of the car. "Be right back."

Zelda stood up in the backseat and turned her head as if she were surveying the parking lot for interlopers. I reached back to pet her. "Let me know if you see anything, okay?"

Zelda wagged her tail and seemed unconcerned by the location, which was a relief. Not surprisingly, only a few other cars were sprinkled throughout the parking lot. It was unlikely that the people who owned this motel had to light up the word "No" on the vacancy sign very often.

Riley returned and got into the car. "I got us a room on the back side, away from the highway, so no one can see the car."

"I suppose a restored classic Mustang like this does stand out."

Riley drove around the building, parked, and we began unloading the car. He seemed to know that I didn't want to stay in a separate room. After the events of the day, I wanted to remain as close to Zelda as possible. There was safety in numbers and Zelda had shown she wasn't all bark. She had a serious bite too.

Once the car was unloaded, I flopped down on one of the beds. Zelda jumped up and laid down next to me. She made a few happy snorty groans as she settled in and rolled over on her back for a tummy rub. I obliged, enjoying the relaxing feel of her soft fur. We'd all had a long day.

Riley handed me a bottle of water and began rummaging around in the bags of groceries. Although he'd gotten all kinds of healthy things like vegetables and fruit, he handed me a box of crackers without comment. Perhaps he was accepting the fact that we had wildly different ideas about food. He set out condiments on the desk and began making sandwiches, which caused Zelda to flip upright and pay attention.

On a positive note, Riley was eating, so I didn't say anything and settled into munching a few crackers. I handed one to Zelda, who gobbled it down greedily. She obviously appreciated their salty goodness as much as I did.

Riley handed me a sandwich and sprawled out on the other bed with a sandwich of his own. I sat up, so my meal would be farther away from Zelda's muzzle.

I reached for my purse and pulled out the notes I'd taken after talking to the people at the bakery. "I think we need to discuss what we should do next."

Riley put down his sandwich. "Go to the circus."

"That doesn't make any sense. I told you, my hallucination was a dream, nothing more. Those guys who grabbed Dean are likely to be in some place with more people, like Los Angeles. Why would they go to a circus in some podunk town?"

"I don't know. Maybe it's irrational, but I have a feeling about it. I've also been thinking about Dean's headaches."

I pulled another cracker from the box. "They don't sound good."

"You found out that they started six months ago. Ernie made it sound like the headaches related to Dean's hearing."

"That's what he said."

Riley nibbled on his sandwich and set it down again. "Don't you think it's odd that six months ago, my sense of smell, your vision, and Dean's hearing all went haywire?"

"My vision isn't affected. I can see fine."

"Except when I'm blue."

"Okay, well, there's that."

"Also the term second sight relates to vision too."

I threw a cracker at him. "Are you talking about me being a prophet again? Because I told you, I'm not buying it."

Riley tossed the cracker to Zelda, who snatched it neatly from the air. "How do you know for sure? I'm just saying it's a possibility. What if you can see things that are far away? Like your mom being with this circus? This whole thing is bizarre, so in a way it makes sense."

"So you think I have x-ray vision like Superman or something? Spare me. I'm quite sure I don't. Otherwise, I'd be seeing you naked, or your skeleton, or the naked guy in the next room. I'm happy to say that you appear fully clothed to me and I don't know what the guy in the next room looks like."

"Although that's a relief, it's not what I meant. Second sight is not the same as x-ray vision. Didn't you read comic books when you were a kid?"

"No."

"Well, you must have watched cartoons or you wouldn't know about Superman." Riley leaned forward and set his sandwich aside. "Anyway, you're missing the point. The point is that all of our senses went nuts at the same time. And it sounds like Dean found some doctor who might be able to help."

"But that doesn't answer the question of where he is. Or Mom. We need facts."

"I know. But I couldn't face going back to Los Angeles." He took another bite of sandwich and chewed for a moment before adding, "How did you feel when you were in LA?"

I shrugged and fed Zelda another piece of cracker. "I was at LAX, then I left. I didn't have time to feel much of anything. I got in my expensive shuttle and left town. I do remember the air quality was pretty bad. The shuttle guy said it was 'marine layer,' but I'm sorry folks, when the air is brown, that's called smog."

"I feel really sick when I'm in Los Angeles. Whatever this problem is that I have, it's worst in LA. That's why I went on the road with Zelda. I thought I was going to die, and I decided I needed to at least see the Grand Canyon and some other national parks before I couldn't drive anymore."

"You didn't say that before."

"I was only back in LA to shut down everything when my Dad called. I'd decided to chuck my life there. When I was on the road, I discovered that I felt better in places like this—places in the middle of nowhere."

"I guess that made it easier to make that turn and go east."

"It was probably another self-serving choice, but yes, it did."

~

I finished my sandwich, put the crackers away, and slumped down on the bed. Zelda curled up closer to me and began to snore quietly.

Riley was equally recumbent on his bed, looking unusually relaxed. He angled his head toward Zelda. "I can't believe how quickly Zelda took a shine to you. That's not like her. Generally, she's pretty stand-offish with new people."

"It's been an intense couple of days, I suppose." I ran my hands across the soft fur on Zelda's head. "I'm starting to agree with you that she's pretty much the greatest dog in the world."

"Told ya."

We were silent for a moment and finally I said, "You honestly thought you were going to die?"

"You think I'm skinny now? It was worse a couple months ago. I gained some weight on my road trip with Zee."

"Hey, you ate a whole sandwich mere moments ago. Impressive."

"It is to me. When you don't eat, you get hypoglycemia with fun stuff like dizziness, headaches, and fainting. Then there's vitamin and electrolyte deficiencies, which cause everything from muscle wasting and digestive problems to depression and mental confusion. Oh, and it screws up your hormones too."

"You mean like testosterone?"

He offered an ironic smile. "Most men, including me, are interested in sex twenty-four hours a day every day. That went to nothing. Less than nothing. Erin wondered what the heck was wrong with me. But all I wanted to do was curl up somewhere and sleep. Except I couldn't sleep well either. She didn't appreciate my sudden lack of sex drive too much."

That was certainly more than I wanted to know about Riley's girlfriend or his sex life, but it did explain why he gave off such a "don't touch me" vibe. "So you're saying no one knows what is wrong with you?"

"Almost everyone thinks I have an eating disorder. But that's not my problem. I *want* to eat. I just can't. So many foods smell too revolting for me to be able to eat them." He gave a dismissive gesture. "It's unbelievably frustrating. Smell and taste are linked and it's not like you can hold your breath forever or something. Then when they started talking about a feeding tube and hospitalization, I said 'no way' and left. If it was time for me to check out, I was going to go on a road trip and see some beautiful places first."

"I can understand that. I've hardly been anywhere."

"The West is full of some amazing country. Glacier National Park, Moab, Arches, and a bunch of areas in between that aren't as well known, but incredible. I had no idea."

"It seems silly in retrospect now that I'm not working, but I never took vacations. I thought I couldn't. That they'd never be able to live without me. Boy, was I wrong about that. I don't think anyone noticed I left."

"Yeah, letting go of my company was hard too. I had to accept the fact that they were better off without a founder who was falling apart and losing his mind."

I bit my lower lip. Did I have the guts to reveal the most humiliating moment of my life? "Well, um, it's not just you. Everyone I worked with thinks I'm nuts. And I'm not talking a little nuts. I mean totally nuts—like certifiable should-be-committed nuts."

"I'm guessing you screamed, didn't you?"

"Well yes, but it was worse than that. I haven't told anybody, not even Mom. I was going to talk to her about it when I came to visit her, but obviously I didn't get the chance."

"What happened?"

I ducked my head behind Zelda's prone form for a moment, collecting my thoughts and wishing I could avoid talking about the whole thing. I propped myself back up on my elbow and cleared my throat. "Okay, this is unbelievably embarrassing, but I think I should tell you because it could relate to what's going on."

Riley sat up and raised his eyebrows, looking expectant. "I'm listening."

"I had a hallucination at work and according to numerous reports, I acted out most of it."

"What do you mean *acted out?*"

"In my hallucination, I thought I was a performer at a circus. Apparently, I acted out some trapeze artist moves, shouted like a ringmaster, and then ran around being a clown. I'm told there were somersaults and other tumbling maneuvers. I found out later that the clown performance was particularly well received." I put my face in my hands. "I know what I thought was happening in the hallucination, but to everyone else, I was marching around, rolling on the floor, and swinging off things."

"You did all this at work?"

"Somehow I managed all this at our extremely crowded newsroom office building. When I acted like I was going to jump off a second-floor landing into the atrium, someone finally stopped me." I took a deep breath. "By the time I came back to myself, the emergency services were there. It was quite the legendary extravaganza."

Riley threw his legs off the bed and leaned toward me. "I'm starting to see why you were so resistant to following the circus."

"I have to tell you that hallucinating about being a clown didn't make me like them any better. I hate circuses and I always have. Clowns creep me out. I don't even like elephants. I think they should stay in the wild along with the lions, tigers, and bears."

Riley just stared at me. It seemed I'd stunned him into silence, so I continued, "I guess what I'm saying is that you aren't the only one with weird issues. Whatever is wrong with me, it seems to be better here than it was at home."

He scratched at the stubble on his chin. "There's also the recurring circus theme. Isn't it possible you *knew* your mom was at the circus?"

"It could have been some other type of tent. And excuse me, aren't we overlooking an important question here? Why would my mom be at a circus in the first place? I think my circus vision is more about some latent clown fear, not my mom."

"Maybe."

"Anyway, now you know. The whole thing has been a huge shock to my system. I went from being a successful journalist with coworkers who liked and respected me to the office lunatic. In the span of twenty-four hours, because everyone thought I'd lost my mind, I was out of work on medical leave."

"Been there."

"I guess you have." I smiled, relieved that he hadn't run screaming out of the room at my peculiar tale. "You're the only person who understands what I'm going through. I haven't been able to talk about this with anyone."

A car honked and a rattling noise came from outside the door. Riley and Zelda both leaped up off their respective beds. Riley waved at Zelda, who remained quiet as he peered out the peephole and turned to me. "You're not going to believe this."

I got up and walked over to stand next to Riley. I looked up at him. "Is somebody messing with the Mustang?"

"Shelby is fine, but there's a clown going through the garbage can."

I shoved him aside and stood on my tiptoes to take a look. A man with orange Bozo hair was examining an aluminum soda can. I put my palms over my face and bowed my head. "This is unreal. I hate clowns. Why does it have to be a clown?" I dropped my hands. "Can you tell what he's doing out there?"

Riley peered out the peephole again. "I think he's collecting cans."

"We're in the middle of nowhere and there happens to be an environmentally conscious clown picking through trash outside our door. What are the odds?"

Riley turned to look at me. "He's leaving, and I'm inclined to pack up and go find this circus."

"It's getting late and we haven't gotten any sleep. I'm more worried about the car. What if he steals it? We can't leave Zelda outside all night to keep an eye on it."

"Stealing Shelby would be difficult."

"Was one of your customizations a special clown-proof anti-theft device?"

"I haven't tested it with clowns per se, but Shelby is difficult to steal. She won't start unless you know how to start her."

"You can't use a key?"

"Well yes, but you also have to type in a code under the steering column. Typing it wrong or not at all kills the engine. Shelby won't go anywhere."

"So you can't hot-wire it either?"

"Well, *I* could, but almost no one else would be able to figure it out."

I smiled at Riley. "I have new respect for you. That's downright sneaky."

"Hey I spent *years* restoring Shelby. I'm not letting her go without a fight." He clapped his hands. "Hey Zee, ready for your walk?"

Zelda sat in front of Riley wagging her tail, and Riley looked at me. "You want to come look for clowns with us?"

"Are you nuts?"

Riley raised his eyebrows. "You mean more than you are?"

"Very funny. There's no way I'm leaving this room and I can't imagine why you want to."

"Zelda needs to go out."

"Having the great outdoors be your bathroom is inconvenient. I plan to lock the door, take a shower, and try not to think about killer clown movies or *Psycho*."

"All right. Suit yourself."

~

Riley and Zelda were gone for such a long time that I started to worry. What if the clown was nasty, like the guys who attacked me? I'd been kidding about the killer clowns. I wasn't being prophetic, was I? That was too absurd to even contemplate, so I took a long, hot shower to try to forget about it.

After I was all pink and clean, I paced around the room and ate almost an entire cellophane-packed row of saltines. I peeked out the peephole approximately four thousand times, and saw no more clowns, but no Riley or Zelda either. Being left alone with my thoughts hadn't been a good choice. Now I was clean, and casting about for something to do. I was going to go stir crazy hanging around all these motel rooms.

If Riley and Zelda were captured, I knew I wouldn't be able to start the Mustang, thanks to Riley's creative security measures. And even if I could start it, I'd have trouble driving it, because a) people who have impromptu hallucinations probably shouldn't be on the road, and b) I didn't know how to drive a manual transmission. Hmm.

If I was going to continue to hang out with Riley, we should talk about that issue. A car that was essentially a gigantic paperweight to me could be a problem. Of course, the odds of him letting me touch his precious car were extremely low. If I had to guess, I'd bet that his mysterious girlfriend had never driven the car either.

I whirled around at the sound of the door opening. Zelda rushed in and jumped up on my bed. I went to her and ruffled her soft ears. "I'm so glad to see you! Did you have a good walk?"

Riley said, "Yeah, we walked over that hill behind this place."

"You were gone for ages. I was getting worried."

"The walk was pleasant and mercifully clown free."

"That's a relief. Do you always take such long walks?"

"I'm trying to build up my strength again. Muscle-wasting and all that." He chewed methodically on a saltine. "How come you look so freaked out?"

"I don't like being alone when there are creepy clowns nearby."

"You don't like being alone at all, do you?"

"I'm used to lots of activity and being around people most of the time because I worked in a busy newsroom."

"Don't you live alone?" He paused. "I mean, I guess I just assumed…"

I put my hands on my hips. "Why would you assume I don't have a significant other or live-in lover? I could have a husband or boyfriend. Or a girlfriend, for all you know. What are you trying to say? That there's something wrong with me?"

"I'm not saying anything. You didn't mention anyone. So *do* you have a significant other or lover of any gender?"

"No." I wasn't going to go down that path with Riley. My romantic life was irrelevant to what was going on and he didn't have a need to know.

"I find being around a lot of people exhausting."

"I'm not a lot of people. I'm one person. You mean being around *me*, don't you?"

"I didn't say that, but you do talk a lot. I'm used to having more quiet time by myself." He shrugged. "Nothing personal. I've always been kind of a loner."

"How could you have owned a company and be a loner? That doesn't make sense." I sat down on the bed next to Zelda. "You had employees, right?"

"Of course. I'm an introvert, not agoraphobic. Plenty of successful entrepreneurs are introverts. Bill Gates and Woz, for example."

"Who is Woz?"

"Steve Wozniak. The co-founder of Apple Computers. How could you possibly not know that?"

"I thought Steve Jobs was the Apple guy."

"Jobs is in the public eye more, but Steve Wozniak came up with the first Apple computer. He's an inventor type like I am. Following their example, I hired an extrovert to deal with sales and marketing while I went off to the lab and focused on product development."

"You said your Dad was a geek, but I'm thinking the pocket protector doesn't fall far from the nerdy tree."

Riley laughed. "I suppose, but I draw the line at pocket protectors. I mean, even when I was a kid I knew they looked ridiculous. But my dad would tell you in a stern voice that after you've had a pen leak all over your favorite shirt, you see the utility of that little plastic thing."

I smiled at the idea of Riley and his father arguing about pocket protectors. Somehow it was all too easy to imagine. "I think I'll like your dad, assuming we ever find him."

"Good thing, because for all we know, he might be your stepdad."

On that conversation-ending note, we got ready for bed. My relationship with my own father was nonexistent. He'd walked out when I was a little girl, leaving Mom to raise me alone. She'd taken countless jobs and gone back to school. Mom was amazing. It took her years to get her PhD, but she did it. I had almost no memory of my father, except for the sound of his voice fighting with my mother.

After those guys attacked me I'd felt exhausted, but now I couldn't sleep. Lying next to Zelda in the dark, I stared at the ceiling, wide awake. We were no closer to finding Mom and the more I learned about the sensory problems Riley and I both had, the stranger it seemed.

Unfortunately, it was also possible that we'd end up killing each other before we found our parents. We had wildly different personalities and had been tiptoeing around each other being polite, because we were stuck with each other. But like any Thanksgiving dinner with lots of relatives in close quarters, people can remain on their best behavior for only so long. Eventually one or the other of us was going to lash out. Probably me.

Somehow, my visit to Alpine Grove to see Mom had turned into a bizarre road trip. In the last forty-eight hours, I'd learned a few things about Dean, quite a lot about Riley, but next to nothing about Mom. I felt guilty that I wasn't doing more to try to find her. But what else could I do?

In the darkness, I listened to Riley's and Zelda's even breathing. Why was I with them? How had I let that happen? And now Riley was making choices without consulting me. He said I made him feel better so he wanted to have me around. And then he decided without asking to head for Nevada and visit a circus in the middle of nowhere. How could that possibly be the best option for finding Mom? We should have searched Dean's house or interviewed people. Why were we going to Nevada?

I scowled at the darkness. Dean had been kidnapped and it was entirely possible Mom had been kidnapped too. What if Riley was kidnapping me? What if he was in on this whole thing and lying about everything? Maybe he was only pretending to help me. And here I was going along with my own kidnapping. I was such an idiot. But I certainly wasn't going to go without a fight.

I sat up in bed and Zelda made a snorting noise, lifting her head to give me a dirty look for waking her up. I threw my legs out from under the covers and Zelda leaped to the floor with a thump. I walked the two steps to the other bed where Riley was curled up on his side, facing away from me. As I thwacked him on the shoulder, I yelled, "Wake up!"

Riley bolted upright, slapping his palms on the mattress. "What's going on?"

"Are you kidnapping me?"

He rubbed his eyes with his fists and tilted his head to look up at me. "What are you talking about?"

"I realized that you're making all these decisions about where we're going and I've been going along with it. Are you kidnapping me?" I pointed my index finger in his face, so that it was practically touching his nose. "If you are and you know where my mother is, you need to tell me right now."

"What is wrong with you? Are you completely insane?"

"All of this could be an elaborate plot to kidnap me. You could be in on the whole thing." I shook my finger. "That's why we're going to Nevada isn't it?"

Riley got out of bed and glared down at me. "No, it's not. And for the record, you are the last person I'd ever *want* to kidnap."

"Then why didn't you talk to me about where we're going?"

"You were asleep, remember?" He spread his arms out wide. "And you would have disagreed and debated my rationale. I didn't want to have that argument, so it was a lot easier to let the sleeping woman stay asleep and keep driving."

"We should have done more investigating. Gone through Dean's house. Or done something." I put my hands on my hips. "But now we're in the middle of nowhere not doing *anything*."

"It's the middle of the night and you want to break into Dean's house? How could embarking on a life of crime possibly be a good idea?"

"It's better than *this*. I'm awake now, so tell me. What was your reason for dragging us here? You said you had a 'feeling' and I'm sorry, but that's not good enough."

Riley gestured toward the dog, who was staring at us with a concerned expression. "Zelda and I sniffed the breeze. We agreed that Dean had gone that way."

"You're saying you and your dog had a little chat? Who are you? Doctor Doolittle?"

"No. She was sniffing the air and her nose was pointed that way." He shrugged. "I kind of understood what she was getting at."

"You are oddly close to your dog."

"My overdeveloped sense of smell, as you call it, has given me some insight into the canine world view."

I sat down on the bed, suddenly exhausted again. "I suppose it would. Zelda is such a great name for her. I guess you named her after Zelda Fitzgerald, huh?"

"Legend of Zelda." At my blank stare, he added, "It's a video game."

"Oh."

Riley sat across from me. "Believe me when I say that I have no idea what's going on. I don't know who the guys in the gray suits are that took Dean."

"You could still be lying. How would I know?"

"My hand still hurts from hitting that guy." He raised a hand and flexed his fingers. "You know, when they punch the bad guys on TV it looks a lot less painful than it really is."

I laughed. "I think you might not be cut out for the whole kidnapping thing."

"I'm glad we cleared that up. Can we go back to sleep now?"

I nodded, crawled back under the covers, and stared at the ceiling again. I was serious when I told Riley that I felt better than I had at home. For the first time in quite a while, the little ache in my temple wasn't there. It had felt like having the tiniest twinges of the beginnings of a headache all the time. And now it was gone. Riley said he felt better too. I couldn't think of any reason he would have made that up or lied about it, so the only explanation was that he was telling the truth.

I squeezed my eyes shut. We were getting nowhere. Tomorrow I'd figure out what to do next. I had to.

Chapter 5

The Not-So-Great Show

The next morning we loaded ourselves into the Mustang and headed for the circus. Riley had grabbed a flyer that indicated the event would be held at a fairground about ten miles away. Zelda and I had reached a tacit agreement about riding in the passenger seat and she happily jumped into the back of the Mustang when I tilted the front seat forward for her.

When we arrived, huge white circus tents were spread out on the ground and people were bustling around getting them set up. The first show wasn't until the following evening, and presumably it took a while to put up those monster tents. The canvas did look similar to what I saw in my vision with Mom. Maybe she *was* here. At that tiny glimmer of hope, I gave myself a mental slap. It made no sense for her to be here because it was a hallucination, for heaven's sake. How had I let Riley talk me into this?

We got out of the car and Riley clipped a leash onto Zelda's collar. Walking through the circus while it was being set up turned out be an experience full of unusual sights and smells. I glanced at Riley. He was wearing sunglasses, so I couldn't see his eyes, but his face was even more pale than usual. So much for feeling better.

Elephants are huge and stinky, and although I hadn't figured out where they were yet, their pungent odor preceded them. If the circus animals smelled this bad to me, Riley had to be miserable. At least the cotton candy machines weren't running yet. That sickly sweet smell mixed in with greasy funnel cakes and popcorn would probably push him over the edge.

A large faded sign was being erected that said we were enjoying "Hector's Traveling Big Top Circus," which led me to the next obvious question: who was Hector? Maybe he was the guy I needed to talk to about Mom.

As we walked along, it became apparent that the circus had been traveling for quite a while. Perhaps many decades. The paint on the carnival and concession stands was peeling and tired. And once we got closer, it was obvious the white canvas of the tent wasn't entirely white. It had greasy dirt along the bottom edges and suspicious brown stains that looked like they had been scrubbed at unsuccessfully.

At night the dingy run-down feel of Hector's circus might be obscured by flashing lights and noisy distractions, but in the crisp morning sun, all the glitzy showmanship was absent, so it was just dirty and depressing. Unlike a lot of kids, I'd never had aspirations of joining the circus. Good thing, since it looked like a lot of long hours and backbreaking labor were spent setting up and taking down the show.

An extremely short man wearing a top hat was jabbing at the air and shouting profanities. He seemed to be having an issue with a bee that was buzzing around him. With a final shriek, he pointed his finger and motioned angrily at the sky.

A man in faded denim overalls, who was standing near the guy in the top hat, yelled, "Cut that out, Myron!" He slapped his hand over his upper arm. "That hurts."

Riley pulled his sunglasses down on his nose and peered over them at me. "That was weird. Did Myron get a bee to sting that guy in the overalls?"

I grimaced. "I don't know. Whatever it was, it hurt. Maybe it's some magic trick they're practicing."

"I haven't been to the circus in a while, but I'm pretty sure Ringling Brothers wouldn't condone that kind of language."

"Maybe Hector runs an x-rated circus."

Riley shoved his sunglass back up on his nose. "I don't want to think about what you mean by that."

"I think we need to find Hector. Even though he's undoubtedly going to think I'm a complete loon, I want to talk to him. In the unlikely event that anyone at this circus knows where our parents are, it's him. And then when he tells me he has no idea what I'm talking about, we can leave."

"Fine by me." He pointed toward the tent. "Let's split up. I want to get as far away from the animal pens as possible."

"I figured you might." I did a backward wave as I turned to walk toward the trailers that were located beyond the vast expanse of white canvas.

The animals were back there too, all crowded together in their stalls and cages. As I got closer, I was thinking Riley had made the right choice, going the other way. The entire area had a dusty, earthy smell mixed in with a whole lot of manure. Mucking out stalls and cleaning up excrement was probably a full-time job for somebody. The potent aroma hung in the air, so it smelled like a the inside of a gigantic porta-potty that hadn't been emptied in a long time.

People of every possible shape and size were milling around next to the trailers. One extremely cute guy seemed to be watching me intently. I flashed a flirty smile at him, which wasn't reciprocated, so I quickly glanced behind me, where a small man teetering on stilts was heading right for me. I quickly moved out of the way and he thumped by. Yikes.

As I approached the cute guy, I went through a mental checklist evaluating why he was so attractive. Athletic build with muscles in all the right places. Check. Broad shoulders. Check. Dark blonde hair with sun-kissed bronze highlights. Check. Lovely warm honey-brown eyes. Check.

All of my analysis didn't go unnoticed, and Mr. Lovely Eyes smiled at me this time. He moved his hand slightly, encouraging me to come to him. No problem. I had questions, and interviewing him was certainly more appealing than trying to talk to the guy on the stilts.

I walked up and put out my hand. "Hi, I'm Meg."

Mr. Lovely Eyes took my hand in both of his and began caressing the tops of my fingers in a strangely erotic way. Maybe it wasn't erotic at all, but I hadn't had a date in so long, how would I know? Clearly, I needed to get out more.

He focused his attention on my eyes and said in a velvety voice, "Meg, it's a pleasure to meet you. My name is Lars. What brings you here? The show is not until later."

I reluctantly pulled my hand away slowly. His hands were so soft. I tried to focus on something other than the arousing sensation of his touch. How was I going to explain this? "I, well, I'm looking for someone. Several people, actually."

"We see many people at the show." He took my hand again and I was transfixed by his voice saying, "Can you describe the people you seek?"

I cleared my throat, belatedly making an attempt to remain professional. I needed to interview this guy, but Lars's thumb was caressing my palm. Along with his liquid voice, the teasing way his thumb moved was utterly distracting and compelling. I said, "Well, one person is my mother, Ellen Jennings. She's a little shorter than I am. Gray curly hair. Another is uh, Tim…Tim O'Shea. I don't know what he looks like, except for one crummy photograph. The other person is a man named Dean. I've seen him. He's, well, um, he's got wavy kind of light brown hair and he's good looking. He might be in a dark blue van with guys wearing gray suits and sunglasses."

Lars narrowed his eyes. "That's interesting."

My focus returned to the sensation of his hand in mine and I gripped it more tightly. "Wait! What do you mean *interesting*? Define interesting. Have you seen my mother? I really need to find her."

Lars tugged on my hand gently and I stepped forward so I was close enough that I could feel his warmth. My heart was hammering in my chest and I looked up at him questioningly. What was happening to me? It hadn't been *that* long since I'd had sex, had it?

He tilted his head as if he were silently responding to my question with one of his own. "Perhaps I can help. I don't remember a woman, but I may have seen the van with the men. I remember that because it's unusual in an area like this to see suits and ties."

"You have seen them then!" I lurched in excitement, stumbled, and mumbled "Oops, sorry."

Lars put an arm around me to keep me from falling into the dirt. Having his arms around me was so overwhelming that I looked at him mutely, stunned into silence.

He inclined his head. "Why are you here?"

"I told you. I'm looking for my mother."

"Why would you think she is at our circus?"

The intensity of his lovely eyes was unnerving and I stammered, "I um, well, we, had a feeling. But you said you saw the guys in the suits!"

"I did."

Our gazes locked and I couldn't look away. His eyes were mesmerizing. We simultaneously moved together and our lips met. Inexplicably, I found myself passionately kissing this stranger at the circus in front of a beat-up trailer. Even as his warm lips moved across mine and I threw my arms around his neck, it was as if part of me was standing to one side, shaking a finger and saying, "What is *wrong* with you?" But the other part of me didn't care.

A few unbelievably pleasurable moments later, we released one another. I pulled my blouse back down and ran my hand over my mussed hair. What was the deal with this guy? It was not my style to fling myself at men and I had no idea what was going on, but it was way beyond time for me to focus. "So, um, as I was saying, do you remember when you saw the men and the van?"

"Yesterday evening. It was parked here at the fairgrounds when we arrived. A number of people were here. It was not unusual. Sometimes people like to watch us unload."

I looked around. "So you're saying the van isn't here now?"

"No, I believe they left last night."

Crap. Another dead end. But after making out with the guy, I couldn't just say, "Oops, thanks, gotta go," and run off. Instead, I went with safe small talk. "So what do you do here at the circus?"

"I'm a clown."

I touched my fingers to my lips. "But you *can't* be a clown. You don't look like a clown."

"Clowns don't always wear makeup, you know." He pulled a balloon out of his pocket, blew it up, tied the end, and with three quick twists turned it into a dog.

"Okay, I believe you. You're a clown." I pressed my hand to my stomach as I stepped back, away from him, feeling slightly queasy. "Nice meeting you, but I've got to go now."

"It has been most enjoyable." He handed me the balloon animal. "I hope I'll see you at the show."

"Yes, definitely. Wouldn't miss it." I waved the balloon slightly as I turned to leave. It was time to find Riley and get out of here.

~

It was difficult for me to not run away from Lars, but I wanted to retain at least a shred of dignity, so I sedately strolled away from the trailers and back to where I'd last seen Riley and Zelda. Maybe they'd had better luck finding Hector than I had.

I was more than a little freaked out at my reaction to Lars. After he touched my hand, it was almost as if I'd been hypnotized. I stopped and looked at the tent, realizing where I was. Circuses were full of magicians, psychics, gypsies, and who knows what else. But were clowns hypnotists? Could you hypnotize someone with your thumb? These were questions I never would have been asking a few months ago. My life had taken a decidedly bizarre turn and it was getting weirder all the time.

As I walked, I lamented the loss my ordinary life as a reporter and the days when my thoughts were focused on my job. Who I was interviewing. My next byline. Squabbles with editors. I missed the camaraderie of the newsroom and going out to lunch with my colleagues, discussing the latest idiotic comment from the mayor or the nuances of some absurd zoning war among landowners who had been fighting for years. All of that felt so far away now.

I walked around the huge tent canvas, which was still lying on the ground. Although many people seemed to be scurrying about, the tent remained flat. I spotted Zelda's furry white form in the distance sitting next to Riley, who was talking to someone juggling apples. A lithe trapeze artist, who had a long black ponytail and was clad in a pink leotard, stopped to join them and I could see Riley laugh as she grabbed one of the apples out of the air from the juggler.

I slowed my pace so I could subtly eavesdrop on the conversation. Riley was describing his father, who was apparently in his sixties, five foot eleven with gray hair, brown eyes, glasses, and a bit of a beer gut. That could describe half the older men I'd ever met, but I wasn't one to talk, since the description I gave Lars of Tim O'Shea was even more sparse.

Even worse, I couldn't describe my own father at all. I had one good memory of the man, but part of me wondered if what I remembered was from a photograph, not real life. In the photo we were sitting on a dock at a lake and my father had his arm around me. The lingering image in my imagination and dreams was like a Hallmark card. It was a glorious sunny day, and I felt warm, safe, and content in my little-girl world. To me, my father was perpetually young, locked in time, with dark hair and horn-rimmed glasses.

Shaking off my uncharacteristic toddle down memory lane, I walked up to the group as the trapeze artist and juggler were resolutely denying having ever seen Riley's father. The juggler grabbed all the apples and turned to look at me. Zelda stood up and leaned on me, requesting some affection. I gave her head a few strokes and said, "Hi, my name is Meg and I'm a, uh, friend of Riley's."

Riley said, "Maybe my stepsister, but we're not sure."

I glared at him. "Did Riley tell you that we're looking for my mother too?"

The two circus performers nodded their assent and my subsequent interrogation led to a big fat nothing. They claimed to know zip about the van, guys in suits, or Dean. After listening to all the denials, I ran out of steam and we said our good-byes.

As Riley, Zelda, and I walked back to the car, I suggested lunch. "I'm tired of crackers. Maybe we could get some real food and compare notes."

"Did you find out anything?"

"I'd rather not talk about it here."

"I bet I know why." Riley grinned widely at me like a little kid bursting to tell a secret. "Jebediah, the juggler, said you were canoodling with a clown. I'm guessing he's the one who gave you the balloon."

"Who uses the word canoodling?"

"Jugglers, apparently. I almost died laughing. Way to get over your clown fear. Was it the guy going through our garbage last night?"

I stopped and put my hands on my hips. "No, it was not. His name is Lars and, um, it was weird."

"Uh-oh. I don't want to hear this, do I?"

"Probably not, but I'd like to go back to the motel and check in with my job. Lars invited me to the show later."

Riley chuckled, "Well, we wouldn't want to disappoint *Lars* now, would we?"

"Shut up."

Over lunch I was able to satiate my need for more substantial food. The truth was that living on sandwiches, vegetable sticks, and crackers wasn't going to cut it. If I didn't score a few real meals, I'd end up with an overwhelming urge to devour an entire box of donuts or mini-eclairs. It was far better for me to eat a normal lunch now to avoid an act of extreme gluttony later.

While I chowed down and watched Riley pick at his typically odd collection of side dishes, I described my interlude with Lars. It was more than a little embarrassing, but Riley managed to keep his snickering to a minimum, which was a relief.

I still couldn't quite believe that Lars had seen the dark blue van. It was possible that he was only saying that so I would jump into his trailer with him. The unfortunate thing was that it almost worked. Now I was going to have erotic dreams about sexy clowns and balloon animals for weeks. How disturbing.

Riley was more convinced than I was that we were on the right track. He thought maybe we'd find Mom or the guys in suits at the show later, but I had my doubts.

After lunch we returned to the motel and Riley went off with Zelda on another one of their marathon walks. I was glad to be rid of them for a while because I wanted to talk to my boss alone. I felt so much better today that I wanted to try to convince him that they should take me back after I found Mom. The fact that my medical leave was so indefinite bothered me, and I wanted to know that I could get my job back when I was deemed healthy again. I'm not good with uncertainty, and having my job up in the air made me feel antsy.

I sat down on the bed and stared at the telephone. As usual, Riley's clothes were strewn all over the place, and I thought again of the lovely pristine hotels I'd stayed at back in DC. What I wouldn't do for a foil-wrapped chocolate on my pillow right now.

With a sigh, I picked up the telephone and dialed the familiar number of the newsroom and asked to be connected to my boss, Leonard Olson, aka Leo.

His gruff voice greeted me and I said, "Hey Leo. I wanted to find out how everyone was doing."

"Good to hear from you, Meg. How are you feeling?"

"I'm great. That's what I wanted to talk to you about. I feel so much better and I'm thinking that I should be able to return to work soon. I have a little thing I need to take care of here related to my mother, but I'm looking forward to coming back to work."

"Well, I guess there's no easy way to say this, but you won't be coming back. I tried leaving a message yesterday, but the number you gave me for your Mom's house wasn't in service. The newspaper has been sold to Archetypal Media. I'm being laid off and so are you."

"What? You can't be serious!" I'd dealt with Archetypal indirectly and my stomach roiled at the notion of that company owning the paper.

"They're cutting back and consolidating. Instead of having a newspaper for each county, it's regional now. We're toast. They're gonna spend our salaries on developing some pretty new web site."

"A web site? That's ridiculous. I don't know what to say." I rested my forehead on my palm. "How can they do that? What am I going to do?"

"I'm sorry Meg, but I know you'll find another job. Maybe you can learn some of that web stuff. Go all high tech."

"But I love journalism."

"I know. If you need a reference, let me know." He paused. "I, uh, won't mention the medical stuff, you know."

"What are you going to do?"

"Retire. I've been in the news game for forty years and I'm looking forward to spending more time working on all the 'honey dos' Mrs. O has been nagging me about since forever."

I laughed. "She must be thrilled."

"Yeah, she's been on me to retire for five years at least. Good luck to you, Meg. I'll miss your enthusiasm."

"Thanks Leo. Good luck to you too."

I set down the receiver and flopped back on the bed. Ever since I'd been a little girl, I'd wanted to be a reporter. With that phone call, my work life as I knew it had ended.

~

By the time Riley and Zelda returned from their walk, I'd had a good long pity party, cried a little, and eaten another row of saltines. Good thing Riley bought the jumbo-sized box.

With a snort, Zelda jumped up on the bed and laid down next to me, sniffing around looking for crumbs. I stroked the fur on her back. "Sorry Zelda, I'm afraid I was pretty thorough."

Riley sat on the other bed and leaned forward to look at my face. "What happened to you?"

"Nothing." I threw a dirty sock at him. "Keep your stuff on your own side of the room."

"Is that what's bothering you?"

"You're a slob."

"I thought you were checking in with work."

"I have no work now. I got laid off." I wiped my eye and looked at the smear of mascara on my index finger. "I'm officially unemployed."

"Welcome to the club. Think of it as career freedom." His mouth curved into a smile. "Now you can ponder what's next instead of what you've left behind."

"But I don't *want* to," I whined. "I loved that job."

"After we find our parents, you can focus on finding a better one."

"The news industry is changing. I'm not sure I'll be able to find another job as a reporter." I sat up and wiped my eyes again. "I guess we should get ready to go back to the circus."

"I'm thinking I should be the one to talk to Lars tonight, since he's less likely to hit on me. Well maybe. I hope not anyway."

"He is gorgeous, but you can always tell him you have a girlfriend."

Riley made a wry face. "I suppose I should call her again. Yeah, well, maybe tomorrow. Or the day after."

Crying didn't do much for a girl's appearance, so I got up and headed for the bathroom. Once I'd pulled myself together, washed my face, and repaired my makeup disaster, we got back in the Mustang for the return trip to the circus.

When we arrived, the tents were up, carnival music was blaring, and crowds were milling around or waiting in line for tickets. All of the performers were in their full circus regalia and sequins and feathers were everywhere. I'd undoubtedly get to see Lars in his clown makeup, which was a thought that made me feel mildly ill again. Maybe I shouldn't have eaten so many crackers.

Riley instructed Zelda to stay in the car and we walked into the fray. A clown walked by me wearing heavy white makeup that made him look as if he had a porcelain mask. He had the classic huge red mouth, heavy black eyeliner, and orange hair. Clad in gigantic shoes, a hideous striped shirt, and baggy pants with red suspenders, he looked like the poster boy for clowns. Bozo had nothing on this guy.

I tried not to shrink away, but moved closer to Riley, who glanced down at me. "You're not quite over the whole clown thing, are you?"

"I hope that wasn't Lars. I'm going to have nightmares about this. I'm sure of it."

"At least it might keep you away from McDonald's. I think Ronald and the Big Macs of the world are safe for the time being."

I shoved Riley's shoulder. "You're hilarious. Let's find Lars or Hector. They've got to be here somewhere. I'm not sure I can face staying through the whole show though."

A performer in a multicolored jumpsuit walked by and Riley said, "Here we are with clowns to the left and jokers to the right. It's like the song."

"And I'm stuck here with you."

"Well yeah, that too."

We continued around the tents and toward the back, where the trailers were. A few clowns tried to give us directions back to the line for tickets to the show. In response, we asked about Hector and Lars.

I grabbed Riley's arm to get his attention and slow him down. "Lars is over there. See the guy with the light brown hair."

"He is hot. For a clown, I mean."

"I'm told they don't always wear makeup."

Riley chuckled. "I can see that."

I moved my hand down to clasp Riley's. "Pretend we're a couple."

"You've *got* to be kidding me."

"This guy has a weird effect on me. Don't let him touch me." I yanked on Riley's hand and looked up into his face. "I'm serious."

"All right, sweetums. Whatever you say."

I reached over with my other hand to give Riley's skinny arm a fierce squeeze as we approached Lars. A trapeze artist gracefully twirled away as we walked up.

"Hi Lars," I said. "This is my friend Riley. We were hoping we could ask you more about the guys in the van."

Lars went to reach for my hand, but I backed away, continuing to clutch Riley's arm firmly. Riley looked down at me, widened his eyes, and silently mouthed, "Ow."

"I'm glad you could make it to the show," Lars said.

Riley said, "Have you seen the dark blue van you mentioned to Meg? Or the men in the suits?"

Lars turned toward the parking area and pointed. "I believe the van is parked over there. I saw the men go into the big top."

"Where is Hector's trailer?" I asked.

Lars said, "Down that way. It has a gold star with his name on the door."

"Great. Thank you. We've got to go," I said, dragging Riley away.

"Perhaps we can meet after the show," Lars said to my retreating form.

I kept walking. Riley shook his arm and hand free of mine, and I looked up at him. "Sorry."

Riley moved his arm and splayed his fingers. "Way to have a death grip. I guess he really got to you."

At the sound of people yelling, I slowed my pace so I could eavesdrop. "That guy in the big hat just said something about people disappearing."

Riley didn't say anything in response and we stopped to listen. Two clowns in checkered pants with suspenders were shoving each other. One had on a dusty beat-up top hat and the other was wearing a bowler. They were furious about something.

The clown in the bowler said, "Do you want to end up like Nate? I don't. We have to do what they say."

"Lars was trying to get the woman, but it didn't work. She split before I could grab her and zap her with the needle," the other clown retorted.

I grabbed Riley's hand. "I think he's talking about me. And needles! I hate needles."

Riley shook his head, but didn't say anything. The clown in the bowler shouted, "Well, George didn't do much better with the skinny guy. You're all a bunch of incompetents."

I squeezed Riley's hand. "We need to leave."

"I think you might be right."

We made a hasty about-face and I looked over my shoulder. Both clowns seemed to realize that we'd overheard them and started after us. I increased my pace and Riley looked behind him. "Run!" he said, and I did.

When you run through a circus, you discover that it's filled with obstacles and people, which is handy if you're running away trying to lose someone—or multiple angry clowns. We zig-zagged through the crowds of people and performers and ducked behind a huge painted wooden cart that appeared to be designed to be pulled by draft horses, or maybe elephants.

The two clowns ran by and once I could catch my breath, I whispered to Riley, "What do we do now?"

"We have to get to the parking lot and make sure Zelda is all right. And I have an idea." He motioned toward the fence. "Let's go that way and circle around the perimeter of the fairgrounds."

I wasn't sure what he was up to, but it wasn't like I had any better options, so I followed him. We tried to look nonchalant, meandering toward the fence. Once we were close to the rows of cars, Riley stopped me. "Do you have anything like a bobby pin or a ballpoint pen in your purse? I need something pointy."

I stopped and we crouched down behind a rusty beige Buick Skylark, so I could rummage through my purse. "Here's a pen."

"Let's find that van."

We walked through the sea of cars and finally spotted the van. I raised my eyebrows at Riley. "Do you suppose it's possible that Dean could still be in there?"

"I doubt it, but let's go up behind it and peek in the back windows."

"And get the license plate number."

"That too."

We took a circuitous route through the parking lot, attempting to conceal ourselves behind big pickup trucks and Suburbans whenever possible. We made our way to the row behind where the van was parked.

Riley held out his arm in front of me. "I'll be right back."

"It figures. There's no license plate. That's just perfect. Why haven't these losers been pulled over? Aren't there cops in this godforsaken place?"

Riley put his index finger to his lips and stooped down low, making his way to the back of the van. He stood up, looked in the back window, then crouched down next to the left rear tire. The van sank and tilted down toward the left. He repeated the process for the right rear tire, then scuttled back to me and said, "Dean's not inside, but I think we should get out of here."

I nodded my assent and we hustled toward the Mustang. When we got to the car, Zelda was thrilled to see us and even jumped into the backseat without any encouragement from me.

Riley started the car and turned to me. "Now what?"

"I'm not sure." I shrugged, "But I have to say I hate circuses even more now."

"I'm starting to share your opinion. This is definitely *not* the greatest show on earth."

~

The Mustang hauled down the highway and when we got back to the hotel room, we hurriedly started packing up everything. This was déjà vu all over again, and my thoughts raced as I packed up toiletries and threw clothes into my suitcase. As soon as we asked about anything, the guys in suits turned up. I did not have any interest in going anywhere with them, but if we kept running away, how were we ever going to find Mom?

Once everything was out of the room and in the trunk of the car, I waited in the Mustang with Zelda while Riley checked out. He returned and drove around the building to the exit.

As we idled, I said, "What are you waiting for? Let's go."

"Which way are we going? That way is toward the circus and Nevada. This way is the direction we came from."

"I vote for anywhere clowns are not."

"All right." He turned and gunned the car into hyper-speed again. Riley had a lead foot like no one I'd ever met .

Glad that I couldn't see the speedometer, I pulled a map out of the glove compartment to distract myself. It whipped in my face as I evaluated our position. Where were we going? I tapped Riley's hand on the gearshift to get his attention and pointed at the map. "Are we going back to Alpine Grove? Gleasonville? What does your sniffer think this time?"

Riley momentarily glanced away from the road at me. "Nothing in particular, but I want to stop somewhere and call my brother. It's possible my father might have talked to him."

"Haven't you been in touch with him?"

"We don't talk much."

"But he's your brother!"

"You're an only child, aren't you?"

"Yes, so what?" I folded up the map. "I'm starting to think that our parents might be hurt or dead."

Riley jerked his attention back to me. "What? Why are you saying that? Did you have some sort of vision again?"

"No, but those guys are out to get us. What they said…I mean, they were talking about jabbing me. You don't talk about *needles* unless you mean business."

"I'm guessing the concept of clowns with needles has tapped into a new level of phobia."

"Maybe, but I'm a little more disturbed that Lars is in on this whole thing. Whatever it is."

Riley smirked. "I guess lover clown isn't so lovable after all."

"That's not what I meant. I was thinking about what you said before. All the odd things that have happened relate to senses. Your sense of smell, my vision, Dean's hearing, and now Lars's bizarre sense of touch."

"Making out with Lars wasn't just because you're horny?"

"Excuse me, but my horniness factor isn't the issue here. I'm not normally in the habit of throwing myself at random men."

"Or clowns, I take it."

"I think you're missing the point. All of this relates to senses that have intensified in some way. What Lars was able to do was not normal."

Riley downshifted as we approached a tiny town. "I gotta tell you that I'd sure rather have Lars's problem than mine. Having women throw themselves at me sounds a lot better than not being able to eat."

"What if these people are after us *because* of our problems?"

"How would they know?" Riley waved a hand toward me. "Sure, I look sick, but that doesn't mean anything. You thought I had cancer. And you don't look any different from anyone else. Quite robust and healthy, in fact."

"Thanks, I guess." Was he using robust as a euphemism for another less-flattering adjective? "What if they are trying to kill us off? Maybe they think we're aliens or something. It's like the X-Files!"

"You can't be serious."

"Hey, you are the one who said some things are hard to explain. Like I said, I'm worried Mom is in serious danger or even dead."

Riley didn't say anything, and given the expression on his face, he obviously didn't want to explore this line of thinking anymore. I sat and gazed out at the desert landscape, lost in my swirling cauldron of distressing thoughts.

We came upon another tiny town that had a gas station and Riley pulled off the highway. I was feeling a little crispy-crunchy from the dry desert wind, so I got out to stretch my legs and dig through the trunk to get some sunscreen out of my suitcase.

After filling up the car, Riley parked the Mustang and took Zelda for a walk in the scrubby field behind the station. When they returned, he told Zelda to get in the car and I waited with her while he used the pay phone to call his brother.

From afar, I could see various emotions alter the expression on his face during their conversation. He appeared to go from annoyance to anger to resignation before finally hanging up the receiver.

He returned to the car and started it. "Talking to Bubba is always such a treat."

I giggled, "Your brother isn't seriously named Bubba, is he?"

"Technically, he's my half-brother, and his name is Robert or Bob. But the story goes that I couldn't say brother when I was little, so I called him Bubba. When you meet him, you'll see that it suits him."

"I'm going to meet him? Since when? Did you make another decision without my input? You know how that pisses me off."

"It's more of a suggestion, because I don't particularly want to visit my brother either. But he might have information that could be useful."

"Where does he live?"

"Las Vegas." Riley reached over my lap for the glove compartment and pulled out the map. "So, we need to go down here, cross over, then hit Interstate 15. After that, it's a straight shot to Vegas, baby."

"Why do you want to go there? What did Bubba say?"

"That Dad left a document for me. Bubba claims he can't read it because it's written in, and I quote, 'that stupid secret code crap you used to do.'"

"I guess Bubba never learned the hieroglyphics."

"Nope."

"Are you sure this is a good idea?"

"Not at all. Do you have a better one?"

I shook my head and folded up the map. "Viva Las Vegas."

Chapter 6

The Rest Stop is History

When you cross the wide open desert in the middle of the night, you experience a unique type of inky darkness. No street lights, no dwellings, no nothing. We were surrounded by velvety black night, unbroken except for the narrow tunnel of light created by the Mustang's high beams and the stars sparkling above us. Riley seemed lost in thought and focused on driving, which was undoubtedly a good thing. Hitting an animal out here in the deepest darkest desert wouldn't do us or the Mustang any good. It could be years before anyone found our shriveled dusty bodies.

Riley said, "You're not having a problem over there, are you?"

"I'm fine. Just sitting here watching the emptiness go by. Why do you ask?"

"You haven't said anything in hours and you're never this quiet for this long. I'm guessing you're worrying about something that you'll yell at me for later."

"No, I'm not, and gee, aren't you in a snotty mood? It just feels lonely out here in the ultra dark."

"I suppose, but check out the stars. They're amazing."

I leaned my head back and looked straight up. "I've never seen the Milky Way before. Too much pollution in Maryland, I guess."

I stared at the stars for a while and then closed my eyes. The next thing I knew, we were pulling into an all-night roadside cafe that obviously catered to truckers. The parking lot was full of semis and the sign advertised hot coffee and air conditioning. I sat up again and looked at Riley. "Everything okay?"

"Zelda needs a walk and I need coffee. Maybe while I walk Zee, you could ask about places to stay."

I went into the coffee shop and sat in a booth with sticky black plastic seats that had been repaired with gray duct tape. All the long-haul truckers must have been hard on this place. The waitress came over and I ordered up two coffees, and since Riley wasn't around to whine about it, some nice greasy snack food for me.

The waitress informed me that Las Vegas had a few pet-friendly places to stay, but most of them were off the Strip and not necessarily in the best areas. I sipped my coffee and thought about my safety or lack of it. I could get mugged, chased by clowns, and kidnapped all in one evening. What was my life coming to?

Riley sat down across from me and put some cream into his mug of coffee. He took a sip and grimaced. "This is vile."

"Drink up. Options are limited at three in the morning in the middle of nowhere."

"What are you eating?"

"Onion rings. Want one?"

"No."

"You're no fun."

Riley took another sip of coffee and set down the mug. "How are you feeling? Like screaming- and hallucination-wise?"

"Okay, I guess." I closed my eyes for a second and opened them. "Well, to be honest, the little ache is back in my head again. Nothing big though. No fantasmagoric light shows or anything."

"Interesting. I guess it's not just me. The smell of those onions makes me want to throw up."

"The waitress said that we might be able to find a place to stay with Zelda, but that it would be off the Strip."

Riley pulled out his wallet, threw a twenty on the table, and grabbed his mug. "Could you pay them when you're done? I'm going to get this coffee in a to-go cup. I've got to get out of here. I'll be in the car with Zee."

"Okay." I looked up at him as he stood up. I could see why Erin didn't find Riley a real fun date anymore.

After I finished my rings, paid, and got the names of a couple of motels, I returned to the car. Zelda was curled up in the backseat. Riley had the front seat reclined and was reaching behind him to pet her.

We took off and when we reached the outskirts of Vegas, we found the sketchy motel that the waitress had mentioned. The room smelled like an ashtray and I wondered if Nevada was the lung-cancer capital of the world. The room wasn't the only thing that was disgusting. Everyone we ran into was smoking or had recently finished smoking, so they carried a noxious cloud around them, like Pig Pen in the *Peanuts* comic strips.

The plethora of bad odors didn't seem to be improving Riley's disposition either. By the time we were finished unloading the Mustang, Riley looked almost as bad as he had when I met him in Alpine Grove. I put my hand on his forearm. "Are you okay?"

"I'm tired," he mumbled as he shook his arm free.

Clearly, Riley was not in a mood to talk, so I retreated into the bathroom. When I came out, Riley was in bed and had curled himself under the covers facing the wall away from me. Zelda was lying alongside his back, presumably providing moral support.

I fell asleep almost as soon as my head hit the pillow. When I woke up, the room was stuffy and Riley was crouched down next to the air conditioning unit under the window. Harsh sunlight was threading around the heavy brown drapes.

I sat up. "What's wrong with it?"

"Bad compressor. It's toast." He stood up. "Let's make some calls and check out. I'll see if we can crash with Bubba. This place is too disgusting even for me, and Zelda and I stayed at some pretty nasty fleabag motels on our road trip."

"I want to try to call a few places where Mom used to go. Maybe someone has seen her. She could have flown back home, for all I know."

"I thought Alpine Grove was her home now."

"What if she and your father broke up? Maybe she left." I turned my palms toward the ceiling. "How would we know?"

"She would have left you a message."

"True, but my calls to retrieve messages from my answering machine have been unsatisfying. I can't believe she'd disappear without saying anything. I mean, come on. No message? She had to know I'd be frantic."

Riley sat down on the bed. "I know. I should call some of my dad's friends too. It's been days now and I think all your worrying is rubbing off on me."

While I showered, Riley made calls and then I did the same while he showered. Many phone calls later, we had come up with absolutely nothing. No one had heard from our parents. Riley reported that his brother had okayed our visit, so our next stop was Casa de Bubba. It had to be better than this dump.

I jammed my toiletries into my suitcase. Laundry was going to become an issue soon. I'd brought warm clothes, thinking I'd be staying in Alpine Grove. The temperatures in the mountains were vastly different from those in the desert, and I hadn't thought to bring my summer wardrobe. With any luck, Bubba had a washer and dryer at his house.

Riley started loading the car again. I suspected that I wasn't the only one sick of all this loading and unloading. Being on the road was exhausting and constantly fretting about being kidnapped didn't help. We needed a break.

Feeling nosy when Riley got in the car, I asked, "So did you call Erin?"

"Talking to her was almost as much fun as talking to Bubba. Speaking of which, he works at night, so he'll be there at the apartment when we arrive. Get ready for extreme fraternal disagreement about pretty much everything."

"Well, you and I disagree about pretty much everything. Did you ever think that maybe it's you? He's your brother. How bad could it be?"

"You're about to find out."

~

I'd never been to Las Vegas, but like most people I'd seen pictures of all the glittery casinos and flashy signs on the Strip. As we drove into the city, I realized that most of the photographs I'd seen had been taken at night. In the starkness of daylight, Vegas seemed somehow faded. Treasure Island, the Bellagio, and the Luxor were all there, but without the sparkle of lights, they seemed a lot less glamorous and a lot more fake.

We bypassed the Strip and cruised toward the residential area where Bubba lived. Off the Strip, Vegas was even less glitzy and glamorous. Even the streets seemed bleached out by the relentless desert sun. With the palm trees and sandy desert soil, the non-touristy areas of Vegas looked a lot like Los Angeles, but without the ocean. And with a whole lot more slot machines and XXX-rated entertainment emporiums.

Like LA, there were upscale areas, suburban family neighborhoods, and significantly less desirable areas. Bubba lived in the latter. Riley pulled the Mustang into the parking lot of a nondescript beige stucco apartment complex and parked in one of the visitor spaces, which were not under a carport. If you wanted a covered spot to prevent extreme automotive paint oxidation, you needed to sign a lease.

Riley put up the convertible top, looking resigned to his fate. He put a leash on Zelda and said, "Let's skip unloading. It's possible we won't be here long."

"Bubba wouldn't throw you out, would he?"

"You never know. When I was a kid, he used to beat me up for no apparent reason."

"I doubt that. He probably had reasons." I gave Riley a dismissive wave. "You can be pretty annoying, you know."

Riley paused a moment to scowl at me, took off his sunglasses, and knocked on the door to apartment 4C.

A huge man opened the door and thrust his arms wide, "Riley, my man!" Bubba was as tall as Riley, but had to weigh twice as much. Although he wasn't overweight, he was an enormous specter of a human being with approximately fourteen million freckles that covered every inch of him. I stepped back out of the way as he enveloped Riley in a massive bear hug.

Zelda made a growly snorting noise and Bubba let go of Riley. He looked down at the dog. "You still have that mutt, I see."

"I'm sure Zelda is thrilled to see you again too," Riley said. He gestured toward me. "This is Meg, Ellen's daughter, who may or may not be your stepsister."

I shot my hand out to shake hands before Bubba could pounce on me with the hugging routine and suffocate me. "It's nice to meet you."

He shook my hand, then yanked me toward him for a hug. "Hey sis! It's good to know you. I always wanted a sister."

I extracted myself, stepped back, and ran a palm over my hair. "Thank you for letting us visit."

"C'mon in!" Bubba said as he stepped aside so we could get through the doorway.

Bubba's apartment was sparsely furnished, but sloppiness appeared to be an O'Shea family trait, and the living room was strewn with remnants of meals and past social events. Old food containers and dirty clothes were scattered everywhere and thoughts of skittering roaches danced across my frontal cortex. The idea of sleeping in this rat hole made me shudder. It smelled like the inside of an old gym sock to me, which meant Riley had to be in sensory overload.

Zelda was more pleased than I was about the abundance of garbage and rammed her snout into a take-out container from a Chinese restaurant. Riley looked down at the dog. "Zee, stop that. *Sit.*"

With a deep canine sigh, Zelda did what she was told, but didn't take her eyes off of the enticing kung pao prize.

Bubba shoved some clothes aside and gestured toward the sofa. "Have a seat."

I perched on the edge of the plaid upholstery and folded my hands in my lap. "So how long have you lived in Las Vegas?"

Bubba turned a chair backwards, threw a leg over, and settled in. He was wearing shorts and I made a point to look at his face. I did not want to know if he was going commando or not. Given how much laundry was strewn about, the odds of him being out of tighty whities was pretty high.

"I moved here about five years ago," Bubba said. "I got sick of LA. Too expensive."

"There also was that little problem of Dad throwing you out," Riley added.

"He did not. I left 'cause I wanted to. The band broke up. It wasn't happening anymore and I needed a change of scene."

Riley didn't say anything, so I volunteered, "Are you in a band here?"

"No, I'm solo now. Being a head-banger was getting old, so I cut my hair," Bubba said. "I decided to switch to the classics."

He had done more than cut his hair. It was virtually shaved off in a crew cut that helped disguise his receding hairline. His hair was probably blonde or reddish, but there was so little of it, I wasn't sure.

"Do you play classic rock?" I asked.

"You know it. The King. I'm one of the understudies at the biggest Elvis show on the Strip."

I tried for a diplomatic polite smile, but it was difficult to envision Bubba dressed up as a gigantic incarnation of Elvis. But the fact was we *were* in Vegas. At least he wasn't a stripper. Or I hoped not anyway. I was already having enough trouble with clowns. The notion of a Giant Freckled Elvis stripping could make my already strange dreams even worse.

Riley said, "Do you have that note from Dad you mentioned? I'd like to see it."

Bubba settled his gaze on Riley and pointed an accusing finger at him. "Speaking of hair, man, what's with you? A ponytail? When was the last time you got a haircut? And you look like death. You were Mr. Uptight Nerd. What happened?"

"I've had some medical problems," Riley said.

"I thought you had megabucks. You can afford doctors. Can't they figure out what's wrong with you? You look like crap, bro," Bubba said.

"Thanks." Riley tightened his hold on Zelda's lead to keep her from creeping toward an old pizza box. "Have you been feeling all right?"

"I feel great! Never better. Hey, Dad asked me the same thing the last time I talked to him. Is he sick too? You're not contagious or anything, are you? Because the show must go on. I can't get sick or they'll replace me," Bubba said.

"It's nothing like that," Riley replied. "What, exactly, did Dad say to you?"

"He wondered if I had headaches or anything else funny going on. He called it 'unexplainable phenomena,' which I mean, come on, that's such a Dad thing to say. I thought maybe he was asking if I got the clap or something, but had to say it in some type of classier way. I mean, if you wanna know, the answer is no. I wear protection, you know."

This was far, far more than I wanted to know about Bubba's love life, although it was heartening that he was being cautious about his potential exposure to sexually transmitted diseases. But eww.

Riley looked down at Zelda, scratched his chin, and looked at me. "Well, Meg has had some unexplained phenomena, so I thought I'd ask. I'm glad you're all right."

"You mean, you got the clap?" Bubba said.

I practically shouted, "No!"

Riley made a half-hearted attempt to suppress a smile. "Well, she's assuming the clown was clean."

"I did *not* have sex with the clown," I retorted.

Bubba unsuccessfully stifled a guffaw. "Oh wow! You got it on with a clown? That's awesome."

"No, I did not." I stood up and put my hands on my hips. "It's a long story and by the way, my sex life is not the issue here. I believe your father was asking if you've felt odd in any way, maybe with one of your senses—like sight, hearing, smell, touch. That type of thing."

"My girlfriend says I eat too much." Bubba patted his stomach. "Does that count?"

"Meg means odd, as in does food taste different?" Riley asked.

Bubba looked confused. "Different than what?"

"Different than it used to taste or smell funny," I said as I sat back down.

"Man, I dunno, you guys. What's with the third degree anyway? Is this some geek research project or something?

Because I don't like being the guinea pig. I mean hey, Riley, I told you and Dad not to do that kind of thing ever again. That was seriously uncool."

"Never mind." Riley said. "Could you find that note from Dad?"

I averted my gaze as Bubba spread his legs even wider as he got up off the chair. He left the living room and disappeared into the bedroom. It occurred to me that his apartment had only one bedroom.

I nudged Riley. "Zelda is crawling toward that pizza box, which is pretty tricky. I didn't know dogs could crawl like that. Shouldn't you take it away from her?"

He reached for the box and set it on a stack of magazines on the coffee table. "Sorry Zee."

"Riley, do we have to stay here?"

"No."

"Thank goodness."

~

After Bubba found the letter and gave it to Riley, there was a knock on the door and a man wearing navy-blue coveralls arrived to fix Bubba's cable. To hear Bubba tell it, life without ESPN wasn't worth living. We stood around watching the cable guy for a while and once all sports channels were restored, the man left.

Although he was overjoyed to have his video input again, Bubba couldn't settle in and enjoy a game because he had to go to work. In addition to being an Elvis understudy, Bubba also worked nights at a casino. From his description, it sounded like Bubba's job was to wander the casino floor watching the roulette tables, supervising game play at the various tables and looking for evidence of cheating or breaking the casino's house rules. Given his size, I certainly wouldn't want to cheat. If he sat on me, he'd break me in half.

We said our good-byes, then Riley, Zelda, and I returned to the Mustang as Bubba drove off into the sunset.

I settled into the passenger seat. "So how come your Dad gave this note to Bubba and didn't mail it to you?"

"I asked him to."

"You knew about this before? How come you didn't say anything?"

"My lawyer has been dealing with my mail because I knew I'd be on a road trip all over the West. I figured I'd stop by Vegas before I went back to LA, but I ended up going to LA first and then Alpine Grove. After everything that happened, I forgot about it until Bubba said something."

I crossed my arms across my chest. "So are you going to read it?"

"I'm not feeling that great. Let's get out of Las Vegas and find someplace to stay outside of the city first." He swept a hand toward the glove compartment. "There's a booklet in there with a list of Motel 6 locations. They take dogs."

I leafed through the booklet and found a Motel 6 east of Vegas near the Arizona border and showed it to Riley. He nodded and kept driving, apparently intent on removing us from the City of Sin.

Because Bubba's bathroom was likely to be a hazardous waste zone, I'd opted to avoid using the facilities during our visit and by the time we'd been on the highway for half an hour, my bladder was starting to let me know that it was time for a bathroom break. The situation was becoming urgent and I badgered Riley for several minutes before he grumbled, "Fine, the sign says the next exit has a gas station."

Riley pulled up to the gas pumps and I hustled out of the car as quickly as possible. I ran around the side of the block building and discovered the ladies room was locked and I needed a key. I danced around in frantic fury for a couple of seconds before running back around the building to the front door. At my panicky request, a surly man with a goatee silently handed me a key attached to a piece of two-by-four with a piece of twine. Out here in the middle of nowhere, he had to be used to having women with urgent needs begging for that key.

I returned to the bathroom, unlocked the door, and took care of business. I felt so much better that I sat there for a moment in quiet relief. The bathroom had the gritty tan patina that old gas station restrooms get when they are cleaned only twice a year, but I didn't care. Any toilet was still better than dropping my drawers in the wide-open desert, which is filled with prickly cactus, scorpions, and snakes. I had enough problems and didn't need that level of additional excitement in my life. As I exited the ladies room, the door locked behind me with a heavy clicking noise.

I was starting back to the car when a massive blast from an explosion roared behind me. Windows shattered, and momentarily stunned, I turned to look at the pieces of glass raining down behind me, then sprinted away from the rushing smoke and fire. A shrill alarm blared, and a toilet seat flew through the air, landing in front of me. I jumped over it and ran for the Mustang.

Riley pointed and shouted something at me, but I couldn't hear what he said. I got in the car and we took off.

I looked behind me and saw smoke billowing out from the bathroom where I'd been moments before. The guy with the goatee stood out in front of the gas station waving his arms.

With a shaky hand, I held the key out to Riley. "I forgot to return it."

"That's not our only problem." He gestured toward the road behind us as we drove up the on-ramp to the highway. "It's the people in the blue van. They're behind us. What is going on? How did they find us again?"

"I don't know." I shook the wooden key chain at Riley. "Have they been following us this whole time?"

"I didn't see them, but I'm getting off the freeway."

"You just got *on* the freeway."

"I have an idea."

"Sometimes I hate your ideas. Where are we going?"

"North. Exit 90 takes us to Route 168, which connects to US93. There's nothing up there. Except in a couple hundred miles, Ely."

"Ely?"

"Yes. Ely, Nevada, which has a Motel 6."

"*This* is your idea?"

"Sorry, it's all I've got. Do you have a better idea?"

"No." I turned to look behind us. "I don't see them back there anymore."

"I might be exceeding the speed limit a little. If I can get around these trucks, we'll be harder to spot when we get off at the exit."

I slumped down in the seat, suddenly exhausted as the reality hit me that ten minutes ago, I'd almost been blown to tiny bits. "I think I'll close my eyes and try to pretend this isn't happening."

Listening to the now familiar purr of the Mustang's engine settled me down until something occurred to me. "Riley, what about Bubba?"

"What about him?"

"We visited him. What if these guys who are after us know where he lives? What if they go back for him too?"

Riley glanced at me. "We watched Bubba drive off in that rusty old Chevy Nova. No one was after him."

"But what if they circled back? We didn't say anything to him about what is going on."

"I suppose that's true." Riley sighed deeply. "Dammitall. Crap. All right. Fine. Up ahead, we can turn and take 93 south instead of north, get back on I-15, and go back to Vegas."

"It's the right thing to do. He's your brother. We have to tell him what's going on."

"I suppose you're right. But we were far enough out of Vegas that I was starting to feel better again. Maybe you're right and it's the smog in congested areas that makes me feel so sick."

"Yeah, my twinge was going away too." I pointed at an old metal building ahead of us in a dusty, weed-infested field. "Stop up there, so you can read the note from your dad first. I want to know what it says. There might be something in it we need to tell Bubba. Plus, I'm hungry."

"You're always hungry."

"What can I say? I'm a stress eater. Almost being blown up is stressful."

"I suppose I can't argue with that."

~

Riley parked the car behind the building and we had a little tailgate party minus the tailgate. The trunk of the Mustang was the next best thing and I rummaged around in the cooler and grocery bags looking for appealing food. Riley opened the envelope and read the note.

I crunched on a carrot stick, which was incredibly unsatisfying. "So, don't leave me in suspense here. What does it say?"

"Nothing helpful." Riley shook the paper at the cloudless deep blue sky. "Jeez, Dad."

"Read it."

"Fine." He held the paper in front of him. "If you've talked to Dean, you know what's going on. Ellen and I are continuing our research. Please get in touch with me as soon as you return from your trip. You said you weren't feeling well and I'm worried. I need to talk to you."

"That's it?"

"That's it." He folded the paper up and crammed it into his pocket. "What research?"

"My mom was on sabbatical from teaching at the university. I know what she worked on generally, but not the specific research she was doing when she left."

"Grab your food and let's go. Every time we turn around that van turns up. I want to keep moving."

I collected some veggies, chips, and crackers and returned to the passenger seat with my impromptu picnic. "I can't figure out how they keep finding us whenever we return to civilization. Unless…"

"Unless what?"

"Back when I had my cellular phone, I was on it constantly, except when I went out of range and couldn't get a signal. One time, I had a story out in West Virginia and I almost lost my mind trying to call it in to my editor. Maybe the guys in the van have a car phone."

"So what? Who would they be talking to? Do they have spies everywhere? Give me a break."

"Well, the guys in the van did reappear when we got to Las Vegas. How did they know that's where we were?"

"This whole thing is pissing me off." He smacked his hand on the steering wheel. "I don't even know what we're running from. Maybe I should let them take me off with them, so I can find out what they want."

"You know that's not a good idea. Dean didn't look happy."

"I know, but this is crazy. I can't believe we're going back to Vegas."

Riley descended into what I thought of as his silent sulky mood and we cruised down the lonely two-lane highway until we reached the turn to go south. Then it was another long haul through the empty desert and wanna-be ghost towns to get back to the interstate.

The sun was low in the sky when we returned to the city. After a terse consultation, we opted to stay at a Motel 6 that was near the interstate and about a mile off the Strip. When we arrived, the lights of Las Vegas were sparkling everywhere. The little twinge at the side of my head returned, and I hoped that the little squiggles of light at the edge of my vision wouldn't evolve into something worse.

Riley was irritable, but largely silent as we unloaded the car. Even Zelda was giving him a wide berth. After we had everything in the room, he said, "All right, let's go deal with Bubba and get that over with."

Zelda wagged her tail expectantly and Riley bent to pet her. "Yes Zee, you're coming too. You get to guard Shelby again."

"Aren't you afraid someone might steal Zelda? She's such a pretty dog."

Riley gave Zelda one last pat and stood up. "I'm not too worried. You saw what she did to the guys at the bar."

"Good point." I ruffled Zelda's ears. "If you see the nasty guys in the blue van, you have my permission to take a big, big chunk out of them."

We drove out to the casino where Bubba worked and went inside. The interior was a sea of flashing lights, smoke, and noise. The hum of voices mingled with a bizarre cacophony of sounds from the slot machines. An elderly woman with blue hair and wearing a pink sequined track suit shoved my hip when I got too close to her slot machine. She croaked, "Hey, this one's mine. Get away from me, Red. Find your own. This one is about to pay out."

I mumbled an apology and tried to focus on Riley, who was walking fast, getting ahead of me, his long legs striding across the purple-and-red patterned carpet. I tried to yell at him to slow down, but a flickering arc of teal blue light washed over him like a wave, and it seemed like my voice couldn't penetrate it. He turned back to look at me as the light morphed around him, moving and swirling, mixing in with the cigarette smoke that permeated the air.

A clown with melting smeared makeup ran past my mother and toward me holding a flamethrower, and then my skin was ablaze. I screamed for my mother as I frantically clutched at my arms, trying to quell the stabbing pain and put out the fire. The clown cast his flamethrower aside and ran up to me, grabbing my arms and dragging me into a dark cavern. The blackness enveloped me, and I felt as if I were sinking down into brackish water. A hand reached to me and I grabbed on, trying not to drown in the inky quagmire.

My body shook a few times and the blackness was suddenly swept away, replaced by the lights and noise of the casino. I gazed into Riley's dark eyes and immediately burst into tears. He put his arm around me and I leaned into his chest. I squeezed my eyes shut and let him walk me along next to him. I heard him say, "Bubba, we kinda need to talk to you about something."

Bubba's booming voice came from behind me, "Yeah, man. What's wrong with your girlfriend?"

"She's not my girlfriend. That's Erin. This is Meg, your possible stepsister, remember?"

"Oh yeah. Damn, our family gets weirder all the time."

Riley walked me into an office and Bubba followed, closing the door behind us. "Welcome to my spy station."

The room was essentially a windowless closet with sixteen monitors that displayed the action at the gambling tables. I sat down in a chair and faked a smile. "I'm sorry I made a scene out there."

Riley sat in the chair next to me and Bubba crouched down to look at my face. "Riley said you're okay, but man, that was pretty freaky. Usually people who do that type of thing are tripping on major drugs. And uh, I know you might be family and all, but if you're on drugs, it's against our policy and I have to throw you out. Sorry."

I finally let go of Riley's hand. "I'm not on drugs. I promise. It's a problem I have with hallucinations."

"And screaming," Riley added.

"Did I scream? I guess that's not a surprise—I was scared. I think all the lights and noise set off the hallucination."

Bubba sat in an office chair in front of the monitors and leaned back. "So, I don't get it. Why are you here? I thought you were getting outta Vegas and weren't gonna stay at my place after all."

"Something happened on the way out of town and we think you should know about it," Riley said.

"I almost got blown up." I gestured toward the door. "It was at a gas station. There are these guys that might be after us. I thought they were trying to kidnap us, but, well, I think it's possible they're trying to kill us. I'm not exactly sure."

"What do you mean you aren't sure?" Bubba narrowed his eyes at Riley. "Are you in some kind of trouble, bro? Does this have to do with that note from Dad?"

"The note wasn't helpful. All he said was that he was working on some type of research and I should talk to him," Riley said. "Did he say anything to you about where he was going?"

"I thought he was with Ellen in Alpine Grove. That was the last thing I heard," Bubba said.

"He not there. Meg's mom called her and Dad called me and they demanded that we meet them there. But they never showed," Riley said.

"The house is empty," I volunteered. "Then Riley found a note that said to talk to Dean Wolfe. We tried, but then Dean got kidnapped. After that, things got a little strange."

Bubba folded his hands and rested them on his brass belt buckle. "Uh, I hate to tell you, but I think it was already strange. So are you saying you think Dad got himself kidnapped or something?"

"We don't know," I said.

"Then there was the whole thing at the circus," Riley added. "The guys who took Dean were there too. Then at the rest stop where Meg almost got blown up. We came back here to warn you to be careful."

Bubba leaned forward and put his elbows on his knees. "I don't know what to say, man. I haven't seen you in years, then you show up outta nowhere with this weird woman…sorry Meg, but you're weird…and you look like death. What's all this about?"

Riley said, "I'm not sure. But Meg, Dean, and I all seem to have developed problems at around the same time."

"What kind of problems?" Bubba said.

I sighed heavily. "I know it sounds off the wall, but it has to do with our senses. Riley's sense of smell, Dean's hearing, and my vision."

"So that's why you were asking me about all that." Bubba stood up. "What do you want me to do?"

"I'm not sure. We just thought you should know." I said. "Please, please be careful and watch out for guys in a blue van wearing suits."

"And if anything happens or you hear from Dad, please let me know," Riley said.

"How am I supposed to do that?" Bubba said, "You don't have house or a phone anymore."

"Oh yeah, I guess that's a problem. We're staying at the Motel 6 here tonight, but I'll check in with you from wherever we end up." Riley stood up and gave his brother an awkward hug. "Take care."

"Sure, man. You too."

Chapter 7

So Many Speeds

By the time we got back to the Motel 6, I was in the throes of what I thought of as "hallucination hangover." Physically, I was exhausted and visually, everything seemed faded, gray, and slightly out of focus. It was the antithesis of the vibrant colors of the hallucination, like when Dorothy went back to black-and-white Kansas after the Technicolor wonderful world of Oz.

I sat down on one of the beds and Zelda curled up next to me on the brightly colored bedspread. I reached over to grab the phone book from the nightstand. Whether Riley liked it or not, after the day I'd had, I needed a serious infusion of carbohydrates. I dialed the phone and ordered a pizza to be delivered as soon as humanly possible.

Riley chewed on a celery stick. "So do you feel better now?"

"I will once the pizza gets here." I leaned back against the pillows. "We need to talk."

"About what? Your constant need to eat?"

"Very funny. No. Somehow laying everything out for Bubba made me realize that my visions aren't just something that has ruined my life. Maybe they can be helpful."

"How is screaming helpful?"

"Don't be obnoxious. I'm serious. We wouldn't have found the circus or Lars or the guys in the van or anything if it weren't for your 'feelings,' or more accurately your sense of smell, and my visions."

"You were the one who swore up and down that you weren't a prophet and the visions didn't mean anything." Riley grabbed a carrot stick. "So what *are* you saying?"

"I think we should take whatever is going on with us more seriously. The vision I had tonight was full of fire. After the explosion and almost being blown to smithereens, I'm not so inclined to write off a fiery vision as nonsense anymore. I think we need to step back and look at this from the beginning."

A loud knock at the door and subsequent ferocious barking from Zelda interrupted whatever Riley was going to say. He got up, paid for the pizza, and handed it to me. Zelda leaped back up onto the bed and hovered over the pizza box like a vulture.

I shoved her away. "If you behave yourself, you might get some crust."

Riley said "Zee" and moved his hand slightly. Zelda jumped back down to the floor and sat in front of me, looking expectant.

I took a restorative bite of pizza and continued. "If you're not going to eat any of this, get a pen. We need to write down everything we know about how my mom and your dad met and what they said about each other."

"Are you thinking that whatever is going on has to do with whatever the 'research' is that Dad mentioned in the note?"

"Yes, exactly!" I flipped a piece of crust to Zelda, who snatched it from the air. "They obviously have something in common, but I don't know what it might be. I mean, Mom teaches psychology at the University of Maryland and does a lot of research related to child development."

Riley chuckled "And you're wondering why she would be interested in a super-geek like my dad."

"Well, yeah, you must see what I mean. Although he sounds like a nice guy, he's an electrical engineer who thinks pocket protectors are the bomb. I'm sorry, but he doesn't sound like my mom's type. What on earth could they possibly have in common?"

Riley got up, dug around in a suitcase, and extracted a pen and paper. "Dad told me he met Ellen at SIGGRAPH, that huge computer graphics conference."

"Mom was on a panel." I reached for my bag that was sitting at the end of the bed and pulled out my reporter's notepad. "She told me about it. They wanted her to talk about a paper she wrote on the physiological and psychological impact of gaming on children."

Riley frowned. "That's quite a topic."

"Mom was way into ethics of design as it relates to gaming addiction in kids. According to my notes, the panel was about visual perception and its applications in computer graphics. Lots of stuff on how people perceive light, color, pattern, motion, texture, shape, and so forth. She said she wanted to learn more about how images are interpreted in virtual environments. She felt that game designers are intentionally including elements that encourage addiction."

"Wow, you take good notes."

"I'm a reporter. Or I was."

Riley paused for a moment, then said, "Well, when I talked to Dad, he said he was going to SIGGRAPH because he wanted to learn more about user-interface design. He worked on communications equipment like military radios for a gazillion years and they had toggle switches and tiny screens. He wanted to make them easier to use."

"I thought he was retired."

"He is, but he's still got a garage full of stuff he tinkers with. Or I hope he still does. I was playing with oscilloscopes when I was six."

"You are such a geek." I chomped some more pizza. "I don't even know what an oscilloscope is."

"It lets you see the change in an electrical signal over time." He waved his hand. "Never mind. The point is, Dad was into electronics. He worked for twenty-five years at a company that made HF and VHF communications equipment."

"HF what?"

"They're radio frequency bands. High frequency and very high frequency. If you've ever seen a war movie, the guy with the backpack radio is probably using one of Dad's radios to call someone to save the day."

"Okay, that has nothing to do with childhood development or addiction. What did they do? Talk about user interfaces? That's lame, even for geeks. Is your Dad addicted to anything?"

"Not that I know of. Maybe they connected on a personal level. Like some hobby maybe?"

I gave Zelda another piece of crust. "Mom likes gardening. And she used to go to yoga classes sometimes."

Riley chuckled. "I can't imagine my father doing yoga. Even the idea is unpleasant. Just say 'no' to Dad in a leotard."

"Does he like to garden?"

"He didn't even mow the lawn. When the neighbors started complaining too much, he'd hire a landscaper to hack down the weeds in the front yard every once in a while."

Having stuffed myself, I closed the pizza box and moved it farther away from Zelda's nose. "So I've seen one kind of blurry photo of your Dad and I have to tell you, he's not a hottie."

"Hard for me to judge, but I doubt most women would think so."

"He's certainly no Sean Connery."

"Nope."

I waved my hand as if I were erasing a blackboard. "Okay, we're getting off topic here. What else did your dad say about my mom?"

"He met her at the conference and she decided to extend her stay in LA." He shrugged. "Maybe they had wild, kinky sex?"

"Ugh, I don't want to think about this, but okay. So for whatever reason they got together. What else did he say about her?"

"That Ellen is a wonderful person and that I'd love her when I met her."

"That's pretty much what Mom said about your dad. And that he has a brilliant mind. If you knew my mom, you'd understand that's a big deal with her. She always said most of the men she met were too stupid to put up with for more than ten minutes."

"Well, Dad is definitely smart." Riley reached for the pizza box, pulled it over to the other bed and peered inside. "It looks so greasy. And smells like…ugh…I just can't."

I took the box back. "Go eat another carrot. So what have we learned so far?"

"That our parents have nothing in common, except that they're both extremely smart and have an interest in computer graphics, although for different reasons." Riley's eyes sparkled with amusement. "Oh, and they might both like kinky sex, but we might be making that up."

"We can only hope." I placed the box on top of the TV, away from Zelda.

"So where do we go from here?"

"I'm not sure. The vision I had was terrifying. If it's real, then Mom and your dad are in serious danger. Fire was everywhere. It was like a horror movie." I closed my eyes. "I don't know what was burning other than me, but that was enough."

Riley leaned back on the bed and rested his head on his elbow. "So far, your visions haven't been literal. I mean, I've checked, and I'm not blue. We also didn't see your mom walking next to the circus tent. But the hallucinations do seem to be representative of something. Maybe the fire isn't bad. It could be a fire in a cozy fireplace or a campfire."

"I suppose that's possible. If the vision doesn't get out of control, I can pay attention and maybe not pass out. When we were in Gleasonville and you held my hand, it wasn't as scary. But this time, you weren't there and everything went sideways incredibly fast. I was so frightened, but then you were there, and I didn't pass out. So that was something."

Riley smiled. "I guess if you start to feel weird, you need to be like the Beatles and let me know that you want to hold my hand."

"I think you might need to be more forthcoming about any odd feelings you have too. Like which way to go." I pointed down at Zelda. "Maybe confer with your dog too."

"All right." Riley sat up. "But what's next? Is there a way we can intentionally use your visions somehow so we can learn something?"

"Are you saying you want to cause one on *purpose*?" I shook my head. "I'd rather not. That doesn't sound like any fun at all."

"What if we went to a casino and sat at a slot machine. Would all the noise and lights do something to trigger a hallucination like it did today?"

"Maybe. I'm a little afraid of what I might see though."

"More clowns?"

"I'm hoping for no more clowns, *ever*. The last clown had a flamethrower. He was one angry pyromaniac and I'd rather not meet up with that guy again."

"It might not be as bad if you know I'm with you."

"Maybe. I guess we could try it. I can't think of anything else to do."

"Me neither. It might be fine. Even better, we might learn something."

I wasn't sure what I might find out beyond the fact that clowns and fire are not a good mix, but we didn't seem to have any other options. We couldn't stay in this Motel 6 forever. "I guess you're right. It's worth a try."

"I promise I'll hold your hand."

"Well, you're no John Lennon, but I guess you'll have to do."

~

If you've never been there, one thing you need to know about Las Vegas is that the casinos are always open and slot machines are everywhere. Need to go to the grocery store, but can't stop gambling? No problem! You'll find slot machines at the grocery store too. And at the airport, restaurants, and pretty much any other open space where someone can jam in a machine. You never know when someone is going to be overcome by the need to gamble, so machines are available any time or any place people feel compelled to heave all their money into a one-armed bandit.

Because of the ubiquity of casinos and gambling, Riley and I could go almost anywhere to conduct our little experiment in hallucinatory fun. We settled on a casino that was off the Strip and near the Motel 6, so we could walk there. Unlike the grocery store, a casino would have all the flashing lights and noise I needed to lose my mind. Terrific.

To say I was not enthusiastic about this idea would be an understatement. I was by turns anxious, scared, and resigned. For months I had spent almost every waking moment trying to figure out ways to avoid having a humiliating hallucination in public. And now here I was, about to get all vision-y on purpose. If I had another terrifying festival of screaming, I was going to kill Riley for suggesting this stupid idea.

Riley fed Zelda and encouraged her to take a nap in the motel room while we were gone. Motels frown on leaving pets unattended, but Riley assured me that Zelda would behave herself. However, I did notice that he moved the grocery bags and cooler to a high shelf above the metal coat rack. Zelda was a dog, after all. Like most canines, when it came to food, she could resist anything except temptation.

Riley and I left the motel and strolled down the street to the Jumping Jack Flash Casino, which had a neon sign of a jester jumping around that did bear a bit of a resemblance to Mick Jagger. Riley was looking ill again. Once we got this over with, maybe we'd be able to go somewhere out of the smog for a while. Of course that was assuming this experiment gave us some idea about where we might look for our parents.

So much had happened, it seemed odd that I'd only known Riley for a few days. We already knew way more than either of us probably *wanted* to know about our various issues, and he undoubtedly was as ready to return to his regular life as I was. But for the time being, we were stuck with each other.

We walked into the casino and it took a moment for my eyes to adjust to the dim, smoke-infused light after being out in the brilliant morning sun. No one was going to confuse this place with one of the swanky new casinos on the Strip. A few die-hard gamblers were hunched over tables fondling their chips, and the jangling sound of slot machines and falling coins filled the room. Considering that people in casinos were supposed to be on vacation and having all kinds of fun, this place was remarkably depressing.

Riley nudged me. "I'm guessing this is where the locals go."

"That would explain the ambiance. This must be a great recruiting spot for Gamblers Anonymous."

"There's a couple of nickel slots over there. Let's go hang out."

We settled into seats in front of the machines and I put my hand to my temple. "These do have the flashing-lights thing going for them. That's obnoxious."

"This music makes Disney's 'It's a Small World' seem like Tchaikovsky."

"Is there a weird light over there on the left?"

Riley looked around as a blue light misted around him. It seemed like his voice saying "Nope" came from extremely far away, so I reached out and grabbed one of his hands with both of mine. I felt a sense of relief at the warmth of his palm when he placed it on the back of my hand.

The slot machine in front of me had a sign that said I could win the jackpot in a hundred-fifteen ways, and then I heard Matt's voice say, "What a rip-off. You won't win."

I looked up. What was Matt doing here? My ex was a media executive who worked in a shiny, modern glass-and-marble office building in DC. His family came from "old money" as he liked to say, so he was unbelievably wealthy. He was fond of pointing out that he enjoyed the finer things in life, and the idea of him being in a run-down seedy casino in Las Vegas didn't compute.

We'd met when I'd interviewed him for a story about how media businesses were embracing the Internet. After telling me how the Internet was a fad that would have no impact on media properties like his, he'd asked me out. I found out much later that Matt was an expert at courting women, but when I met him I didn't know that. He'd swept me off my feet with flowers, wildly expensive dinners at swanky restaurants, and evenings at luxurious hotels.

In the beginning I'd felt like Cinderella, or Julia Roberts in *Pretty Woman*. By the end of our time together, I was more like Endora in *Bewitched,* wanting to cast an evil curse on him. Matt used to harp on the fact that I didn't trust men because of my father's ignoble exit from my life, but I considered his opinion a steaming pile of crap. I didn't trust Matt because he was a lying, cheating, arrogant jerk.

Part of my mind knew I was actually sitting at a slot machine, holding Riley's hand in a seedy casino, so I was stunned into silence for a moment. But after our incredibly acrimonious breakup, I had to say something to Matt, even if he was only a figment of my hallucination. In my most snide sarcastic tone, I said, "Why Matt, this is a surprise. What brings you to the bright lights of Las Vegas?"

Matt gave me one of his patented snooty looks and replied, "Don't you know? I thought you knew everything that was going on with DC-area businesses. You said you were the eyes and ears of the community, keeping your readership informed with all the news that may or may not be fit to print."

"Why don't you enlighten me?"

I felt a tugging on my hands, but ignored it as Matt sat down at the slot machine next to me. He gave me a self-satisfied smile. "We're merging with an up-and-coming Internet property."

"I thought you were all about television. You proclaimed to me and anyone else who would listen that cable channels… and I quote…provide an *unprecedented* level of selection and everyone has all the entertainment they could ever possibly need…unquote."

"You do so love to throw my words back at me, don't you, Meg? I'm sure I may have said that, but technology marches on. If we send out complimentary CD-ROMs to people, we can get everyone onto the Internet and sell them advertising online."

"Eww, you're merging with *that* outfit? Ninety-nine percent of those horrid CDs end up in the trash. Did you see the article about the guy who papered his room with them? Landfills are going to be overflowing with CDs. Environmentalists hate that company."

Matt scowled. "You have no vision."

I laughed. "That's not true. I have lots of visions. And it turns out sometimes you're in them!"

There was a crashing noise and the guy in blue coveralls who had fixed Bubba's cable walked by. He gave me a friendly wave and said, "How's that ESPN working out for ya?"

Something yanked on my hand and I blinked a few times. Riley's face was about six inches from mine and he said, "Who's Matt?"

"Matt?"

"You were talking to someone named Matt about CDs."

"I need to talk to Leo. He'd know about this."

Riley released my hand. "This what? Who is Leo?"

"I told you. He's my boss, or he was before we were laid off. In my vision, I found out that a media company I used to, um, know quite a bit about is merging with an Internet company. In fact, it's the cable company Bubba uses for his seven-thousand TV channels. The repairman was there in my hallucination too."

"You didn't answer my question. Who is Matt?"

"My ex-boyfriend."

Riley made a face. "I'm thinking that trying to figure out your visions isn't going to work out. Did we come over here to this dive of a casino so you could have sex fantasies?"

I crossed my arms across my chest. "Why do you assume I was having sex fantasies?"

"You were smiling."

"I was not." It was more likely I was sneering, and I waved my hand to brush off the comment, "That's not the point. You said your father is into electronics and communications. Media and communications are related. What if the cable company has something to do with, well, something."

"That's a stretch." Riley moved a shoulder half-heartedly. "And it gives us less than nothing to go on. As far as I know, Bubba has his ESPN again and order has been restored to the sports-viewing universe. So what?"

"It felt connected." I stood up. "You have your feelings; I have mine."

"At least you didn't scream. I guess the sex with Matt wasn't that good, huh?"

I squinted up at him as I yanked open the door to leave the casino. "You're fixating on this sex thing, aren't you? I think maybe you should call your girlfriend again. Perhaps a little phone time with Erin will settle you down."

As we stepped out into the sunlight and began walking, Riley grabbed my hand and swung it between us. "No thanks. She'd gripe at me for not eating enough. Plus I'm having way too much fun hearing about your sexcapades right here."

I let go of his hand and shoved him to the side. "For the last time, there were no sex fantasies, okay?"

A woman walking by gave me a sidelong look as she passed and I raised my eyebrows at her. "Well, there weren't!"

She shook her head and hustled away from us.

Riley chuckled and clasped his hands behind his back. "Well, one good thing is that there was no crying or screaming this time. I think that's progress. We've now demonstrated that you can have a vision without the people around you feeling compelled to call nine-one-one."

"I agree, that's a plus. But here's the thing. If we've decided to believe my visions, we can't write off what I saw as random. Matt was there for a reason and so was the cable guy. I want to get back to the room and call Leo. If I can get more dirt on this merger, maybe I can find some type of connection to what's going on with our parents. There's got to be one. I *know* there is. I can feel it."

"Yeah, well, we'll see. Now we have child development, computer graphics, electronics, sexy clowns, and the cable guy. It's like some reading game on Sesame Street." He added in a sing-song voice, "Let's all shout out our favorite words!"

"You're hilarious, you know that?"

"Just trying to keep things light, so I don't get too depressed. I'm worried about Dad. If anything has happened to him, I mean, I just can't…"

"I know. I feel the same way. We'll figure something out."

"We'd better."

~

Back in the room, Riley made a feeble effort to straighten up the small space while I looked up Leo's home number. Neatness wasn't exactly Riley's forte, but it was considerate of him to try.

He dug Zelda's leash out from under a pile of clothes and held it up. "I'm going to take her for a walk."

I waved good-bye and settled in next to the telephone. First, I called my answering machine, which had a message from human resources letting me know that I needed to fill out some forms. Who knew that being laid off could be so bureaucratic?

I called Leo and talked to his wife briefly. I'd only met her a couple of times at holiday parties, but we exchanged a few pleasantries. Leo was reportedly digging up rotted fence posts in the backyard and she went to retrieve him. It sounded like Lou's "honeydo" projects had already begun. Hopefully retirement wouldn't kill the guy.

Finally, he came on the line, breathing heavily. "Hi Meg. What's up?"

"I have some questions for you about Matt and Archetypal Media."

"I guess you heard already? That was fast. I didn't think the story would spread so quickly since nothing's been officially announced."

"What story?"

"Well you already know about the layoff, but it's bigger than that. The rumor mill has been flying, but the word is that Archetypal Media is being gobbled up by OSU."

"Online Systems United is merging with them?" I put my hand to my chest. My vision was true. How creepy was this? Was Riley right? Was I some type of prophet? I didn't want to be a prophet. Things usually ended badly for those guys.

"The executives are the ones responsible for consolidating our little newspaper group. So if you happen to talk to Matt, say thanks for chucking my decades of journalism experience out the window."

"Matt and I broke up quite some time ago." I suspected Leo remembered that, but wanted to get a little jab in. He'd taken an instant dislike to Matt, which had annoyed me at the time. Of course, in the end, it turned out that Leo had been a far better judge of Matt's character than I had been.

"Word is that the new company will be called Archetypal Online Systems. From the sounds of it, your buddy Matt had a little temper tantrum about naming at a meeting." Leo snorted. "So typical."

"I'm sorry about this, Leo."

"The newspaper biz is changing fast and I knew that this type of thing was inevitable. That doesn't mean it doesn't still piss me off. Yesterday afternoon, the bigwigs from Archetypal even had the gall to show us their new commercial. Talk about rubbing salt in the wound. They don't care about actual writing anymore, but they're recruiting like crazy for advertising reps and people to install cable and Internet."

"That's interesting." Matt's comments in my vision about the CDs and selling advertising fit in like a little corner in a thousand-piece jigsaw puzzle.

"The jobs are pretty sweet if you're into that type of thing. They're offering all kinds of perks like free company car, free Internet, cellular phones, gym memberships, discounts to restaurants, bonuses. They've got a huge list of benefits."

"I guess you don't want to install cable for a living?"

"No, I'm too set in my ways. I've always been a news hound and I'm not interested in changing careers at this point in my life. And, well, this is going to sound sorta funny and I might be biased, but the new company kinda gives me the willies."

Given the events of the last few days, I was half afraid to ask, but I couldn't help myself. "What do you mean?"

"The commercial reminded me of those old black-and-white propaganda newsreels from World War II. The voice-over is kinda over the top."

"In what way?"

"I'm probably reading too much into it because I'm so pissed off about everything. But the commercial felt manipulative. Like technology is going to be the savior of the future and it must be protected and expanded. Like I said, kinda over the top. I mean, it's installing cable TV, not a religion, for heaven's sake."

"That does sound odd. I'm not sure what to say."

"I know you were upset, but now I think the timing of your medical leave might have been a blessing in disguise. Nobody's doing any work here, we're all biding time until the office closes and we pick up our final paychecks. Be glad you're missing it."

I wished Leo well and hung up the phone. The information he'd shared with me was disturbing in many ways, but it hadn't led me to any conclusions as far as what I should do next to find Mom.

The twinge at the side of my head was back and I hoped it was only a plain garden-variety headache. I went to the bathroom, got an aspirin, and crawled back onto the bed. I rolled onto my back and stared at the ceiling. The air conditioner was making the heavy drapes move and flashes of sunlight danced on the walls. Lou had said that the commercial was like a propaganda film. How freaky was that?

I closed my eyes, waiting for my aspirin to take effect. Then I was alone in a darkened room, but it wasn't the motel anymore. A voice echoed above me telling me to watch the important information about Archetypal Online Systems. Wait! I didn't want to see this. I sat up and everything was still dark. Where was the Motel 6? Where was Riley?

Sappy music played and a soothing voice said, "Technology will connect us, make us one, and help us work together to solve the world's problems. We are at the cusp of a new frontier, and you have the opportunity to be a part of it. Are you brave enough to join us? This can be your future, but only if you make the commitment." Images appeared of beautiful places, loving couples, and happy parents playing with their children. My muscles relaxed. This wasn't so bad. Maybe I could deal with a vision without having Riley around. That would sure make my life a lot simpler.

A photograph of the Grand Canyon at sunset segued into a family arguing at the dinner table. The sappy music changed to hard death metal with screeching guitars. Even worse, the little girl was me. Mom was there shouting at my father, overwhelming the soothing voice of the narrator, who was still calmly explaining the virtues of technology. Fire came through the doorway from the kitchen and my mother waved her hand at it. "See, this is where I am!"

We'd never had a kitchen fire when I was growing up that I remembered, but this was a bad one. If we didn't do something, the whole house would burn down in minutes. I screamed at my mother to get out of the way. The flames were lashing around her as she continued to shout at my father. They'd had a bitter divorce and I knew she was yelling at him, even though I couldn't see his face. It was just like old times.

The inferno enveloped the dining room table, but my mother seemed oblivious to both the flames and my desperate screams imploring her to get away from the fire. The man moved, catching my attention. I turned my head and to my shock, it wasn't my father. It was Dean Wolfe. What was he doing here? He pointed and I looked back at my mother. I tried to grab her, but my outstretched hands couldn't quite reach her. She moved back into the flames and was enveloped by the blaze.

I was crying and shaking, curled up on the bed, until something licked at the tears on my cheek. I moved and found myself looking into Zelda's nut-brown eyes. I snuffled, wiped the drool off my face, and reached out a hand to pet her. "Oh Zee, I've never been more glad to see a dog in my whole life."

I sat up and found Riley sitting on the bed clutching my forearm. He studied me with an uncertain smile and released the grip he had on my arm. "I'm guessing this hallucination didn't go too well."

"It was awful. I'm afraid something bad is happening." I wiped my eyes. "But I don't know what. I think it has to do with Matt's company, but I have no idea how it all fits. And there was fire again. I hate fire."

Bringing up the fire launched another wave of shaking, and Riley fumbled to put his arms around me. He patted my back and said, "It's all right."

I sat there silently weeping into his shirt for a while, until I was cried out. I moved away from Riley and made an effort to collect myself. "I'm sorry about this."

"Why don't you tell me what you saw this time?"

I went through the conversation with Leo and my vision. Riley listened without saying anything until I was finished, his only movement to scratch at his chin a few times. When had he completely given up on shaving? I hadn't been paying attention. Now he looked like a scruffy, skinny vampire. The stubble was long enough that it had to be getting to the itchy phase.

When I finished my tale of weirdness, he said, "Maybe we should get out of Vegas. If you keep having visions like this, you'll have a nervous breakdown. Or I will." He shrugged. "Hard to say which one of us will fall apart first."

"I need to call Matt. Everything points to him being mixed up in this somehow."

"Are you sure it's not about losing your job? Now you know your ex-boyfriend is responsible for you being laid off. That might have brought up some personal stuff and you're expanding on what you learned from Leo."

"That doesn't explain the fire though. Reliving one of my mom's and dad's fights was bad enough. Throwing in some more fire was icing on an already disturbing cake."

"Except it wasn't your dad. It was Dean. Look at the bright side. At least there were no clowns this time."

"My mom was there and in danger, which is a recurring theme."

"Along with clowns and Dean. I think we need to find out how this circus and your boyfriend's company are related."

"He's not my boyfriend." My eyes widened and I looked into Riley's face. "But you're absolutely right. There has to be a connection. I'll get Leo to fax me everything he's got on the company and the merger and I'll call Matt."

"We never did talk to Hector of Hector's Traveling Big Top Circus either. That's another avenue we can investigate."

I widened my eyes in exaggerated surprise. "I'm impressed. You're starting to think like a reporter."

"I'm not sure if I should be flattered by that or not."

~

I called Leo again and asked him to get all the information he could about the merger. It was Saturday, so he wouldn't be able to do anything until Monday, but he promised he would do it as soon as he got to the office. Riley was fairly insistent about getting out of Las Vegas and to a rural area. I couldn't remember the last thing he'd eaten, so I suspected he was feeling even worse than he was letting on. I was ready for a break from horrific visions, so I wasn't about to argue with him about it.

Riley dug out the circus flyer, and although the prospect of seeing clowns again pained me, we looked up where Hector's band of creeps and freaks were going to be next. The circus only stopped at locations away from major metropolitan areas because they needed a wide-open space like a county fairground to set up their big top.

The circus was currently at the Churchill County fairgrounds, which according to the flyer was notable for being the home of the Heart 'O Gold Cantaloupe Festival. Who knew there were cantaloupes in Nevada? The circus's next stop was Ely, which was a decent destination for us. It was about two hundred and fifty miles from Las Vegas, located in the middle of nowhere, and as Riley had mentioned before, it had a Motel 6 where we could stay.

I tried calling Matt, but I got a low-level Archetypal flunky who sounded like she'd turned sweet sixteen mere days ago. She said in her best grown-up voice that Mr. Eskridge was not available on the weekend. When I vowed to call him back on Monday, Little Miss Perky seemed unimpressed, but she didn't know what an incredible pest I could become.

While I made my calls, Riley packed up the room. I still hadn't taken time to do laundry, and tonight I was going to have to wash a pair of underwear in the sink, which was a bleak prospect because I didn't even have soap. Wherever we ended up staying, I absolutely had to deal with my laundry disaster. Zelda seemed to appreciate my stinky, sweaty, dirty clothes, but I was grossed out.

Once the car was loaded up, we set out to say good-bye to Bubba. We hadn't heard anything, so we assumed he was okay, but I wanted to ask him a couple of questions about his cable company before we left town.

We left Zelda with the Mustang and knocked on Bubba's door. He answered wearing nothing except boxers with little red hearts on them. There was a lot of freckled Bubba to see and I tried not to gape. He leaned against the doorframe. "Hey Ri, I thought you guys left town."

Riley said, "Not yet. Could we come in for a second?"

Bubba made a welcoming gesture with his arm and I walked inside. It was obvious he had not cleaned since we'd been there the previous day. In fact, it looked like the detritus was reproducing. An unwelcome thought entered my mind that he might be entertaining a guest in the other room. Ugh. I decided not to make any attempt to clear a space to sit down. Instead I clasped my hands in front of me, trying not to touch anything. "So I wanted to ask you about your cable."

"My cable?" He slammed the door. "My damn cable sucks. How did you know? I'm so pissed. The guy said he fixed it, but it's still not working. I was gonna watch the game and Bambi is a major fan. She even has a cheerleader outfit. But she left because we couldn't get the TV to play anything. Just a bunch of static. She said she needed the game for inspiration, so there was no cheering anywhere, least of all by me when she bailed."

"Isn't it odd that your cable is broken again?" I gestured toward the TV. "Did you call them about it?"

"Of course I did. They gave me a window of time when they *might* come by to fix it. I mean, it could be now, or could be later. I don't know. I figure I'm not putting on pants if they aren't going to tell me." He whacked the top of the old television set. "And I gotta go to work before too long. This stinks, man."

Riley raised his eyebrows at me, giving me a significant look. "Meg, I think we should leave before the cable guy arrives, don't you?"

I understood what he was getting at. "Yes, I agree. We'll call you when we get to Eee…I mean when we get where we're going."

"Where are you going?" Bubba asked.

"Not sure yet," Riley said. "But we should let you get ready for work. We're really leaving this time. I need to get out of the city for a while."

"Yeah, man, find a doctor somewhere would ya?" Bubba said. "You look even worse than you did yesterday. What happened to Erin, anyway? Maybe you need a little action to cheer you up and get the blood moving."

"We're, um, taking a little break right now, but thanks for the advice," Riley said. "I'll call you soon."

We left then, and as we walked back to the car I shoved at Riley's arm and flashed him a lascivious grin. "So hey, I guess I'm not the only one who thinks you should get a little action from ole Erin, huh?"

"Shut up."

We took off and retraced our route on Interstate 15 to US 93, which wound north through an endless expanse of desert. As someone who had spent my entire life living in cities on the east coast, I had trouble wrapping my mind around the fact that there were so many places where you could drive hundreds of miles and see almost no one. Not even other cars. Our only companions were flocks of crows that clustered on the side of the highway, picking at long-dead corpses of creatures that had attempted to cross the road at the wrong time. As we approached, the birds flew off briefly, then returned to their task. Intellectually, I knew that it was all part of the circle of life and all that, but eww.

The late-afternoon sun was warm and glaring, so my entire body relaxed to the point that I was half dozing in the warmth.

The car swerved and I swiveled my head to look at Riley. He shook his head, took off his sunglasses, and rubbed his eyes with his thumb and index finger.

I leaned over to look into his face. "Are you okay?"

"I didn't sleep much last night. Or eat much of anything. I feel sort of spaced out."

"How about we pull over?"

"Yeah, I'm kind of tired. All this driving and running is wiping me out."

He pulled onto the shoulder and we got out and walked around with Zelda for a few minutes. I said, "Why don't I drive for a little while? There's no one out here."

"I thought you said you couldn't drive a stick shift."

"So teach me. How hard can it be? And it's not like I'm going to hit anything. There's nothing here to hit."

Riley smirked. "I'm more worried about Shelby than about us."

"Oh, come on. You need a break. Bubba was right. You look like death."

"Thanks. You have no idea how uplifting it is to have people keep telling me that."

I shrugged. "Well, it's true."

"All right, fine. But as soon as we find a place to get coffee, I'm driving again."

"Works for me."

Riley got in, started the car, and then we traded places. After I adjusted the seat and mirrors, he leaned over and pointed at the floor. "On the left, that's the clutch. You know about that, right?"

"I'm not an idiot."

"If you can wiggle the gearshift around like this, you know you're in neutral. The pattern is printed right there on the knob. Remember that you always start the car in neutral. Then when you're ready, push in the clutch and shift into first. Never shift without pushing in the clutch."

"Yeah, yeah, I got it."

"Pay attention to the tachometer. You shift up at around thirty-five hundred rpms and downshift at twenty-five hundred. It roughly corresponds to speeds. First gear is more or less zero to twenty-five, second is twenty-five to thirty-five, third is thirty-five to forty-five and fifth is fifty-five and up. Most of the time on the highway, you're in fifth and you can put on the cruise control, hang out, and steer. The cruise is over there."

"Okay, fine." I put the car in first and it made a horrible screeching sound.

Zelda whined and Riley shrieked, "Push in the clutch. Use the clutch! That's the first thing I said! You're stripping the gears!"

I pushed in the clutch and the car immediately stalled. Riley put his face in his hands. "This might not be a good idea."

"Settle down. I'll get the hang of it, if you'd relax. So how do I start it?"

I pushed in the clutch, put it in neutral and Riley gave me the code for his extra-special security measure that allowed the Mustang to start. I clapped my hands together. "Yay!"

"Don't get too excited. We still haven't moved. Push in the clutch this time. Then put it in gear, *slowly* let out the clutch, and when you feel it engage, press on the gas."

"Engage?" I looked in front and behind me. No one was around and the highway was empty, except for a couple of crows.

"You'll feel some friction. That's the gears engaging."

"Okay, here we go." I followed the instructions and the car moved. Then I gunned it and it moved a lot faster. "Holy crap. This thing really goes."

"Shelby is not a thing. She's an extremely customized precision automobile. What gear are you in?"

"Gear?"

Riley pointed at the knob. "Shift gears for God's sake!"

I pressed in the clutch and shifted to second without incident. "Yahoo! This is fun."

Riley leaned back, pulled off his sunglasses, and covered his eyes with his hand. "Slow down or consider third gear, please."

"Oh yeah. Check me out. I'm in third gear!"

"Fantastic. Shift."

"How do you know I need to shift? Your eyes are closed."

"Listen to the engine."

"Five speeds seems like a bit much. Why are there five? This would be simpler with fewer speeds."

"Then it would be an automatic."

"Oh yeah, I guess so."

Riley groaned, "I'm so sorry about this, Shelby."

Befuddlement

Riley was right that once I was at cruising speed, driving his car was as boring as driving any other car. Just when I was getting the hang of shifting too. We listened to the stereo at high volume for a while as we crossed miles upon miles of empty Nevada desert.

About twenty-five miles outside of Ely, Riley demanded that I pull over. I managed to downshift successfully, then when I stopped on the shoulder, the car immediately stalled out. It was an ignoble ending to my driving experience and Riley glowered at me as the engine noise faded away. And I'd been doing so well too.

We got out, traded places, and Riley shoved the seat back with a clank. He patted the dashboard. "Thank God that's over."

"You're welcome."

He started the car and glanced at me. "I think I'll buy a thermos and keep it stocked with coffee from now on for situations like these."

"Too much caffeine without eating anything will make you jittery."

"Watching you drive makes me jittery."

I crossed my arms. "The car is fine, but I'm hungry."

"We'll see about that. I plan to look over Shelby."

Ely, Nevada, is located at the intersection of three highways and is hundreds of miles from any form of civilization. Although it may not be the *actual* middle of nowhere, it's pretty close. We drove in on US93, passing by the Motel 6 because Riley was desperately seeking coffee. We turned onto US50, which is the main drag that runs through town. The area was surrounded by craggy hills dotted with sagebrush, and the vast blue sky seemed to go on forever. The teeming masses of people and bright lights of Las Vegas seemed like a lifetime ago, which was a relief in many ways. Not only was I less likely to have any screaming visions, but odds were good that people in Ely weren't living a fast-paced hard-driving lifestyle and I might be able to relax a little.

Riley pointed at a sign for the Economy Drug and Old Fashioned Fountain. "That'll work."

He parallel parked and ran inside while Zelda and I waited in the car. In addition to the drug store and fountain, there was a J.C. Penney and a multistory brick building adorned with a neon sign and a gigantic miner. Apparently the Hotel Nevada and Gambling Hall had been around when mining was a big deal. As it was, not many citizens of Ely were out and about, and a dust devil swirled down the desolate street.

Riley had mentioned that US50 was referred to as the "loneliest highway," and it was easy to see why. Although during our journey across the desert I might have gotten a sunburn, the little twinge at the side of my head had disappeared. The thought of having a hallucination-free evening was appealing, even if it was in the middle of nowhere.

Riley returned with a huge to-go cup of coffee and a blueberry muffin, which he handed to me. "This should tide you over until we get to a grocery store. The lady at the counter said it's homemade."

I took a big bite out of the muffin, which was excellent. "Mmmfff, this is great! Thank you."

"I have enough coffee to make it through checking in at the motel and going to the store to get food, but then I'm done. If you have any ambitious plans to chase after clowns tonight, I'm opting out."

"Fine with me. I think I'll pass on the Ely nightlife too."

After we checked into the motel, Riley took Zelda for a short walk, then we went to the grocery store. Riley was adamant that I should attempt to eat some decent food and I was equally adamant that he eat anything at all.

I pushed the grocery cart down the aisle and pondered the deli section. Without cooking facilities, our options were limited, but we did score a microwave and refrigerator in our unit, so that helped matters a little.

Riley threw healthy things like granola bars and more carrots into the cart. I tried to repress a sigh as they flew by. Once we made it to the baked-goods aisle, I threw in a package of Hostess cupcakes to balance out the vegetables. I wasn't a rabbit, for heaven's sake.

Riley reached in, pulled out the cupcakes, and read the ingredients list to me extremely slowly, enunciating each chemical name precisely.

I grabbed the package from him and put it back on the shelf. "Okay. Fine. Be that way."

"You'll thank me later."

After we got back to the motel, I nuked my frozen dinner and settled in for the evening. I chewed on my pasta alfredo and watched Riley prepare his latest strange compilation of food. Tonight's delight was a pile of raw almonds, applesauce, a piece of bread, and a frozen dinner that seemed to be mostly rice. At least he was eating something, even if it was weird.

Zelda moved back and forth between the two beds, begging for handouts. I tossed her the corner of a piece of bread, which she snatched from the air. She had amazing eye-mouth coordination.

Riley leaned back on the bed and set his paper plate aside, away from Zelda's inquisitive nose. "So I need to tell you something. I think Dean is here somewhere."

"Here, as in here in Ely? Are you kidding me? How do you know?"

"I smelled pie and baked goods again."

"Are you sure it wasn't my cupcake? Hey, I put it back!"

"Pie and prefabricated cupcakes don't smell anything alike. Dean smelled like all different types of pies. It's hard to explain, but it's like layers of scents. I'm guessing he hasn't washed his coat or shirt or something and it still smells like the bakery."

"You're positive it's him? How can you be sure?"

"It's difficult to describe. Imagine trying to explain the color red to someone who can only see in black and white."

"Hmm, yeah, I guess that would be tricky. But how did you pick that smell out of, well, everything else that smells in Ely?"

"It's easier to isolate scents here. Las Vegas was like an olfactory kaleidoscope. It was confusing and muddled and I felt so bad I could barely think. But here, I can pick things out more easily. I'm sure he was in that grocery store not too long ago."

"Do you think he's here with the circus? I mean, I thought he was kidnapped. What's he doing in the grocery store?"

"That's the million-dollar question. Maybe the guys in the suits got hungry. I mean, circus people have to buy food somewhere, right?"

"So you can detect people? That's incredible." I swirled some noodles around in the cheesy sauce. "Do you think we're safe? I mean, you know they're here. But do they know we're here?"

"I have no idea."

"I hate to ask this, but can you smell Lars? Because I'm hoping I don't run into him again. It would be great if you could point me in the other direction."

Riley popped a raw almond into his mouth, chewed, and then grinned. "I'm not sure I can do that, but if he gets near you, I'll be able to smell your pheromones."

I dropped my fork. "What? You didn't tell me that before."

"I thought you might think it was a little weird."

"Well, yeah, I do. But you're saying I have pheromones? Like sex signals? You can actually *tell* that?"

"Everyone has a different scent. To me, it's almost like a fingerprint. Every person is different. And like I said, for whatever reason, you smell good, although I will say what you eat can have an effect on that too. I may be somewhat selfishly encouraging you to eat less junk. And then when you're aroused, pheromones come into play."

"I don't want to know about this. It's embarrassing."

"Even if Jebediah hadn't told me you made out with Lars the sexy clown, it was pretty obvious. When you came back, I knew *something* had happened." He tilted his head toward

Zelda, who was sitting in front of him like a model obedient canine, listening intently. "I'm sure she knew too, along with any other critter with a halfway decent sense of smell."

"I detect a bit of olfactory snobbery in your tone." I sat up straight and pointed my fork at Riley. "Okay, so tomorrow morning, we need to get you and Zelda over to the big top to sniff these people out. Maybe for once we could find them before they find us."

"That would be a nice change." He reached down to stroke Zelda's head. "What do you think, Zee? Wanna go find some bad guys?"

Zelda wagged, stood up, and looked ready to head out. Riley smiled as he ruffled her ears. "Not yet, girl. Some of us didn't spend all day snoring in the backseat like you did."

"Hey you could have slept while I was driving. You had ample opportunity and I promise you wouldn't have missed much, except a whole lot of desert."

"Never again." Riley leaned back onto the pillows and closed his eyes. "I'm going to look Shelby over in the morning and make sure nothing is wrong with her."

"Hey, my driving was fine."

"We'll see. Unlike people, machines don't lie."

~

After having the best night's sleep in what felt like forever, I got up and chomped on an absurdly healthy granola bar for breakfast. It tasted like tree bark, but the thought that I smelled revolting to happy woodland creatures, dogs, and Riley because of my nutritionally questionable eating habits gave me pause. Sure, a Big Mac tasted good going down, but I was feeling a little self-conscious that I might be grossing out the universe afterward. I wished Riley hadn't told me that. Ick.

After we were fed and showered, Riley and I went out to the fairgrounds to snoop around. This time we were going to be a lot more cautious at the circus. I also was going to make it my mission to talk to Hector. Riley parked the Mustang behind an enormous desert shrub near the parking lot so the car wouldn't be visible from the fairgrounds.

As before, the big-top tent was spread out on the ground and circus trailers littered the area.

Worried that we might run across Lars again, I reached for Riley's hand. "So what do we do this time if we see the guys in suits? Do we get brave and confront them? Because I hate to break this to you, but I'm kind of a coward."

"I am too. Maybe we play it by ear." He squeezed my hand in a show of gutless solidarity. "At least Zelda isn't a wimp. She'll protect us."

"Good point."

Lots of people were milling around, and we tried to look casual as we steered clear of the animal pens. I nudged Riley. "Getting anything?"

He inclined his head toward a pair of clowns that were walking hand in hand. "Over there. Do you think they're a couple?"

"I support the right of anyone to choose to be with anyone they want to be with, even if they are clowns. With that said, could the guy on the right be Dean in a wig and makeup? He's about the same height and build."

"That's what I was thinking."

I stopped, let go of Riley's hand, and we moved around so we were behind the end of a trailer. The clown couple had stopped and I didn't want to get too close.

"Does your nose agree?" I looked down. "What about you, Zee?"

Riley nodded and Zelda wagged happily.

"Now what?" I said. "It looks like Dean has found a clown friend. Do you think he could be Dean's captor or kidnapper?"

"I suppose so."

"Or what if we're wrong about everything and Dean just ran away and joined the circus to be with his gay clown lover? Maybe he got sick of delivering pies and living a lie."

Riley shook his head. "I think you're making up stories. We do know he didn't look happy about being grabbed and stuffed into the blue van. It seems more likely that he ran away after he was kidnapped and decided to join the circus. Or the kidnappers are here too. Maybe the circus and kidnappers are in cahoots."

"Cahoots? Who says that? Sherlock Holmes? I guess we do know the van was near the circus before. I suppose that could be it. Maybe they were looking for Dean or dropping him off. Okay, so what are we supposed to do now?"

"No matter why Dean is here, we still need to talk to him. As far as we know, he's the only person who has any idea where our parents went."

We crept up to hide behind the next trailer in the row, and Riley turned his head, scanning the area. He walked a few steps and picked up a slinky magenta silk scarf that looked like it might have belonged to a trapeze artist. "We need a distraction."

"Like what?"

"Could you go over to the one of the cages and open a door?"

"Like a lion or a tiger? Are you nuts? No way."

"I was thinking of something less dangerous and more domesticated. Maybe a horse or a pony? Any equine would be thrilled to have an outing. Then get back over here as soon as you can. I'll need your help."

"I think I can deal with a horse. I took some riding lessons a few years ago, and horses seem to like me. What are you going to do?"

"I'll watch Dean and his friend while you go liberate a suitable equine."

"Okay." I turned and left Riley and Zelda in their hiding spot behind the trailer. As nonchalantly as I could, I walked over to where the animals were kept. A bear paced back and forth in a cage and I scuttled by. He was huge and brown with ferocious teeth.

The horses were set up in portable stalls with metal gates across the front. A pretty white Arabian nodded her head at me, which I took as a good sign. I looked around and found a big bucket of grain hanging on a hook. I grabbed the bucket and went up to the gate. "Hi there, pretty horse. Lookie, I have food."

I examined the locking mechanism and opened the gate, holding the grain out in front of me. The horse was clearly interested and seemed to like the idea of free grain. I gave her a handful and walked away with the bucket. The horse followed me out of the stall and I grabbed a last handful of grain before locking the bucket behind the gate.

With my hand outstretched in front of me, I led the horse away from the stalls, let her eat my handful, then walked alongside her, patting her back. When I reached her hind quarters, I slapped her rump hard and said, "Go have fun!" and ran the other way.

I looked back to see the beautiful white horse galloping across the field toward the parking lot. She was having all kinds of fun, kicking up her heels, and whinnying with joy. I giggled as I made my way back to the trailers, attempting to hide behind a series of props and buildings while other people ran after the horse.

Breathless, I returned to the trailer and found Riley and Zelda right where I'd left them. I grinned with pride. "Mission accomplished."

"No kidding. Nicely done. Let's get closer."

The clown with Dean was shouting at the people who were trying to catch the horse and was waving his arms. Meanwhile, Dean looked confused. Worse than that, he was handcuffed to the other clown and we heard him say, "Billy, how come there are three of you?"

We stopped behind another trailer and I turned to Riley. "What are we supposed to do now? They're *attached* to each other!"

Riley scowled. "This is not good."

Billy was shrieking and trying to drag Dean toward the horse, but Dean didn't seem to want to go. Dean also had to weigh twice as much as Billy. As the clown ranted about Dolly the Wonder Horse, I come to the conclusion that Billy was a nut job. He was like a bratty little boy who had lost his toy, trapped in an adult body and wearing a clown suit. Billy threatened to hurt Dean, who seemed unfazed by the talk of violence.

I nudged Riley. "Something is seriously wrong with Dean."

"Maybe they drugged him."

"Well that's bad, but even worse, I think Billy is a psycho. He may be small, but he's scary, which isn't doing much for my clown phobia."

Riley waggled his eyebrows. "Dream about Lars; you'll feel better."

"Shut up. What's your plan?"

We turned as Billy burst forth with a massive, expletive-laced rant against Dean, the circus, God, and the larger universe as he fiddled with his handcuff. He shook his hand free and turned to Dean. "You stay right here, or I'm gonna kill you. I mean it—if you're not here, I promise you I will hunt you down like the nasty little mutant mongrel you are. Without that horse, I don't have a unicorn for the show." And with that, he ran off toward the parking lot after everyone else.

I peered around the trailer to check on the situation. "Dolly is one wily unicorn. She's having all kinds of fun. Ha, look at that! She jumped over that railing like a champion. Good girl!"

Riley tugged at my shirtsleeve. "Focus. This is our chance. Come on, Zee."

We ran over to Dean, who now was crumpled on the ground like a sack of potatoes. Riley crouched down. "Dean! Are you all right? We need to talk to you."

Dean looked up and his head bobbed as he focused on Riley, then me. "You look. I know. What? Them. Farg."

"Farg?" I said. "Dean! What is farg?"

"Toadstool!" Dean said.

I looked at Riley. "I think we have a problem. Those must be some serious drugs they gave him."

Zelda licked Dean's face and he patted her head. "Dog!"

"Can we get him out of here without being seen?" I asked.

"I'm not sure." Riley dragged Dean to an upright position. "Jeez, how much does this guy weigh? Can you help me?"

I put my arms on the other side and groaned as Dean's muscular body began to list in my direction. "Help! He's going to squish me!"

We set Dean back on the ground and Riley glanced at the steps up to the trailer. "Wait. Hold on for a minute." He ran into the trailer and I could hear him throwing things around. He threw a wide-brimmed sombrero, a gigantic rainbow afro wig, and a three-panel folding screen out the door of the trailer.

I raised my eyebrows. "Okay, so what are we doing with this stuff?"

Riley put the huge floppy hat on his head, picked up the wig, and plopped it on my head.

I rolled my eyes up, peering at the rainbow hues above my eyebrows. "You can't be serious."

He bent down, hauled Dean up into his arms, and boosted him into a reasonably upright position. "Take that scarf and tie him to me, so gravity doesn't take him down again."

I did as instructed, wrapping the scarf under Dean's arms and diagonally across Riley's chest and shoulder. "Okay, what am I supposed to do with this screen?" It was the type of fabric screen used to divide an area like a dressing room or closet from a larger space, so it wasn't heavy, just awkward to hold.

"You carry the screen to block us from view. We'll go to the perimeter of the fairgrounds and sneak our way around to the exit."

"What about Zelda?"

Riley let go of Dean's floppy form with one hand and moved it slightly to point at the dog. "Shelby."

Zelda took off like a shot and disappeared from view almost immediately. My jaw dropped. "Riley! What did you do?"

"Don't worry. She'll be waiting for us in the car. Pick up the screen and let's do this."

"Holding up a screen seems sort of lame. I hope this works."

"Me too. This guy weighs a ton."

~

Riley half dragged, half carried Dean's limp body slowly across the fairground while I held up the screen. I was mildly worried that Riley would collapse or have a heart attack from the exertion. The poor guy was breathing heavily and he wasn't in the best health to begin with. Because Dean wasn't participating in his rescue much at all, it was like Riley was hauling a stoned walrus.

We slowly made our way around the fairgrounds and went behind the exhibit buildings, so we were mostly obscured by them by the time the circus performers had rounded up Dolly the Wonder Unicorn.

Riley sputtered, "I gotta rest for a second."

I stopped, shoved my shoulder under Dean's armpit, and waited while Riley stood there breathing for a moment. He looked down at his shirt. "I'm covered with clown makeup. This is nasty. I liked this shirt too."

His t-shirt looked like it was covered in white snail slime, and it was unlikely to recover from the gooey stains. I patted Dean's chest. "Come on Dean, it would be great if you could cooperate here. We're trying to help you."

Dean mumbled, "Goat tails, snarkleaf, moose cockles."

I moved out from under Dean's arm and attempted to loop it over Riley's shoulder. I looked up at him. "I think you're on your own."

"All right. I think I can cope with more dragging now."

Once Riley started moving, I held up my folding screen. "Just a little farther."

I was lying. It was a lot farther. Slowly, we made our way across the parking lot and outside the fairgrounds to where the Mustang was parked. Zelda was patiently waiting in the backseat and stood up to greet us with a happy wag.

Riley stopped next to the passenger side. "Get him off me."

I worked on untying the scarf and finally Dean slid down Riley's chest and into a heap on the ground.

Riley bent and put his hands on his knees. "Thank God that's over."

I kicked at one of Dean's big red clown shoes. "I think we still need to pour him into the car somehow."

"I know. Give me a minute." Riley stood up again. "Dragging two-hundred-fifty pounds of dead weight wouldn't have been such a problem six months ago. I'm so tired of feeling like this. Everything is ten times harder than it used to be."

I reached up to pat Riley's shoulder. "Sorry. Let's introduce Dean to your car."

Riley opened the door and we both shoved, pulled, and dragged Dean into the passenger seat. I got into the back with Zelda and Riley settled in to drive. He paused to turn around and look at me before he started the car. "Should we take him back to the motel? What if someone already knows we're there?"

"Maybe we could drive a ways out of town and find a patch of desert to prop him up in until the drugs wear off."

Riley shrugged and turned the key in the ignition. Dean was slumped down in the passenger seat, which was probably a good thing, since that made him harder to spot. I put my arms around Zelda and gave her a hug as we took off. If I never saw another clown in my life, it would be too soon.

After getting off the two-lane highway, Riley parked at the side of a dirt road and we waited around in the sun for a while, watching Dean sleep. Whatever they'd given him certainly was potent.

Zelda yawned loudly and Riley turned in his seat to look at me. "Do you want me to put the top up? We could crispy fry to a crackly crunch out here. Or maybe we should give up on this idea and take him back to the motel. I could stand a shower. Maybe we could hose him down too. Watching Dean's clown makeup melt is kind of gruesome."

Riley's comment reminded me of my hallucination with the flame-throwing clown and I grimaced. "Fine, let's go. I don't want to think about melting clowns."

We went back to the Motel 6 and dragged Dean out of the Mustang and into the room. Riley wasn't interested in trying to get Dean up on the bed, so we left him sprawled on the floor. The guy had to wake up sometime. I stepped over his body to get to the snack foods we had in the room. Kidnapping or rescuing or whatever we'd done had worked up my appetite.

Riley grabbed some clothes and retreated to the bathroom, but before closing the door, he threw a washcloth at me. "If you want to try to scrape off some of that makeup, feel free."

"Yeah, the cleaning staff is gonna love us. That red mouth is going to permanently stain this towel. They're going to think we performed some type of ritual sacrifice in here."

Zelda supervised as I knelt down next to Dean and pulled the tangled orange wig off his head. I smoothed his light brown hair away from his face. In addition to being ugly, that nasty wig had to be uncomfortable. Poor guy. It was unlikely that he'd asked to be made up as a clown.

As I wiped off the heavy, slimy makeup, the fact that Dean was an extremely good-looking man started to become apparent again. When we'd seen him for those few minutes at the diner in Alpine Grove, I'd thought he was a complete hottie.

I leaned over and said, "Dean, come on, it's time to wake up. I'm starting to get a little worried here because I have no idea what drugs they might have given you."

His lashes fluttered, and when he opened his hazel eyes they were filled with alarm. "Glerk!"

"Dean, it's me, Meg. I met you in Alpine Grove. Remember?" Although to me it felt like a lifetime and thousands of miles ago, it had only been a few days.

"Meg," he mumbled, then closed his eyes again.

I sat back on my heels and stroked the fur on Zelda's head. "We're not getting anywhere with this guy, are we?"

Zelda didn't seem to have any input on the matter, so I got up, put my makeup-saturated washcloth on the nightstand, and sprawled out on the bed. Zelda jumped up next to me and I closed my eyes, enjoying the small respite from running around and clown-cleanup duty.

Riley came out of the bathroom rubbing a towel on his wet hair. He looked down at Dean on the floor. "Well, he looks a little better, I guess."

"He said my name before he passed out again. I think that's progress."

Riley sat down across from me on the other bed. "I hope there's not something seriously wrong with this guy. I mean, I guess there's a hospital here somewhere, but I doubt it's state-of-the-art or anything."

"Is Las Vegas the closest real city?"

"Probably. Reno is three-hundred-fifty miles away."

Suddenly, Dean sat up and both Riley and I looked at him. I said, "Dean? Are you okay?"

"What happened? Why am I on the floor?" He wiped his palm on his cheek. "Yuck. What is that?"

"Makeup," Riley said. "You were at a circus. Do you remember why you were there?"

"Who are you?" Dean said.

"Riley O'Shea. We met a few days ago. You said you know my father, Tim. Remember?"

Dean's eyes clouded and the expression on his face was one of complete befuddlement. "Tim? Yes, Tim O'Shea. I know Tim. He's a great guy. Really smart."

I crouched down on the floor next to him again. "Do you remember my mother, Ellen Jennings?"

Dean said, "Yes. She's doing research."

I flapped my arms and practically fell over with glee. "Yes! Yes! What was the research about? But more importantly, *where is she?*"

"Doing research." Dean's eyes widened and he moved to get up. "Don't feel…good."

He did look a little greenish under the remaining makeup. I made a sweeping motion with my hands. "The bathroom is over there. Can you make it?"

Dean half crawled, half walked to the facilities and pushed the door partway closed behind him, presumably to access the commode. A few horrible retching sounds came from within and then a flush. He crawled back into the room and splayed out face down, like a dead fish on the floor.

I stood up and made a face at Riley. "Poor Dean. He's a mess."

"Maybe we should try to take him to a doctor." Riley reached for the phone book on the nightstand. "Let me figure out where the medical facilities are."

Riley reported that the hospital was on East Aultman Street, aka US 50, aka the main drag through Ely. Given the size of the town, we were only a few minutes away. He closed the phone book with a snap and crouched next to Dean. "Do you feel any better, Dean? Should we take you to a doctor?"

Dean moaned, but didn't move. I nodded my head and Riley sighed. He reached under Dean's arms and dragged him up onto the bed. "Come on Dean, work with me here. We need to get you back in the car."

Riley rolled Dean over and motioned to me to help. Zelda followed us as Riley and I hauled Dean back to the Mustang.

Once we had Dean back in the car and mostly upright, I got into the backseat again. I reached over the seat and tapped Dean on the shoulder. "It's going to be okay, Dean. We're taking you to the doctor."

Riley started the car and drove the ten blocks to the hospital, which proudly proclaimed it had been in existence since 1905. Riley said, "I hope they've done some upgrades since then."

Zelda waited in the car while we dragged Dean into the hospital. Unlike many emergency rooms, this one was largely empty. Maybe everyone was at the circus. A nurse at the reception desk handed us some forms and told us to wait in the reception area before she loaded Dean into a wheelchair and carted him into the back.

I tilted the clipboard toward Riley. "I don't even know the correct spelling of Dean's name. Is it Wolf with or without an e?"

"No idea."

"Do you suppose he has insurance?"

Riley widened his eyes and raised his eyebrows. "How the heck should I know? I met him when you did. Why are you asking me?"

I sat down on one of the hard plastic chairs with a thump. "I don't know. I hope he's okay."

"Can you handle this stuff? I'd like to walk around a little with Zelda. It's been kind of a long day."

"I'm guessing you need some alone time, don't you?"

"You have no idea."

Chapter 9

Dogs and Crazy People

I sat in a chair perusing the stack of hospital admittance forms. I lifted my pen and wrote "Dean." That was it. Everything else was a mystery to me. I set the clipboard on the chair next to me. Once Dean was coherent, he could fill out his own inane paperwork. I stood up and began pacing around the room. Where was everyone? The woman at front desk eyed me suspiciously as I wandered around the room.

With an exasperated sigh, I snatched an ancient magazine from a stack and sat down. Waiting was not one of my strong suits. I flipped through the magazine, scanning the headlines. For the first time in years, I hadn't seen the news in days. What had happened in the world? I had no idea, which was sad for a former news hound like me. I used to pride myself on being up on current events. Now I was sitting around waiting to see if a stoned clown could tell me anything about my mother. Sometimes life is strange.

I looked up at the sound of Riley returning through the front door. He sat down next to me. "What are they doing with him? This is taking forever. I mean, is he dead? What is going on?"

"You're right. I was trying to be patient, but I'm not good at that."

"You don't say."

"I'm worried and I don't care what the receptionist said. I'm going back there." I marched over to the swinging double doors and stood on my tiptoes to peek through the window. No one was there.

Riley came up next to me. "Where is everybody?"

We both pushed through the doors and walked into the small emergency room. The beds were empty, but behind a white fabric screen two nurses and the receptionist were sitting in a row of chairs with wads of cotton rammed into their mouths. Their wrists had been tied behind their backs with gauze and their ankles were tied to the chair legs.

One of the nurses uttered a muffled squawk and I rushed to pull the cotton out of her mouth. "What happened? Are you okay?"

She nodded at the exit "There was an awful clown!"

I looked at Riley, who was pulling cotton from the mouth of the receptionist. She burst out, "He was an evil little gnome-like guy with such a potty mouth! Even though he was whispering, I couldn't believe the words he used. It was disgusting."

"Billy, the psycho clown," I said as I pulled cotton from the mouth of the second nurse.

Riley nodded. "Did you see where the patient went? His name is Dean."

The three women started talking at once and the consensus was that Dean was gone and Billy was a nasty little troll. I couldn't argue with that, but the fact that Dean had been taken again worried me. I asked the nurse, "Did you find out if Dean was okay? What was he drugged with?"

"We're not sure, but he was starting to come around and when he saw the clown, he ran out the door."

I almost shouted, "You mean Dean is *gone*?"

The nurse tilted her head to indicate the emergency exit at the back of the room, "Yes, he ran out the door while the clown was tying us up."

"How could you let that happen? There are three of you!" I demanded.

Another nurse moved her hands in a 'calm down' gesture. "He tackled Cindy, then when I went to see what was going on, he jumped me from behind. Then he tied us up. When Anna came in from the reception office to ask a question, he jumped her too."

Riley said, "We've already seen that Billy is a wiry little dude."

I stomped my foot in abject frustration. "I can't believe Dean is gone again!"

"Ely isn't a huge metropolis, so he can't have gotten far," Riley said, then grabbed my arm to still my temper-tantrum gestures. "I think it's time for us to go."

"Fine."

"Wait! Shouldn't we call the police?" Cindy said.

"Do whatever you want to do, but we need to find Dean," I said.

Anna added, "But I'm sure they'll want to question you."

As he grabbed my hand, Riley said, "Gotta go."

We hurried out to the car and spent two fruitless hours driving down every single tiny side street in Ely. It was entirely possible that Billy had caught up to Dean and taken him right back to the circus.

Finally I said, "So now what? Clearly Dean is not wandering the streets of Ely. We've been everywhere."

"I'm hungry. Let's go back to the motel and get something to eat."

I held out my palms in front of me. "Stop the presses! You're *hungry*? I don't believe it."

"It's been a long day and I didn't eat anything before we took Dean to the hospital."

I couldn't argue with that because as usual, I was hungry too. Of course, that was nothing new. I was always hungry, and nuking up another fabulous frozen dinner sounded appealing. I pushed back a guilty little thought. The fact was that I should be doing everything in my power to find my mother, but I wasn't.

I should bravely run back to the circus and perform a heroic act of Dean-o rescue. But I didn't want to. Going back there again had zero appeal. From the expression on his face, it appeared Riley was equally depressed at the idea of trying to retrieve Dean *again*. Even Zelda looked glum.

After spending time with Dean and learning almost nothing, it was entirely possible that he didn't know anything about where our parents had gone. The only thing we'd established was that Dean knew who our parents *were*. We did not find out if he knew where they *went*. It was an important difference. Had we rescued the guy for nothing?

My circular thoughts weren't helping my mood, and by the time we got back to the room, I was sweaty and grumpy. I tore open the box for my frozen meal and peeled the plastic off the enchiladas. The little halo of ice crystals on the gray tortillas looked particularly unappetizing. I threw it into the microwave and slammed the door.

Riley looked up from his container of yogurt. "Something wrong?"

"I'm tired of this."

"This what?"

"All this running around looking for Dean. We went to all this effort and we are no closer to finding our parents than we were days ago."

"I think we've had this conversation."

"I know. But what I really care about is Mom. Where *is* she?" I sat down on the end of the bed and leaned over to pet Zelda. "Half the time, I feel like crying. The other half, I'm mad. And then I'm sad and worried."

"That's more than two halves."

I lifted a hand off Zelda's head, so I could point at him. "Hey, don't get technical. I'm just saying I'm tired of the circus, tired of motel rooms, tired of driving around, and tired of thinking about these awful visions that involve fire. And don't get me started about clowns."

"I share your passionate dislike for them." Riley took a spoonful of yogurt. "In more mundane news, the t-shirt that is now covered with clown makeup was the last clean one I had. I need to wash some clothes in a bad way."

I sighed and flopped back on the bed. "I know. Me too. I'm sick of this. All of it."

"Yeah, I know. Me too."

I rolled over to face Riley. "What are we going to do?"

"In the absence of any other ideas, I vote for visiting the Motel 6 laundry facilities." He took a bite of yogurt. "I can't face going back to the circus tonight. They're here for another day anyway. If that's where Dean went, he'll probably still be there tomorrow, right?"

"Maybe we could have an evening in and go over everything again." I sat up. "Is that too pathetic? I mean, if I were some brave super hero, I'd be insisting that we go back to save Dean. Batman would go save Dean. But I'm not Batman. I also feel like we're missing something."

"I know what you mean."

"Okay, let's do laundry and think. Tomorrow is Monday and everyone will be back at work and I can start making those calls and getting faxes."

"Sounds like a plan."

"That's the type of thing I'm actually good at."

Riley put down his spoon. "It beats dragging clowns around the desert."

"No kidding."

~

When I woke up the next morning, Riley and Zelda weren't in the room. Presumably they were off on a nice Monday morning excursion through the desert. Their jaunt was good news for me, because I had phone calls to make. Nevada is on Pacific Time, which meant it was three hours later in DC. By now, everyone I needed to talk to would be up and at work, so I could start my campaign of long-distance harassment.

I called the front desk to get the fax number for the motel and then called Leo. One thing that has always endeared me to my now-former boss was his enthusiasm for digging up dirt. He loved a challenge and was thrilled to report that he had fifty pages of information he wanted to fax over to me. I thanked him profusely and told him I hoped to see him soon.

It was the truth. I missed my life back East. To be fair, by the time I left, things weren't going particularly well professionally or personally, but I still had my apartment. I missed my knickknacks, photos on the wall, my closet. My many pairs of shoes. And an actual kitchen with a full-sized refrigerator stocked with all my favorite goodies. I missed it all and I desperately wanted to go home.

I called the front desk again and warned them that I was going to receive a large and important fax, so they needed to load up the machine with paper. They assured me that they would handle my correspondence with the tenderest of loving care.

I waited a few minutes before toddling down to the office and retrieving my pile of papers. Leo had done an amazing job of amassing every recent news report on Archetypal Media and Online Systems Unlimited. He'd also enclosed all the information that had been provided to employees about the merger and layoffs. Because I was technically an employee, some of the documentation might also be sitting at the post office near my house. My mail was being held there because of my trip to Alpine Grove, so I'd undoubtedly missed out on some educational separation paperwork.

I suspected there was gold in the massive stack of paper that the fax machine had spewed out, but next on my phone agenda was calling Matt, and I didn't want to put it off. He was a creature of routine and I knew his schedule. Now was the perfect time to interrupt his o-so-important business.

When I called Archetypal Media, I ended up talking to Little Miss Perky again. She did her best to pass me off to someone in public relations, but Little Miss Perky didn't know me. The reason I had been such a good reporter is because I was willing to call anybody at any time and have uncomfortable conversations with people who didn't want to talk to me. That was how I met Matt in the first place.

I had gotten over any fear of rejection and cold-calling people long ago and it had served me well. I pointed out to Perky Girl that I was calling Matt's private line, so clearly I knew who he was and he knew me. There was a pause and I could almost hear the gears in her brain computing how much trouble she would get in with Matt if she put me through. Finally, I said, "So is Matt there or not?"

"Um, well, I think so, but I'm not sure he's available."

"The office is glass and I know you can see him sitting there. Put me through."

"I'm not sure…"

"It is ten twenty, which means he is leaned back in his chair with his feet on the desk reading the *New York Times.* Put me through."

"Fine! Have a nice day."

I allowed myself a small smile of satisfaction until Matt's voice greeted me. At one time I'd enjoyed the sound of his suave, velvety voice. Now it made my skin crawl. I cleared my throat. "Matt, I'd like to ask you some questions."

"Why are you calling me? You aren't a reporter anymore and I have nothing to say to you. I have a meeting."

"No you don't. You've blocked out the next forty minutes to read the *Times.* That's not a meeting. Your next meeting is a visit to the men's room at eleven."

"What do you want? I thought you were still on what some might euphemistically and politely term medical leave, but which I like to think of as your personal trip to crazy town."

"As it happens, I *am* on a trip; however, I do know that I've been laid off. I don't care, except that I think you're an idiot for laying off Leo. That's a mistake that you'll regret."

Matt paused. "It's hardly surprising you'd think that. You've always had some strange hero worship for that old relic."

I took a deep breath, trying to tamp down my anger. He was baiting me. Matt knew every trick to press my buttons, but I wasn't going to let him get to me. "I'd like the truth. Why is Archetypal Media merging with Online Systems United?"

"It's quite simple. If we can get everyone onto the Internet, we can sell them advertising online."

My stomach lurched. It was almost exactly what he'd said in my vision. I said evenly, "What about cable? You said that television was what everyone wanted."

"We want to expand our advertising footprint. Technology marches on."

I tried not to think about the fact that I'd heard him say that before too. Something clicked in my mind, and I said, "As you may remember, my mother was studying visual perception and how it is used in computer graphics."

"Vaguely. So what? Are you doing research for your mother now that you're unemployed?"

"No, but I was wondering if you were adding more gaming into your media portfolio."

"That is a possible avenue we're exploring. I can't comment further on forward-looking ventures."

That was executive weasel-word code for yes they were. I continued, "Leo told me about your recruitment video.

It sounded like the images were…interesting. And quite compelling."

"What are you getting at, Meg?"

"Nothing. I was just curious about it. Did you do it in-house?"

"No."

"Who created it?"

"Centerfield Technologies, based on our creative brief. What is your point? You're wasting my time. You know I'm a busy man."

"One more question. Do Online Systems United or Archetypal Media have anything to do with radio?"

"Don't be dumb. This isn't 1934. Radio is old news. We're into television, cable, and the Internet. We're exploring bundling, and of course other communications ventures as well. You'll be able to get TV, phone, and online services all in one package. After the merger, approximately half of the homes with any type of media access will be working with us. It's going to be huge!"

"Nothing to do with frequencies or anything like that?"

"Frequencies? What are you talking about?"

I was fishing and had no idea where I was going with it, but I bluffed anyway. "Like high frequency or very high frequency. It's techie stuff."

"Obviously, radios, television, and some types of phones use frequencies. I'm most familiar with TV, which uses the VHF and UHF bands. So what?"

"UHF?"

"Ultra high frequency."

"Okay."

"Meg, honestly, what are you rambling on about? Are we done here?"

I was lost now and needed to stop and think. "Okay, Matt, yeah, thanks for your time. Enjoy your newspaper and potty break."

"Always a pleasure, Meg."

I hung up and stuck my tongue out at the phone. What a jerk. Thanks to the merger, now he'd be worth even more money, which would make him even more of an arrogant prick. Ugh.

The door opened and Riley and Zelda walked in. Zelda jumped up to sit next to me and I gave her a hug as Riley sat down on the other bed. He nodded at the piles of papers next to me. "What's all that?"

"Leo's fax."

"Did you learn anything good?"

"Maybe. I'm not sure yet." I shook my head. "I talked to Matt. The whole merger thing is a big deal. Elements of it relate to your dad's expertise and my mom's as well."

"You mean the computer graphics stuff?"

"And frequencies. I guess TV uses ultra high too?"

"Yes, UHF. Remember the knob on old TVs?"

"Oh yeah. Did your dad do anything with that?"

"Yeah some of the radios he worked on were UHF, and lots of work with antennas too."

"In addition to TV and the Internet, the new company is going to be offering games. What if they are wanting to suppress my mom's research or something? I mean, who would want to play a game you're going to get addicted to?"

"On the other hand, you'd sell a lot of games when addicts tell all their friends and then *they* get hooked. I don't know what they could do to ensure that someone is addicted. If you drink alcohol, there's no guarantee you'll become an alcoholic."

"Yeah, I don't know." I stroked the fur on Zelda's back, trying to gather my thoughts. There was something here, I could feel it. "I suppose playing a game doesn't necessarily mean you'll be addicted, unless they've figured out some new subliminal stuff to get you hooked. Wait! What if that creepy video Leo told me about has subliminal messages in it? I mean, he said it had a bunch of images and I think I saw them in my vision. Then it turned bad. Maybe it's not literally fire. Maybe it's that people are being brainwashed!"

Riley gave me a doubtful look. "That's a stretch. I'm not sure I'm buying this idea. So you're saying the merger is a gigantic conspiracy to control the minds of humanity through TV?"

"I don't really know. But something weird is going on."

"So your ex-boyfriend Matt is like Lex Luthor trying to take over the world?" Riley chuckled. "Wow, you've got some seriously bad taste in men. At least Lois Lane was smart enough to go for Superman, not Lex."

"You're a laugh riot. I'm serious." I picked up the papers. "If you're not going to help me think this through, you need to be quiet. I've got a lot of stuff to read."

"Right." Riley got up and rummaged around a grocery bag, then turned around. "Wait. If we're all being brainwashed, what does that have to do with our sensory problems? We haven't seen any videos, signed up for cable, or accessed the Internet. The closest we got was Bubba's cable, which was broken. All we've done is drive around and annoy clowns. We've barely even listened to music in the car or watched the three TV stations we can get here. How do *we* fit into any of this?"

"I don't know." But I was determined to find out.

~

I spent the rest of the morning reading the fax, taking notes, and then passing the pages over to Riley, who was reading on the other bed. The only sound was the flipping of pages and Zelda's snoring. It was convenient that she was such an adaptable dog, ready to either nap or go off on an adventure at a moment's notice.

I handed the last sheet of the fax to Riley and scribbled my final notes. Everything seemed to come back around to the merger and the video. Once the dust settled, Archetypal Online Systems was going to have a vast network connected both online and physically with thousands of cable installers across the country. Maybe the cable guy who'd been at Bubba's place *was* there to spy on us. We'd thought it was absurd, but maybe we were wrong. My mind swirled at the possibilities and implications.

Riley set the last page aside, grabbed some clothes, and disappeared into the bathroom. The shower started and I grabbed the pages off his bed. I went over my notes and the information again. Why was I in Nevada, of all places? We had no indication that my mother was even here. We still had absolutely no clue where she was, and it was looking more and more like chasing Dean had been a huge waste of time.

I thought about all those cop shows that said the first forty-eight hours were crucial to solving a case. We were well beyond that window now. I wanted to cry in frustration. What if the time we'd wasted running all over the countryside meant Mom was lying dead in a ditch somewhere? It would all be my fault. And Riley's too.

After reading through everything yet again, it was obvious to me that Mom's research was connected to the merger. Whether it was brainwashing or gaming or something else, Matt was behind it. I was sure of it. Even though he'd been disdainful and pretended not to remember my mother's research, we'd talked about it countless times, and as a media mogul he naturally had been interested in her findings.

The door to the bathroom opened and Riley strolled out. "All yours. I think I can handle returning to the circus now."

"What are we doing, Riley?"

"Well, I don't know what you were doing, but I was taking a shower. I'm guessing that next we're going to the circus to find Dean, right?"

"Why? Why are we doing that?"

Riley opened a granola bar and chucked the wrapper onto the desk. "To get answers about what's going on with us and your mom, blah, blah, blah. You know why. We've talked about it. It's not like we can call the clown police and ask them to set Dean free."

"We have no answers. We're going in circles."

"I suppose maybe a little. The conversation with Dean might go better if he isn't stoned the next time we get to chat with him. It would also be nice if there were fewer clowns."

"This is absurd. Who goes around Nevada getting chased by clowns?"

Riley chewed more slowly. "Well, *us*, apparently."

"That's exactly the problem. What are we doing? I mean come on, yesterday we were sneaking around a circus, freeing a unicorn, and running off with a stoned clown. This is nuts and what's wrong with my life right now. I mean what in heaven's name is wrong with us?"

"Hey, we had our reasons to run off with the stoned clown, you know. Your visions, for one thing."

I flapped my arms in exasperation. "And your nose. Dogs follow scents. Dogs and crazy people."

Riley shook the granola bar at me. "Hey, watch who you're calling crazy, Ms. Screaming Hallucination."

"This is ridiculous." I gave my best game-show hostess gesture. "Look at us. We're in another crappy, cheap motel room. Then there's the filthy truck stops, restrooms that blow up, bad coffee, and repulsive diner food. *This* is what my life has become!"

"Mine too, in case you hadn't noticed."

"And it stinks! Do you really want to be stuck in that car with me forever, driving all over the West after this circus? I know I don't want to. You drive too fast, you never eat, and being around you twenty-four hours a day every day could drive me insane. The best thing about you is your dog. Let's face facts. This isn't working."

Riley sat down on the bed and leaned forward. A muscle in his jaw twitched and his expression hardened. "Fine, if that's the way you feel. But let's set the record straight here. Hanging around you twenty-four hours a day hasn't been a picnic for me either, you know. You...oh my God...you never shut up. And your eating habits! Do you have any idea what that does? You inhale a pile of onion rings and I have to live with the noxious evil fumes for days. It's like riding around with a seething nuclear-waste dump all the time."

Zelda moved to sit in front of Riley, staring up at him and whining quietly. He looked down at her and ruffled her ears with both hands. "Shh, it's all right, Zee."

"Is that so? Well, you were the one who said I smelled *good*." I pointed at the tiny refrigerator. "And if you weren't so unbelievably weird about food, I wouldn't have to go on these junk-food binges in the first place."

Riley let go of Zelda and stood up. "Fine. Forget it, then. We don't go to the circus. What's your big, brilliant master plan supposed to be?"

"I don't know, but we're done here. *I'm* done. I'm done with the clowns and the circus and the desert. You can keep driving around in circles if you want, but I need to go home. Back to DC." I got up, moved Zelda aside, and grabbed the phone book from the shelf on the bottom of the nightstand. "What's the closest real airport?"

"Las Vegas."

"How fast can we get there?"

"Do I have your majesty's permission to exceed the speed limit?"

I flapped the phone book at him to cover up the fact that my hand was trembling with anger. "You can drive as fast as you want. The sooner I get out of this godforsaken desert, the better. But if you get a speeding ticket, it's on you."

"Fine. Then a couple of hours." Riley started collecting clothes and ramming them into suitcases. "And I'll be just as happy as you are to be done with all of this. The joy of silence will be such a welcome relief."

"Fine." I picked up the phone and called the only travel agent in Ely. "I need to book a flight for tonight from Las Vegas to Washington, D.C."

Riley stomped around the room packing up, and I stroked the soft white fur on Zelda's head while I negotiated with the agent about times and connections.

The long drive back to Vegas was quiet and strained. Zelda curled up in the back of the Mustang and napped while Riley and I stared out at the highway, barely acknowledging each other's existence. I'd said some things to Riley I wished I hadn't, but it was unlikely I'd ever have to see him again, unless our parents stayed together. I hoped I was wrong and they hadn't actually gotten married. That could make next Thanksgiving more than a little awkward.

Of course, there was still the ugly fact that we hadn't found our parents yet, and Thanksgiving would be a big no-go without Mom. At this point, I had no concrete evidence that she was alive, dead, kidnapped, in a fire, or anywhere else. For all I knew, she and Tim O'Shea were hanging out in Maui sipping Mai Tais, having completely forgotten to let their offspring know where they were.

If I was lucky, maybe I'd pick up my mail from the post office and find a pretty postcard mixed in among my separation papers and junk mail. But who was I kidding? Mom was notorious for never, ever writing letters or postcards. She didn't even give me birthday cards. Email had been the one written-communication medium she'd embraced, and that was limited. Because I'm a writer, I'd send my mother long, involved, thoughtful, detailed ruminations on the state of my life and times. In response, I'd get the same standard eight-word message: "So nice to hear from you. Talk soon!"

Although written communication was iffy, Mom was a phone person. Before she met Tim, we regularly had long, enjoyable conversations talking about everything under the sun. Hours later, I'd hang up and the warmth of Mom's love would make me happy for the rest of the day. I missed her friendship and encouragement more than I'd ever imagined I could. Like the old saw went, you never truly know how much you'll miss people, until they're gone.

Where was she? I had to find out what was going on. I *had* to.

Chapter 10

Theories

On the trip back to Las Vegas, I learned that it's difficult to maintain a serious level of anger when you're driving through blazing sunlight across hundreds of miles of empty desert. It's like the mad melts out of you.

By the time we drove into Las Vegas rush-hour traffic, I was feeling even worse about the things I'd said to Riley. Based on the expression on his face, my guess was that he might be feeling the same way. We'd both hurled a lot of nasty insults at each other, but he had driven me around and paid for my food and lodging with little complaint. And even held my hand when I freaked out or cried. Not everybody would have done that and even though we were extremely different people, I did appreciate all he'd done to try to find our parents.

McCarran International Airport in Las Vegas is one of those airports that is almost always busy, day or night. We slowly wound our way through the traffic to the passenger drop-off area. Taxis and limos swirled around, and pedestrians waving and shouting things like "party time" and "viva Las Vegas" were everywhere. It appeared that more than a few people were having trouble letting go of their vacation and had not sobered up before preparing to fly home.

Riley wormed the Mustang into a slot next to the curb, got out, and retrieved my suitcase from the trunk. After I

195

exited the Mustang for the last time, I leaned into the backseat to give Zelda a final hug. As I wrapped my arms around her fuzzy body, I whispered. "I'm going to miss you, Zee. You be sure to take care of Riley, okay?"

Riley held out my now rather dusty Hartmann to me.

I grabbed it and put the strap over my shoulder. "I, um, well, thanks for everything."

"Have a safe trip."

I let the suitcase slide off my shoulder and thump to the ground. I looked up into Riley's face. "Look, I'm sorry about the things I said before, but I think I'm doing the right thing going back home."

Riley took off his sunglasses. "I know. I'm sorry too. If I learn anything useful about our parents, I'll give you a call."

"Promise?"

He twirled the sunglasses by the earpiece with a smile. "I promise."

I lurched forward and gave him an awkward hug. "Thanks for everything. Eat something, okay?"

He put his sunglasses on and stepped away from me. "I'll work on that. Getting back out of Vegas will help. Take care."

I picked up my suitcase and moved away from the car. Riley got back in the front seat and I waved as they pulled away into the pulsing throng of cars and shuttles. Zelda woofed good-bye and I waved at her. My long, strange trip was ending, but I still had a lot of work to do.

I planned to spend most of the plane ride going over my notes and thinking, so I made sure I had everything in my tote bag. The older woman next to me had a gigantic handbag that taxed the limits of under-seat storage. Once the plane was in flight, she yanked it out and began knitting something that was large enough to cover a football field. The multicolored yarn was a hideous mix of browns and tans.

She clacked her knitting needles a few times and then nudged me. "What are you working on?"

I didn't want to talk about what I was actually working on, so I went with, "A research project."

"What's it about?"

"It's classified." I decided to go on the offensive. The gigantic knitted artifact far exceeded the boundaries of her middle seat, which was a breach of airline etiquette. The man in the aisle seat had already pushed some brown yarn off his knee twice. I offered a polite I-don't-want-to-talk half-smile. "What are you knitting?"

"It's a sweater."

"I looked down at the massive expanse of tangled brown yarn. Was it a sweater for Big Foot? "How pretty. I'm sure the recipient will love it."

"It's my first one and it's taking forever to finish. I had no idea knitting patterns involved so many instructions. Ks and Ps and W-Ss and R-Ss. It's a bit confusing. Do you knit?"

"No, but I'm sure the sweater will be beautiful." I looked back down at my notes as a signal to close out the small talk, mentally willing her to be quiet. My grandmother had taught me how to knit when I was ten, but I wasn't volunteering that information. I had bigger problems than oversized sweaters to think about.

After four-and-a-half hours of flight time, I got into Dulles airport and caught a shuttle back to my apartment in suburban Maryland. By the time I got home, it was almost four in the morning. Of course, because I'd been on Pacific time, to me it was only one, which was small consolation.

I turned on the lights and my nose told me that although my apartment looked the same, it smelled mildewy, as if it had been closed up for a month. Maybe the plumbing had leaked. Perfect.

I crawled into bed and when I finally opened my eyes again, the clock said three thirty. It took a moment for my mind to compute that I'd slept for almost twelve hours. All my desert adventures had been exhausting.

After going about my morning routine a wee bit late, it was time to deal with mundane realities like going to the grocery store and picking up my mail. At the neighborhood Safeway, I went a little nuts, cruising down every single aisle and throwing items into my cart that I hadn't been able to eat for what seemed like forever.

When I got home, I put everything away and then pulled the Pepperidge Farm chocolate cake I'd just purchased back out of the freezer. I'd grabbed it at the store because it reminded me of Mom, who always admonished me not to eat too much cake. A little slice would tide me over while I figured out what to cook for dinner.

Here's a little confession: when it comes to chocolate, I don't have much control. Okay, make that no control. Whatever they put into that Pepperidge Farm chocolate icing is like crack. By the time I finished the entire cake, I remembered why my Mom didn't let me do this. I dropped the fork on the molded styrofoam plate. I hadn't even gotten a real china plate out of the cabinet, just dug in.

I certainly wasn't hungry anymore, but I felt sluggish and dull. Given my sugar stupor, I opted for going through my mail, since it didn't require much brain power. It was a demoralizing collection of bills, junk, and the information

I'd expected related to losing my job. I heaved a sigh as I ripped open a medical bill and added it to the pile. Soon I wasn't going to have health insurance anymore.

I turned my head to look at my apartment. It wasn't much. A standard one-bedroom, one-bathroom place in a nondescript square brick building that was indistinguishable from countless other equally nondescript complexes in suburbia.

Most of the time I'd lived in my apartment, I'd been too busy with work to do much about decoration. I had a cast-off sofa that Mom gave me years ago when she'd decided to get a new one. It was not something I ever would have picked out for myself, but it was reasonably comfortable and the price was right.

I walked over to the window and looked outside at my view of the street. It was full of newly leafed maple trees and the late-afternoon sun dappled the sidewalk as a light breeze wafted by. Spring in the DC area is beautiful, full of cheerful yellow daffodils and forsythia blooms and a rainbow of other flowers bursting forth everywhere. When I'd moved in, the lot across the street from my building had been filled with daffodils and they'd returned every year until this one. The lot was now a gaping hole, destined to be turned into yet another apartment building.

Over the last year or so, thanks to increases in rent prices in suburbs that were closer to the District of Columbia, my neighborhood had become almost mildly trendy. Never missing an opportunity, developers had swooped in and the amount of construction in my little corner of the world had soared. It was only a matter of time until they raised my rent.

I turned around and scanned my apartment. Everything was exactly as I'd left it, even down to the pile of old newspapers that I'd forgotten to ditch on the way out of town. Although the apartment hadn't changed, I had. Before I'd left to visit Mom, I had been wallowing in my medical leave, cursing my fate, and railing against the reality of my situation.

Tonight wasn't the first time I'd consumed an entire dessert. Mini-eclairs had been my favorite when I wanted to take my pity party up to the thousand-tiny-violin level. It hadn't been pretty, and now in hindsight, leaving town might have been a good thing as far as shaking me out of my medical-leave malaise.

I leafed through a few of the newspapers in the stack. My entire journalism career was literally old news. Most of the writing I'd slaved over was in a landfill, recycle pile, or moldering in someone's garage.

My peerless prose was destined to be heaved aside without a glance by some surly teenager who had to clean the garage because he'd stayed out too late. All my most cherished works were now some kid's punishment or the receptacle for bird droppings at the bottom of a cage.

Although I didn't have a job and my career was currently going nowhere, I did have a mission. Tomorrow I'd go to meet Leo at work. Or what used to be work. Dropping off my separation paperwork was a reasonable reason to stop by, but what I really wanted to do was watch the video he'd told me about. Although I needed to watch it, part of me was terrified, because there was the distinct possibility that it would bring on a vision. And this time Riley wouldn't be around to hold my hand.

~

The problem with sleeping until mid-afternoon is that returning to a regular sleep schedule is tricky. I stayed up late watching bad TV, but still spent hours awake staring at the ceiling, trying to will my mind to shut up.

By morning, the only thing the insomnia had given me was an idea about how to avoid distressing my former coworkers with another hallucination event at my old workplace. I called Leo, told him I would be stopping by, and asked him to make a copy of the videotape for me. That way, I could watch it in the privacy of my own home rather than in a crowded office.

Returning to the newsroom was jarring. It was like being thrust back into a world that I knew but that now seemed far away. For years I'd come in, grab a cup of bitter coffee, and immerse myself in the latest news of the day. I'd scan through images, videos, wire feeds, and printouts from every possible source with information about the news stories that had broken overnight.

I'd riffle through stacks of papers searching for every scrap of information for a story, make phone calls, and do research, frantically trying to meet a deadline. I was constantly talking to sources, readers, editors, and other reporters. It was a never-ending stream of information that kept my brain occupied on countless subjects every day.

I'd thrived on the stress, until I didn't. Although I hadn't wanted to admit it, even before the hallucinations began, the stress of my job had been taking a toll. Over the winter, I'd had a cold that I couldn't shake, which had turned into bronchitis. When my doctor dispensed a third course of antibiotics, he started asking questions about my stress level.

Even my friendships started to suffer. I spent so much time at work that I had no life outside of it.

I took consolation in the fact that I was doing what I'd gone to school to do. I was a respected journalist, and as someone with a short attention span, I got to enjoy a constant stream of information. My finger was on the pulse of what was going on all the time. I was the ultimate news junkie, enjoying a constant river of words and images that were filled with ideas, rants, emotional appeals, and opinions.

When I was writing, I wasn't making any noise except for the clicking of keys on a keyboard, but my mind was noisy. It was occupied with such a cacophony of ideas and facts for stories that I never spent much time thinking about anything else.

Coming back to this environment was surreal after spending so much time at home and then riding across vast open spaces with Riley and nothing but the sound of the wind and my own ruminations. It was like accidentally walking into a heavy-metal concert when you thought you were going to be listening to a violin quartet. The cacophony of voices and ringing telephones was raucous and even offensive. I recalled Riley telling me how annoying it was to be subjected to my endless chatter. Perhaps this was what it felt like.

After stopping by human resources to hand in my separation paperwork, I walked to Leo's office and tapped lightly on the doorjamb. He was on the telephone, but gestured for me to come in and take a seat. After he hung up, he said, "Welcome back to the nuthouse."

"Thanks. It hasn't changed much."

"You okay?" He leaned forward. "You look a little pale."

"I'm fine. It's a little strange to be here and not in the thick of things, I guess. I feel like an outsider."

He waved off my comment. "Hey, we're all about to be outsiders in a couple weeks. Don't worry about it."

"Were you able to make a copy of the video?"

"Sure did." Lou bent down to access one of his desk drawers. He retrieved a videotape and handed it to me with a flourish. "Have fun with that."

I stuffed the tape into my bag. "I appreciate this, Leo."

"Hey, there's gonna be a big good-bye bash the day before we lock the doors for the last time. You want to come?"

"Thanks for the invitation, but I don't think so." The twinge at my temple had returned and I moved to get up. I didn't want to have a massive meltdown in front of Leo.

"All right, but if you change your mind, you know you're welcome to come, Meg. I mean it."

"Thanks, Leo." I walked around the desk and gave him a quick hug around the shoulders. "You're the best."

"Hey, you know you can always use me as a reference."

We said our good-byes and Leo said that after the layoff thing was done, he'd invite me over for dinner with Mrs. O. I knew he wouldn't, but it was still nice that he'd made it sound like we'd keep in touch. The reality was that I'd never see most of these people again. Work friendships didn't tend to endure unless you had something in common outside of work. I found that out the hard way when I'd gone on medical leave. All the people who said they'd call me and "do lunch" never called. And I'd been too mortified and demoralized to initiate contact. Some days I hadn't even gotten out of bed.

I got into a taxi and went back home. Taking a cab wasn't exactly fiscally prudent, given my current lack of income. I could have taken the subway, which would have cost less, but I was a little concerned about having a hallucination underground and throwing myself onto the tracks or something equally horrific.

Fortunately, I had sold my car before I left to visit Alpine Grove, so at least I didn't have a car payment anymore, but my Visa bill was going to be startling. Changing my flight reservations and getting a last-minute flight out of Las Vegas instead of Los Angeles hadn't been cheap. I was going to have sit down and take a hard look at my finances and figure out what I was going to do.

By the time I got back to my apartment, the twinge in my head had evolved to a little flicker of light at the edge of my vision. I went to the refrigerator and pulled out a bottle of wine Leo had given me as a going-away present. He had said I should open it when I got my next job.

I wasn't going to wait that long. And who would hire me anyway? I needed liquid courage now to face watching the videotape. What if it brainwashed me? Then what?

I poured half the bottle of wine into a tumbler. Because I wasn't much of a drinker and was too busy to entertain, I didn't even have wine glasses, which seemed a little pathetic.

I popped the tape into the VCR, sat down on the couch in front of my TV, and took a huge gulp of wine before pressing Play on the remote control.

The video was basically what Leo had described. It matched my vision with lots of pretty images and the slick, silky voiceover. Then there was the photograph of the Grand Canyon at sunset and the family at the dinner table. But they weren't arguing. A little boy said he'd gotten an A-plus on his math test. The little girl said she'd won the spelling bee and that having the Internet helped her do her homework. More shiny, happy people extolled the virtues of having information at their fingertips. There was no fire and no screaming. At the end there was a phone number or web site people could use to get more information.

I pressed the Stop button and leaned back on the sofa. The video wasn't scary. Okay, it was a little over the top, particularly at the beginning about building a new frontier. But mostly it was typical boring advertising pabulum.

I gulped down some more wine. Maybe the subliminal images were inserted between the visible frames. Wasn't that how it worked, so you couldn't tell you were being brainwashed? I pointed the remote at the screen, rewound, then stepped through frame by frame. The Grand Canyon was still the Grand Canyon. It was all the same. If there was something sneaky or nefarious in the video, I couldn't find it.

My stomach made an unhappy gurgling noise, suggesting that perhaps the wine hadn't been such a great idea after all. I clicked off the TV and went to my bedroom to lie down. I kicked off my shoes and crawled under the coverlet. The light from the window came in through the sheer curtains, making patterns on the wall that seemed to dance wildly.

I squeezed my eyes shut and the fire was all around me. I could see Mom walking away from a tent and I screamed for her in terror, then there was blackness.

When I woke up, I looked at the clock. About ten minutes had passed. My stomach was still quite unhappy with me and the light on my answering machine was flashing. I sat up and pressed the button. It was my neighbor Ralph telling me to turn down my TV because he didn't like all the screaming in the horror movie.

Neither did I.

After erasing the message, I stared at the phone. Maybe Riley was still at Bubba's house. He'd given me the number and it wouldn't hurt to talk with him to tell him what happened in the video.

I dialed Bubba's number and he answered with, "Yo, this is Bob."

I paused for a moment because I'd forgotten his name was actually Robert. "Hi, um, Bob. This is Meg. I was wondering if Riley was there."

"Nope. He stopped by, said my place smelled like a sewer in Guadalajara, and rolled on out. I thought that was a little harsh. I mean yeah, I could clean more, but…"

I interrupted, "Do you know where Riley went?"

"Some little crap town in Nevada. I forget the name, but it's the same place he was before."

"Did he leave any contact information?"

"Nope. He said he'd check in every once in a while to see if I'd heard from Dad."

"I don't suppose you've heard anything?"

"Nope. Nothing. Dad's still going for major radio silence."

I thanked Bubba and hung up. Radio silence was an ironic choice of words, given Tim O'Shea's occupation. With a heavy exhalation of breath, I leaned back on my fluffy pillows. I didn't need Riley to tell me my hallucination wasn't useful. Fire and blackness provided zero clues to anything.

Even so, my apartment seemed especially empty. I was utterly alone and on my own when it came to finding Mom.

I had absolutely no idea what to do next, but it was time to figure that out.

I got up, went to the kitchen, and sat down at the table. I stared at my notes again. Something was going on here in DC and I was determined to find out what.

~

After going through my information for what seemed like the seven-hundredth time, I kept coming back to the fact that the research my mom had been doing related to technology. More and more studies were showing that technology was influencing behavior. Subtle things programmed into software could reinforce actions and trigger basic human instincts, like responding to peer pressure.

Mom was interested in how the power of computers could change behavior and beliefs and how it might be used to improve the world in some way. She loved to talk about the possibilities. Maybe computers could help people quit smoking or heal from life-altering issues like post-traumatic stress disorder. Of course, she was worried that this power to influence children, in particular, could be abused as well.

The effects of the increasing use of technology were already all around me. I didn't participate in online forums, but I knew people who had joined Prodigy or CompuServe because they felt left out. All their friends were chatting away on those forums, and they joined so they wouldn't miss anything. What if the mega merger meant Archetypal Online Systems became the place to be? With advertising, creative programming, and maybe even a dash of subliminal messaging, they'd have a huge opportunity to convince people to do almost anything.

Sure, it was possible that my past association with Matt might have made me a little cynical. He was a greedy little sociopath and it wouldn't surprise me at all to find out he was behind the idea. To be fair, he didn't own Archetypal, but even if it wasn't his idea per se, he was high enough in the corporate hierarchy to know what was going on. First I was going to talk to Centerfield Technologies and see if I could get more information about that creative brief for the video. Then I was going to talk to Matt again.

The next morning I felt better, and even made myself a healthy breakfast. It was time to turn over a new leaf. My chocolate cake and wine binge hadn't helped. I decided to brave the subway and took the Metro down to Farragut North. I walked down to K Street, where the Centerfield Technologies offices were located. It was a swanky glass building that also housed dozens of firms teeming with lobbyists and lawyers. Earnest yuppies scurried about in their Brooks Brothers suits with their brand spanky new cellular phones pressed to their ears, trying their best to look extremely important. There were a few things I didn't miss about the DC area. Being exposed to so many self-aggrandizing political social climbers was one of them.

I took the elevator up to the sixth floor. I could have called, but I knew this was one of those situations when the folks at Centerfield had absolutely no good reason to talk to me. I'd found over my years as a reporter that it's a lot easier to blow someone off over the phone than it is when she's making a nuisance of herself in your lobby.

The Centerfield offices were opulent, ostentatious, and utterly silent. It was about as far away from the hustle and bustle of a newsroom as you could get. The company did corporate videos, and from the looks of things, charged mighty hefty fees. The leather couch in the lobby had to cost more than the Toyota Corolla I'd recently sold. Clearly, I'd been in the wrong line of work. This place was where the big money was being made.

A clean-cut man wearing a dark suit and tie was stationed at the gigantic marble reception desk underneath the shiny silver Centerline logo that hung on the wall. He wore a telephone headset and was quietly typing. Even the keyboards were quieter here. I walked up and asked to see the account manager for Archetypal Online Systems.

With a forced polite smile, he said, "Do you have an appointment?"

"No. I only need five minutes of that person's time."

"May I ask what this is regarding, ma'am?"

I tried not to grit my teeth. Yes, it's courteous, but being called ma'am by a twenty-two-year old makes me feel ancient and that made me cranky. "It's about a video your company did for Archetypal."

"Are you affiliated with the company?"

Dating an executive probably didn't count. "Not in any meaningful way."

"We don't share our client information."

This wasn't going well. Time to make something up. I leaned my elbow on the desk. "Well, I'm not supposed to say anything, but I'm with a video-awards committee and the video was brought to our attention as an excellent example. I was hoping to find out more about how it was created."

The young man perked up at the word "awards" and said eagerly, "You mean the videographer awards?"

I turned my head, pretending to look at someone walking by in the hallway, and uttered a mumbling noise that could have been interpreted as an affirmative. I turned back to face the man. "So may I see the account manager? I'd love to gain some insight into the creative brief you were working from."

He picked up the phone. "Let me see if Christine is available."

After a brief discussion with Christine, he led me back through a long row of offices where people were working behind glass like rodents in cages. I saw an editor in front of TV monitors splicing together film, and several people squinting at computer screens.

I shook hands with Christine as the receptionist left, closing the door behind him. She said, "I'm delighted to meet you. How can I help?"

"I was curious about the goals of the video. I mean, obviously it's about recruitment, but who was the target audience?"

She folded her hands in front of her on the dark mahogany desk. "Professionals between the ages of twenty and fifty who are looking to make a change and a difference."

Wow, that was some serious marketing speak. "Were there any underlying messages that you were trying to share?"

"I'm not sure what you mean. We wanted to inspire people to be part of the future. That new technology will change lives."

"You mean in a good way?"

"Yes, of course in a good way. The video shows a positive and hopeful view of the future." Christine picked up a pen and pulled a folder from a stack in her inbox. "What are you getting at?"

Oops, time to back off. "Nothing. I was impressed with the visual complexity and was curious if there might have been other themes you were exploring. The Grand Canyon, for example, perhaps as a metaphor for the vastness of human knowledge that now will be at our fingertips." Yeah, I was laying it on thick now.

Christine looked thoughtful for a moment before replying. "Ah, I see what you mean. That's an interesting perspective. I like it."

We chatted about the various images and how they related to the theme for a few minutes, then I decided to get back to the things I wanted to know. I asked, "Who did you work with on the project? I'm hoping to talk to that person as well."

"Matt Eskridge. He's in marketing."

I wanted to shout "Aha!" but I controlled myself. "I believe I've heard his name before." I reached across the desk to shake her hand as I stood up. "It's been a pleasure to meet you. Thank you so much for your time."

I walked out of the office and waved to the receptionist on the way out. Everyone had been extremely pleasant and polite to me, considering they didn't know me from a hole in the ground. They also seemed incredibly innocuous, not even the least bit nefarious. Could people this bland be in bed with criminal masterminds trying to take over the world? At this point, it didn't seem likely. They seemed more like people just doing their jobs.

With a sigh, I stepped onto the escalator to ride down into the deep, dark depths of the Metro. So far, despite all my convictions and suppositions, I wasn't getting anywhere with this line of investigation.

~

After I got home, I stewed about calling Matt and realized that the odds of him being willing to talk to me again were next to zero. I'd managed to successfully inveigle my way into the Centerfield offices, so I decided taking the direct approach and strolling into Matt's office was better than hassling with his assistant again. It also meant I could put it off until tomorrow because Matt's office was in Virginia and I'd had enough time on the Metro for one day. I mentally apologized to Mom, wherever she was, for procrastinating.

I decided to embrace healthy food and made myself a real dinner, then spent a relaxing evening watching re-runs on TV. It was the first time in quite a while that I'd been able to loaf around by myself, being a video-droning couch potato.

The next morning, refreshed from my evening of sloth, I was raring to go. I put on a grossly expensive conservative navy suit from Nordstrom's, my favorite matching pumps, and looked in the mirror. I was ready to face the executive suite.

I swapped the pumps for sneakers and put the high heels in my tote bag with my notebook. I walked to the subway station and got on the Metro for the trek out to Virginia. After some quality time on the Orange Line, I took a bus to get to the Archetypal offices. In the old days, I would have taken a cab, but now that my employment status had changed, saving money was more important than saving time. For the foreseeable future, I'd better get used to public transportation.

I'd allowed a lot of travel time so I would arrive at Matt's office during his newspaper-reading session. All I had to do was brashly dodge his perky assistant so I could confront him.

When I arrived at the building, I took the elevator up to Matt's office and looked around. People were scurrying around and stacks of banker's boxes were everywhere. Books were stacked on desks and the whole place was in disarray. It hadn't occurred to me that because of the merger Archetypal might be moving.

Thanks to all the hustle and bustle, no one noticed when I walked down the corridor to Matt's glass-encased corner office. As I'd predicted, Matt was leaned back in his huge leather office chair with his perfectly polished Florsheims resting on the corner of the glass-and-chrome desk. The *New York Times* spread in front of his face blocked my view, but I could imagine the slight furrow in his brow as he scanned the news.

I opened the door and walked into the room, which had a fantastic view of the city below. As I approached the desk, a row of pigeons enjoying the vista from their perch on the metal building framework flew off.

Matt put down the paper to look at the birds and jerked his head to look at me. "What are you doing here?"

"Just stopping by to say hi. I have a couple of questions." I sat down in the visitor's chair and gave Matt the type of intent fixed stare that I knew made him uncomfortable. He dropped his feet to the floor and rearranged himself, adopting a more professional pose and sitting straight in the executive chair. I hadn't seen him in months, but it was annoying to note that he was as gorgeous as ever. With his perfectly cut and coiffed straight black hair and sexy brown eyes, he looked like he should be a model for *Suave Wealthy Yuppie* magazine.

"Why are you annoying me again?" He leaned forward. "The last time we chatted I told you about the merger. If you want to know anything else, go talk to the people in PR."

"No, this is about the recruitment video that Centerfield Technologies created."

Matt rolled his eyes melodramatically. "Oh, for heaven's sake. Not this again. I already told you they created it based on our creative brief. So what?"

"I'm curious if there are any extra messages in there. I know you were interested in my mother's research."

"What research?"

"I mentioned it before. My mother was studying visual perception and how it relates to computer graphics. She did a lot of research on persuasion techniques as well."

"And again I say, *so what?*" He threw his hands upward in a theatrical display of exasperation. "I don't know what you're talking about."

It was time to lay it on the line. "Matt, when we went to Lake Louise, we had a long conversation about her research. You said it was fascinating."

"I did?" He curled his fingers in front of his face and examined his cuticles. "Maybe it was. At the time, I suspect I wasn't listening. We went to Lake Louise right after I'd met Buffy."

"Buffy? Who is Buffy? I'm assuming you don't mean the vampire slayer from that crappy movie with the guy from *90210*, right? I heard they turned Buffy into a TV show recently too." I slapped my palms on the desk. "Yeah, I'm thinking that's not who you're talking about. Was this yet *another* woman you slept with when we were together?"

His eyebrows rose and he bestowed a superior smile on me. "Perhaps."

What a complete jackass. On the one hand I was surprised, on the other, I wasn't. A tiger doesn't change its stripes. Who knows how many women he'd been sleeping with? Obviously, I hadn't had a clue. I took a deep breath in an effort to rein in my fury and retain control. "So in my mother's research, she worked with computers. What do you remember about it?"

"That you could use them with kids? Education maybe?"

"Brilliant, Matt. I'm impressed by your stunning recall. But returning to the point, did you use any, shall we say, questionable techniques in that video?"

"What techniques? You mean like dissolves? Those are video transitions. How could you not know that? The video had pictures of pretty places like the Grand Canyon, and one image dissolves into the next. The idea was for it to look happy and appealing." He crossed his hands and set them on the desk as if he were a teacher patiently dealing with a slow pupil. "You see that type of thing every day on TV. What's your point?"

"That perhaps you're a slimeball, but not in the way I thought you were." If he knew that Mom was interested in interactive computer technology experiences that could motivate and influence users, he sure was hiding it well. And coming off like a dolt, which wasn't his style. Matt always wanted to be the smartest person in the room. Even when he didn't know what he was talking about, he'd do a credible job of faking it. This was pathetic.

Matt stood up. "I think it's time for you to leave now."

I stood up, pushed my bag onto my shoulder, and gave him a dismissive wave. "So do I. You have your date with the men's room. Good-bye, Matt."

The long ride back on the subway left me far too much time with my thoughts. Had I been wrong about everything? All my theories seemed to fit together, but now all my assumptions were suspect. I knew Matt well enough to know that he truly had no idea what I was talking about when it came to Mom's research.

Matt had particular "tells" when he was lying, which I'd discovered during a rather rousing round of strip poker. When he was lying, a corner of his mouth turned down in a particular way. That knowledge came in handy when our relationship imploded and I asked him about the various other women he was seeing.

I stared out the window as suburban Virginia whizzed by. What was Riley up to right now? Was he still in Ely or out on the road again, following the circus? By now he might have run across some new leads. Or maybe even talked to Dean. It still frustrated me that we'd gotten nothing from the guy. Closure would have been nice.

Mom's research had to come into play somehow. It was time to go to the source. A bunch of her colleagues were at the University of Maryland. Just because she'd gone on sabbatical didn't mean all the research in her department had stopped. When I got home, I'd make a few calls and see what I could find out.

Satisfied that I had finally come up with a decent plan, I yanked the *Washington Post* out of my bag to get caught up with current events. Federal Reserve chairman Alan Greenspan was getting married and a few economists were predicting that the nation's unemployment rate was dropping and it might fall below five percent. Apparently they hadn't included me in those figures.

I scanned a few more stories and Matt's words, "so what?" kept popping into my head. Finally I put the paper away. Somehow I couldn't muster up my typical enthusiasm for reading the news. I found I didn't care. Being a news junkie had been a huge part of my identity for years. What was going on? How could I suddenly not care about current events?

The obvious answer was that because my mother was *still* missing and I was no closer to finding her than I had been when I left Las Vegas, so everything else seemed trivial.

Chapter 11

Ideas and Tenacity

By the time I opened the door to my apartment, I was tired, grumpy, and irritated with my fellow humans. Being crammed next to the teeming masses of humanity to get anywhere was bringing me down. I missed my little Corolla and being able to drive where I wanted without having to coordinate twelve timetables written in four-point type.

I made myself something to eat and sat at the table. Almost the entire time I'd been on the road with Riley, all I'd wanted was to come back here. I'd felt like Dorothy in *The Wizard of Oz*. "There's no place like home!"

But now, as the excitement of being back at home was wearing off, I had no idea what was next. My post-medical-leave descent into depression had been interrupted by my trip. I was no longer wallowing in self-pity anymore, but I was restless.

Without a job, my life here in DC felt empty. Because of my ever-so-strange limitations, I wasn't sure if it was even possible for me to go back to being a reporter again. I couldn't drive and I might break out screaming. These are not skills you want to include on your resume. In the unlikely event an intrepid publication was willing to hire me, I wasn't sure I could do the job. Worse than that, I wasn't sure I wanted to.

219

But if I didn't work as a reporter, what was I supposed to do to earn a living?

The people I'd worked with were undoubtedly all doing the same things they'd done before. They'd be off enjoying their new jobs without me. They'd go to the same bars and go to work, but in a different location. And what would I be doing? Washington, D.C., is one of those cities where what you do is critically important. It's the first thing anyone asks. In DC, what you do is who you are. Now I was doing nothing. What did that mean? DC had the same uptight yuppie vibe it had always had, but I didn't feel the same at all.

I had an urge to go off and do something important. Saving Mom, for example. And after that, maybe save the world somehow. That feeling was difficult to articulate to anyone, except maybe to Riley.

Although I wasn't sure what I wanted to do, the idea of trying new things was more appealing than failing miserably at my old life as a reporter. I felt so limited by my visions. There were so many things I couldn't do anymore. Even riding the bus and subway was worrisome.

Riley was the only person who truly understood how much my problems had upended my life. I missed having a sympathetic listener. Although I could try to reach him at the motel in Ely, after our big blowout I wasn't sure if he would be interested in hearing from me, unless I had news about Mom.

Here I was at thirty-two years old, and my life was a complete shambles. I'd thought I had everything figured out. Boy, was I wrong. My life had been going on an even keel according to plan, then in the span of six or seven months all the things I thought I had dialed in—career, family, relationships, everything—had fallen apart. I had huge student loans and almost no savings. It was only a matter of time until I would be utterly broke.

My God, I didn't even have a *dog*, for heaven's sake. Even Riley had a dog. I could rot here in this apartment and no one would ever notice or care if I disappeared. I crossed my arms on the table and rested my forehead on my arms. Closing my eyes, I tried not to let the heaviness of depression swamp me again. I was a smart woman and there had to be something out there I could do.

I jolted awake at the sound of the telephone and jumped up to answer it. A woman's voice said, "This is Christine Dawson from Centerfield Technologies. I talked to you the other day."

Had I left her my number? I was pretty sure I hadn't, after our conversation had made it clear she didn't know anything about subliminal messages. "Hi, it's nice to hear from you."

"You're probably wondering why I'm calling, but I talked to Matt Eskridge."

Uh-oh. "Really? How is he doing?"

"Fine, I suppose. He dated my sister for a while, and I suspect that helped us get the Archetypal video job."

"That's interesting." Why was this woman talking to me?

"After talking to him, I know you think he's a jackass. I do too. And you don't want to get me started about how he treated my sister. But he's also a past client, so I felt comfortable asking him for your phone number."

"How did you know that I know him?"

"Your name sounded familiar. After you stopped by, I did a little research and found a photo of you and Matt at a charity event. I had forgotten you were a local reporter, but I looked up some of your articles. You did outstanding work at the newspaper. I remember that piece you did on municipal corruption. That was some tremendous investigative research."

"Thank you." I was pretty proud of that series of articles. It had even won a few local journalism awards.

"Obviously, I also know about the merger and layoffs. Are you looking for a new job or have you already found something?"

My mouth opened involuntarily in stunned surprise. "I, uh, no. Nothing yet."

"I know the industry is changing and it's not as easy to get a reporting job as it used to be."

"Tell me about it."

"I was wondering if you'd be interested in a slight career shift? We're looking for a researcher to help us with some documentary projects."

"That sounds interesting, but to be honest, I've never worked on a documentary."

"You have skills that would transfer well. If you're interested that is."

"Very!" I blurted out without thinking. Wow, way to play it cool. Desperate much?

Christine laughed. "I was hoping you'd say that. Could you come by on Monday for an interview with our leadership team?"

"Yes. What time?"

"One in the afternoon would work for us. If you could bring some of your clips and your resume, that would be great."

We finalized the details and I hung up the phone. I couldn't believe it. I had gone in to Centerfield Technologies, and in my reporterly way had made a complete pest of myself and ended up getting a job offer out of it. Sometimes the world moved in mysterious ways.

I spent most of the weekend at the library at the University of Maryland, where my mother had taught before she went off on her sabbatical and subsequently disappeared into thin air. Although her colleagues weren't around, I was able to sit in the library and read through virtually everything she had written over the last few years. Mom was scary smart in an academic way that I wasn't. Even though some of the reading got a little dense and technical, I plowed through, determined to figure out what was going on in her head before she'd disappeared.

Some of what I learned was more than a little frightening. As more and more computers and technology became available and integrated into peoples' everyday life, more products were being designed to alter what people think and do. Designers could target certain behaviors and devise ways to achieve their goals through technology.

Most of mom's research assumed that the goals of this technology were altruistic and ultimately beneficial to people. She had many promising ideas for how computers could be used in education. Software could be designed to help increase children's focus and interest in reading and help foster new creative ideas. But what about when the goals weren't necessarily good?

Although email had only been widely used for about a decade, now people's lives revolved around it. Like most people, when I was at work I checked my email a ridiculous number of times a day. According to research, I did that not only because I was afraid of missing something, which I was, but also because of a concept called intermittent variable rewards. Sometimes you checked, and you were rewarded with an email. "Woo hoo! You've got mail." And sometimes nothing happened at all.

The concept was akin to using slot machines, which I'd seen a lot of lately. All those people glued to their chairs at the casinos became addicted to the slots because they offered variable rewards. You yanked on the lever and you got a match, a prize, or absolutely nothing at all. According to what I was reading, the addictiveness of something is highest when the rate of reward is most variable. Hmm.

Although maybe my behavior regarding checking email had been manipulated, that seemed fairly innocuous. What if people were using Mom's research to hijack people's minds for truly nefarious reasons? What if these psychological techniques were being used to exploit human vulnerabilities and weaknesses? The more I read, the more worried I became.

This line of thinking is what had brought me back to DC in the first place, although it didn't appear that the video or Matt were involved with Mom's disappearance after all. Much less Riley's father or Dean. But it still seemed like something more was going on here. What was I missing?

~

Late Monday morning I took an extra-long shower so I'd be squeaky clean and have smooth, freshly shaved legs for my job interview. Having to put on pantyhose would be worth it if they decided to hire me. I stood in front of the mirror combing my hair. All the time driving around in the blazing desert sun hadn't done much for the color. The Nice 'n Easy

Natural Radiant Auburn had evolved into a shade that not even Clairol could create. It was definitely not a color that occurred in nature. Zelda and Riley were lucky they didn't have to worry about these things.

A distant voice said something and I turned my head to listen. Was that Riley? The last thing I needed was to start hearing voices. If that happened during the job interview, I was doomed. I could easily imagine it. "Don't mind me, I might be a prophet who has a little problem with hallucinations. Oh, and by the way, today I started hearing voices."

I pressed my hand to my chest in a futile effort to convince my heart to stop thumping like a drum at a million beats per second. Slowly, it dawned on me that the voice was coming from the other room. I yanked open the bathroom door and heard Riley's voice from the answering machine saying, "Zelda, come on, stop that! I guess I'll try you again later. Bye."

I ran to the phone and picked up the receiver. Crap! Slamming the phone down on the cradle, I pressed the Play button on the answering machine.

There was some type of commotion or traffic noise in the background and through the din Riley said, "Hi Meg, it's Riley, um, Riley O'Shea. I was hoping to talk to you. Something, well…Zelda, cut that out would you? Anyway, I found out something I wanted to talk to you about. Zelda, come on, stop that! I guess I'll try you again later. Bye."

I scrutinized the machine as if it were its fault that Riley had left such a useless message. It was almost as lame as the note his father had left with Bubba. Maybe leaving cryptic messages was a genetic thing with the O'Sheas. The worst part was that I wanted to talk to Riley too. I had about a million ideas I wanted to discuss with him and he hadn't left a number. The caller ID didn't know where he was either. "Out of Area" was not helpful. I already knew Riley was out of my area. From the message, it sounded like he was standing in a pay phone in the middle of a traffic circle with Zelda yanking on her leash.

Patience isn't my strong suit, but there was nothing I could do except hope that Riley really would call back later. I had a job interview to go to. Although I was relieved that the voices I'd heard were on the answering machine and not in my head, I might have to diplomatically explain my little problem with hallucinations. Doing that might be complicated, but I had some time on the subway to consider the best way to delicately introduce the topic without blowing the interview.

Decked out in my best professional attire, I returned to the shiny Centerfield Technology offices. This time I had an appointment, which made my conversation with the receptionist a lot simpler, although it occurred to me that my little lie about the video awards might come out eventually. Uh-oh. I hadn't thought about that before. Oh well. Even if I made a fool of myself during this interview, I wouldn't be any worse off than I was now.

Christine came out and led me back to a glassed-in conference room with a long black table surrounded by office chairs. Four men and three women were sitting and chatting amiably. Christine introduced me and sat in one of the empty chairs. I shook everyone's hand and sat down next to her. A man with short graying hair sat at the head of the table. His name was George Centerfield and not surprisingly, he was the founder of the company.

The interview was fairly standard, with the typical questions about who I was and what I'd been up to during my professional life. They wanted to know about my background, how I dealt with challenges, and why I thought I'd be a good researcher. I talked up my tenacity and ability to interview people and they seemed reasonably accepting of my answers. Lots of nodding and a few chuckles at my stories about how I'd managed to get my foot in the door for some of the interviews. I opted not to mention the little fib about video awards, although given the other stories I did share, no one would be shocked if Christine or the receptionist mentioned it.

Things went well because I *have* had a lot of practice with job interviews. After I got out of graduate school, I had grand aspirations of going to work at the *Washington Post* or *The New York Times*. Maybe even the *Los Angeles Times* or *Chicago Tribune,* although the idea of living in LaLa Land or the windy city hadn't appealed to me. Sadly, that was not to be. I didn't even get interviews at those places.

In addition to large student loans, my grotesquely expensive master's degree in journalism netted me a couple of chats with HR flunkies at second-string newspapers that subsequently rejected me after five-minute phone conversations. By the time I did get a job, I'd sent resumes to almost every tiny regional paper in the United States. I was on my fifty-sixth interview and had answered every possible interview question when I finally managed to impress Leo enough that he hired me.

As it turned out, the job had been a fantastic fit, yet it had been dispiriting to find that I wasn't going to set the journalistic world on fire right out of graduate school. I had to pay my dues.

Although now I had quite a few years under my belt, all those big papers would have reasons to reject me today. Staff cuts, moving to the Web, shrinking ad revenues. I knew that's how it was out there in newspaperland. Working as a documentary researcher sounded a lot easier and less stressful. In fact, it sounded somewhat boring. But maybe with a less stressful job, my hallucinations would stop, or at least subside. The possibility that they were the result of too much stress was as good as any other explanation. No one knew what my problem was, least of all me.

As the interview wound down, Christine asked a question that I needed to answer honestly. She leaned forward, widened her eyes, and said, "Is there anything that would prevent you working for us?"

I knew that the question behind the question was whether I had other resumes out there at swanky publications that would snap me away right after I started at Centerfield. Although that wasn't the case, I did have something else going on. I placed my palms flat on the table. "This is a great opportunity and to be frank, I haven't sent out resumes yet. It's not like I would bail out on you and take another job two days after I start here. This is the only interview I've had since I was laid off."

Christine smiled in obvious relief. "I'm extremely glad to hear that."

I continued, "But there's something you might hear through the rumor mill, and I want to be up front about it. I know you're not allowed to ask about personal matters, but I have a bit of an intermittent but chronic problem with migraines. Well, sort of like migraines. That's what the doctors say, anyway. It's not life-threatening as far as I know."

"Is it manageable?"

"I believe so. It shouldn't affect my ability to do research, but I'd like to hold off starting the job until I go to the doctor again for some different medication." The pills they'd given me before made it impossible to think and I'd refused to take them, but there *had* to be something else out there.

Christine raised her eyebrows. "I'm sorry to hear about your health problems. How long do you need?"

I put my hands back in my lap. "Maybe another week or two? I need to see when I can get an appointment with my doctor."

Christine glanced across the table at George Centerfield, who nodded. She said, "A week or two is not a big deal for us. We're prepared to offer you the job. We can hammer out the details in my office and figure out your official start date after you talk to your doctor."

I grinned like a goof. This was unbelievable. "Thank you. I appreciate your patience."

Everyone stood up and we all milled around shaking hands and smiling as they filed out of the room. It was like we all breathed a collective sigh of relief that the interview was over. And against all odds, I got the job.

The next couple of hours were a whirlwind of paperwork and introductions. I met video editors, directors, writers, accountants, and a bunch of people in human resources. It was all such a blur that I knew I wouldn't remember anyone's name when I returned for my first day of work.

It seemed to take forever to get home, and by then the adrenaline rush from the interview was long gone and I was exhausted. I nuked up some celebratory frozen macaroni and cheese. After a successful interview I deserved to indulge in some serious carbo-loading and bad TV.

The phone rang and I set my cheesy dinner aside with a sigh. Maybe Centerfield forgot something. I picked up the phone and was startled to hear Riley's voice. He said, "Meg, I need to talk to you."

Maybe it was the serious tone, but he sounded different. I pressed my palm against my stomach, which was suddenly queasy. "Are you okay?"

"More or less. We need to talk."

~

Something about hearing Riley's voice brought everything home to me. Amid the excitement of the job interview and the potential for having income again, I'd forgotten that I was supposed to be looking for Mom. What kind of selfish, awful daughter was I?

My thoughts were interrupted when Riley said, "Meg, did you hear what I said?"

"What?" All the horrible things I'd yelled at him before I left came rushing back. "Sorry. I, well, Riley, I know I said this before, but I've had a lot of time to think about the fight we had before I left. And I said some things I regret."

There was a pause and he said, "I know. Me too. Can we set that aside for a second?"

"I just wanted to put that out there."

"Right. Thanks. Did you get anywhere with the idea that there were subliminal images in the video?"

"No." I was dying to tell someone, and I added, "But today I got a job with Centerfield Technologies!"

"You got a job? Wait. Isn't that the company that made the video? Are you going undercover or something?"

"Well, no. It's a regular job doing research. I talked to people at Centerfield and I couldn't find any connection with Mom." I scooped up a macaroni noodle and took a nibble. "They decided they liked my tenacity and offered me a job. It might be kind of boring, but I don't have a lot of options. I wanted to talk to you about it, but it sounded like you were in a phone booth when you left the message. Are you in Ely?"

"Not anymore."

"Why didn't you call?"

"First, I was too pissed off."

I made a wry face. "I suppose that's fair."

"Then I had to drive two-hundred-fifty miles to get from Vegas back to Ely. Since then, I've been either driving or attending the circus shows at night. I've been trying to sleep during the day and I figured you didn't want to hear from me at three in the morning."

"*Trying* to sleep? You're doing the whole not sleeping thing again, aren't you?"

"Well, no, I'm not sleeping particularly well."

"Are you eating anything?"

"Jeez, Meg, now you sound like Erin. I don't need a lecture. That's not why I called."

"Hey, don't get all touchy on me." I chomped another piece of macaroni. "So why *did* you call?"

"By sneaking into the circus at night, I can briefly talk to Dean. They lower the amount of nasty drugs they're giving him so he can perform his drunken-clown act. He's still stoned, but a little more coherent."

I sat up straight and put my fork down. "You *talked* to him?"

"Several times. It's sort of confusing, but I'm getting the impression that our parents are at some type of facility somewhere. Dean calls it a retreat."

"What? That's new! You mean like a church retreat or corporate retreat type thing?"

"I think so."

"Where?"

"I don't know. He also keeps saying the word 'specialists.' Have you run across that term anywhere?"

"No." I didn't want to tell him how little I'd learned. It had been more than a week and all I'd discovered was that my subliminal-images theory was bogus.

"What did you find out about the video? Is it connected? Dean has been mumbling something about waves. I don't understand what he's getting at. Are there oceans in the video? Or have you seen any waves in your visions?"

"Nope. No surfing, lakes, oceans, or waves." I let out a sigh. Time to confess. "I was wrong, Riley. Totally wrong. I got a copy of the video from Leo and I stepped through it, frame by frame, multiple times. I talked to Centerfield and Matt at Archetypal. It's nothing but a recruiting video. The video has a beach with waves, but it's nothing sinister. There's nothing interesting I could find at all. In fact, it's downright dull."

"So no subliminal images? What about the big conspiracy? You're saying there's nothing at all?"

"Not that I can find. I spent all weekend at the University of Maryland library reading everything my mom has written recently. It's interesting and potentially creepy, but I can't figure out any way it's related."

There was silence and finally Riley said quietly, "All right. Wow. I guess I was hoping you'd have something that would help make sense of some of the things Dean is saying."

"Sorry."

"So are you giving up? You're going to take that job and move on?"

"No! I would never do that." I paused. Was that what I was doing? "I'm, well, not exactly sure what line of investigation I should take next."

"Do you have any ideas?"

I paused. "Of course." Who was I kidding? I had nothing at all.

"Have you had more visions? If you saw something, maybe that would help me figure out what Dean is talking about."

"I had one after I went to the newsroom to pick up the videotape."

"What did you see?"

"Not much. My mother was walking away from a tent and I screamed for her, then I fell into the black hole."

"That's it?"

"That's it. I've felt sort of iffy since I came back here, but it was particularly bad when I went to the newsroom. I could tell it was going to happen, but fortunately I managed to get out of the office and back home before it did."

"So no screaming?"

"One of my neighbors thought I was watching a horror movie. I had wine, which I had hoped might help settle me down. That was a bad idea."

"The black hole is what you said used to happen."

"I know. Before I met you, after my meltdown at the office, the hallucinations turned scary. I kept thinking the black hole meant I was dying. It was awful."

Riley heaved a large sigh, but didn't say anything.

I jabbed my fork at a wayward piece of macaroni and chased it around the plate. "I'm going to go to the doctor and see if he has anything better that will make the visions stop."

"It won't work."

I scooped up some macaroni, which was now getting cold and solidifying into a plastic blob. "What do you mean, it won't work. How do you know?"

"Have you tried medication before?"

"Well, yeah, but there's got to be something else."

"You'll either end up unable to think or maybe paranoid, anxious, and dizzy with constant thoughts about death and dying. Or it won't do anything at all, but you'll get to suffer through a bunch of unpleasant side effects like nausea and diarrhea."

He wasn't wrong about not being able to think. I'd had that experience. But every drug couldn't be like that. Paranoia didn't sound good. I pointed my fork at nothing. "Since when are you such an expert?"

"I told you before. We talked about this. I thought I was going to die, so I've been tested every which way possible. I tried every horrible drug they gave me because I was motivated to figure out what was wrong with me. My company was at stake. My whole life, really."

"But we don't have the same problem. It's not the same thing."

"I think it is. And whatever it is also is the same thing that's going on with Dean. You thought so too for a while, until you went on the whole tangent with your ex-boyfriend and subliminal messages."

I set the fork down. He was right. "What are you going to do? Can you get Dean away from the circus?"

"Not by myself. That nasty clown Billy is always watching him, except when he's in the ring performing his act. That's when I can sneak over and talk to Dean while he's waiting for his turn to perform. When they dim the lights, it's harder for Billy to see the audience."

"I hate that little troll."

"I think I'm getting closer to finding out what Dean knows, but it's a slow process because I can only talk to him for about ten minutes and during the first five, he's trying to figure out who I am. It's frustrating. I was hoping you'd be able to tell me something."

"Where are you now?"

"Arizona. I'm not sure what to do. At this point, I'm afraid I'm never going to see Dad again."

"I know." The sick feeling in my stomach wasn't from the cold mac and cheese. I couldn't merrily go on with my life until I knew what had happened with Mom. "Can I be honest here?"

"You don't seem to have big problems holding back your feelings."

"Yeah, yeah, you're hilarious." I waved my arm at my empty apartment. "Like I said, I'm not getting anywhere here. I'm out of ideas. Everything I thought was right turned out to be wrong. I don't even have good hallucinations anymore."

"Good?"

"You know what I mean! When I held your hand, I saw things. It wasn't just a bunch of screaming and blackness."

"I suppose that's true."

"And you sleep better when I'm around."

"Also true."

"I think I should go back out there. Centerfield said I didn't have to start immediately. But I have this huge problem."

"Is something else happening with your hallucinations? Are you feeling all right?"

"No, it's nothing like that. My credit card bill from flying at the last minute is gigantic. I've got student loans, rent, and no income. I can't travel all over the place with you because I can't afford it. If I go back out there, I can't stay long. No matter what happens, I have to return and take this job, or I'll go bankrupt."

"You're saying money is the problem? That's *it*?"

"Yes. It's a huge problem and there's no way around it. I probably should have saved more, but…"

Riley interrupted me. "Meg, it's not a problem."

"Weren't you listening? Yes, it *is*. I'm broke."

"I'll wire you the money."

"You can't do that. I'm not taking your money. I already feel weird about freeloading off you before."

"Finding Dad is more important than money. Name a number. You'll have it in the morning."

"But that's ridiculous. You can't do that."

"Meg, I don't care how much it is. I can afford it."

"You're retired, so you should save it. What if you outlive your retirement? That happens all the time. Plus, you've been sick. What if you need it for treatment? What if you end up in the hospital again?"

"I told you I sold my company."

"Riley, don't be ridiculous. I'm talking about *thousands* of dollars here. Thousands! It's not like paying for some diner food and a few nights at a Motel 6."

"Believe me when I say I can afford it. I got a lot of money for the company. I told you before, they wanted the patents."

"Patents? How much could those be worth?"

"I was the majority shareholder, so I got twenty-six million dollars. "

"What?"

"You heard me. I can pay off your student loans, Meg. It's no big deal. And I'm more than happy to do it if you can help me find my father. Lots of things are more important than money."

"That's easy to say when you have millions. This feels too weird."

"Think of it as a brother helping out his little sister, if it makes you feel better. I need your help and you need mine. Family should stick together. When can you get a flight to Phoenix?"

I laughed. "Okay bro, if you're paying, I can fly out the day after tomorrow."

We made arrangements for Riley to wire me enough money to pay my rent and pay off my credit card. He insisted on paying off my student loans too. If our parents were, in fact, married, maybe having a brother wouldn't be so bad after all.

Chapter 12

Lost and Found

The flight to Phoenix was long, but uneventful. I looked out the window at the crisscross of roads across the reddish desert as we landed at Sky Harbor airport. Although the city is surrounded by mountain ranges, Phoenix itself is completely flat, except for a couple of mountains that poke up in the middle of the city. They were bare, brown, rocky islands in a sea of housing developments.

For this trip, I packed significantly differently than I had last time. I tried to plan ahead with lots of changes of underwear and more comfortable shoes. There was no reason to dress like an urban professional if I was going to be chasing clowns around the desert again, so I opted for significantly more casual attire.

Riley and I had agreed to meet at a short-term parking lot near Terminal 2 and I milled around, following the crowd out the exit, trying to ignore the twinge in my head that was making itself known again. It had been my constant companion since Riley and I had returned to Las Vegas. The only time I got a break was on the plane ride itself. Maybe the canned air kept hallucinations at bay.

I was looking forward to returning to the wide open spaces, so my head could have a little respite for a while. Constantly worrying that I was going to melt down into screaming blackness was getting me down. I was particularly pleased that I'd made it through my job interview without making a fool of myself. It was better that I'd told Centerfield about my issues, rather than having them find out the hard way.

Even if I only lasted a week at the job, Riley had wired me the funds to pay off my debts, which gave me a little breathing room to find something else. Maybe there were jobs where screaming was encouraged. Perhaps I could embark on a new career as an extra in slasher movies.

I crossed the street where cars and shuttles were picking up and dropping off passengers and made my way to the parking lot. I heard Zelda bark and turned to look. I waved at Riley, who was leaning on the side of the Mustang with his arms folded across his chest and his legs crossed at the ankles. His long, dark wavy hair flowed over his shoulders and when he lifted a hand to return my greeting, a rush of relief washed over me. I hadn't realized how badly I wanted someone to talk to about my hallucinations without feeling like a nut case.

I hurried over to the car and stretched my arms out for a big hug. "I'm back!"

Riley laughed and said, "I noticed." We hugged and I leaned into the backseat to give Zelda a hug while Riley stashed my suitcase in the trunk.

I got into the Mustang and put my hand over Riley's on the stick shift to keep him from starting the car. He pulled off his sunglasses and I could see that the dark circles under his deep-set eyes were more pronounced again, indicating that he hadn't been exaggerating about the insomnia problems. He folded the ear pieces of the glasses and set them down. "Something wrong already?"

"Where exactly are we going again?"

"Away from Phoenix to a town called Holbrook. The circus is heading there next. It's off Interstate 40 east of Flagstaff and Winslow."

"Winslow, as in standing on the corner in Winslow, Arizona? The Eagles? That Winslow?"

Riley put his sunglasses back on and turned the key in the ignition. The familiar sound of the Mustang's gigantic engine purred as he said, "That's the one. I hate to break it to you though, it's not such a sight to see. In fact, it's almost invisible."

"Oh well, another illusion dashed. But I'm still going to look for a flatbed Ford."

"Good luck. There's not much in Holbrook either. From the interstate all you see is an enormous power plant. But it's on historic Route 66, so if you're lucky, you might be able to get your kicks on Route 66."

"You're like a walking greeting card here, aren't you?"

"There are also giant cement dinosaurs in Holbrook. Zelda thought they were great and wouldn't stop barking at them."

"Now you're making up stuff."

Riley turned out of the airport and merged into traffic. "I don't need to. You'll see. It's shorter if we take 87 through Payson or up Interstate 17, but we're going for the scenic route through Globe and Show Low then Arizona State Route 77 up to Holbrook."

"You do realize that means nothing to me, don't you?"

"It means I want to get away from Phoenix and out into the open desert as quickly as possible. I don't want to take

87 because it's under construction and the traffic on I-17 is a nightmare."

"Okay, I'm on board with this idea."

Something I hadn't known about was that Phoenix traffic is horrible and best avoided. I'm not sure what's wrong, but something is. Maybe cramming all those people in with all that concrete and desert heat makes them hot and angry. It was a relief when we finally were out of the city. Once we hit the open highway away from all the surly drivers and were heading toward the small town of Globe, my mood improved dramatically. The twinge at my temple finally disappeared and I enjoyed the sensation of the warm sun on my face and the wind in my hair.

North of Globe, we wound our way up and down the Salt River Canyon. The road has approximately four-thousand twists and turns as it drops down to the river and crosses it. Then there are four-thousand more twists and turns as the road ascends the opposite side. It was a good thing Zelda and I weren't prone to carsickness, because it was one seriously winding road.

As I watched the scenery go by, my thoughts returned to the topic of money. After I'd mailed my final bill payments, I stopped by the library to do a little snooping. I'd spent a whole lot of time with Riley and knew next to nothing about him. Maybe I'm hard-nosed and cynical, but realistically, who *gives* you money? On the other hand, who has twenty-six-million dollars, either? As it turned out, Riley did. That was another thing he hadn't made up.

As I read article after article about Riley in the business press, it blew my mind that this was *Riley* they were talking about. The same weird, long-haired dude with bizarre eating habits I knew had been the "wunderkind" who had taken the technology industry by storm, sold out, and then totally disappeared. A photo of him that had been repeatedly used didn't even look like the person I knew. Talk about cleaning up well. No wonder he was so sensitive about his appearance. Back when he was healthy, he'd had a geeky cuteness factor that I never would have suspected.

From the reports I read, it sounded like Riley had taken dropping out to a new level. There was lots of speculation that he'd gone insane à la Howard Hughes. The theory was that he was locked away in an enormous mansion or on a private island somewhere counting his money. Of course, I knew he wasn't. He was driving across miles of Arizona desert in a thirty-year-old car with his dog and possible stepsister who had a teensy-weensy problem with hallucinations.

I glanced at Riley, who looked significantly more relaxed now that we were away from the city. I tapped his forearm. "So tell me more about what Dean said. We need to compare notes."

"There's not much to tell. The poor guy is so messed up from whatever drugs they're giving him that it's hard to talk to him. My guess is that they're keeping Dean drugged up until they get wherever they're going and hand him off." Riley moved his hand off the steering wheel and gestured toward the sky. "But where or to whom, I couldn't tell you. And why? I have no idea."

"Maybe we can find out."

"That's what I'm hoping. You're much better at interrogating people than I am."

"Aww, shucks, thanks. It's good to be missed."

"Speaking of interrogating, tell me what you learned in DC, other than nothing. You were going to talk to a bunch of people."

I leaned back and gazed up at a fluffy white cloud. "I did. Matt is still a prick of the highest order, but clueless on subliminal messages. He had no idea what I was talking about."

"You're sure? How do you know he wasn't lying?"

"I'm sure."

"All right. You also said the video isn't interesting, Centerfield didn't know anything, and your vision was basic black."

I sighed. I felt like I had the word "failure" flashing in neon letters above my head. "That pretty much sums it up."

"It sounds like there's nothing there. Let's go over your visions where something did happen."

"Well, I had some flashing-light stuff and some blackness before the bad one. The one that put me on medical leave was about the circus. In that one, I was in the circus being a performer."

"But your mom wasn't there."

"Nope. The next one was right after I met you. It was during the lightning storm, and nothing much happened, except you were blue. Then the blackness."

Riley took his eyes off the road for a moment to look at me. "I do so love being blue."

"It's a pretty teal color. You'd like it. After we stopped by the bakery, there was the one when you were blue again. I saw the van that took Dean and then Mom was walking next to a tent."

"The next one was in Vegas, right?"

"Yeah, when we went to meet Bubba at work at the casino to tell him that I'd almost been blown up. That was the vision with the clown with the flame thrower that tried to drag me into a cave."

"Good times."

I put my arm out the window, letting the wind rush through my fingers. "Then the next one at Jumping Jack Flash Casino had Matt and Bubba's cable guy. That sorta set me down the wrong path, I think. Matt was being such an arrogant jerk, it might have caused me to lose a bit of objectivity."

"Just a little bit."

"Okay, yeah, well, moving on. Then there was the scary one with Mom and the fire when you and Zelda went out for your walk."

"As I recall, that one wasn't good."

"Looking back, it was a big reason I left. All that fire convinced me something terrible must be happening."

"And then you had another black vision in your apartment."

"Yes. With wine. Ick." I shrugged my shoulders noncommittally. "I don't know what any of this means, except I hate clowns, fire, and black holes."

"What if we look at them from a different perspective? You said that in the first one, you were a circus performer, not observing the show. We focused more on the vision where your mom was walking by a tent because it was your mom. But the first hallucination you had at work was significant too. It was just from a different point of view."

"So?"

"The worst one was with your mom fighting and being engulfed by flames. At the time, you were crying and upset, so you didn't talk about it much. But what if you thought about it again from a different perspective? What if the fire isn't something dangerous? What if you're part of the fire, so you're not scared of it?"

"Huh? Um, no. Being in fire, near fire, or on fire doesn't appeal. I'm done with fire."

"But what if you're seeing something from that perspective? Like you're sitting around a campfire or something innocuous like that, as opposed to being *on fire*. What was there?"

"Mom shouting at Dean. He was green."

"Green? You didn't say that before."

"I didn't realize it until just now because I was so focused on the fire. He had a green light around him kind, of like the way you get that pretty teal blue. It's like an aura that surrounds you. In the vision, Mom said, 'See, this is where I am.' She was pointing at something, but I don't know what it was."

"Interesting."

"If by interesting, you mean weird, then yes, it's interesting."

Riley was quiet for a while, then finally said, "When we get to the motel, we should make a chart with all your visions. We need to write down when they happened, what had happened before them, who you were with, and where we were geographically. Something must tie them together, but I can't figure out what."

"Something other than clowns with a bad attitude and fire?"

He cracked a smile. "Yeah, maybe something other than that."

~

A few hours later we made it to the Motel 6 in Holbrook and unpacked the car. Riley had stocked up on healthy food and I tried not to groan. Maybe I'd lose some of the weight I'd gained from my chocolate binges. Or turn into Bugs Bunny. No one could eat that many carrots.

I sat on the bed and chomped on carrot sticks while we went over the visions again. Riley sat at the desk and wrote everything down.

When we were done, he sat with an elbow on the desk. He was resting his chin on his palm, staring at the list and tapping his pen against his lower lip. I walked over and looked over his shoulder at the chart. "You have ridiculously good handwriting."

He put down the pen and looked up. "That's all you've got to say about this?"

I pointed my carrot at the paper. "One thing that's obvious is that you take me to a major city like Las Vegas, and I've got real problems."

"We already knew that. What else?"

"I should avoid flashing lights."

"We knew that too."

I walked back to the bed and Zelda hopped up next to me. She spun around a couple of times and curled up into a furry ball. I stroked the fur between her ears. "The worst visions happened right after I talked to Leo."

Riley turned around. "Right. That's a good point. You said before your major meltdown at work, he'd given you an assignment. What was it?"

"Well, I never got the chance to write it, but now that I think about it, the story was going to be kind of a puff piece on Online Systems United. How they were making it easy to connect to the Internet by sending all those millions of CDs in the mail. I guess that's sort of a coincidence, given the whole merger thing."

"What if Leo knew it was coming?"

I didn't like where this was going. Leo was my friend and mentor. He was one of the few people I trusted, other than my mother. "I already told you, all the stuff in DC was a bust."

Riley looked back at the chart. "Maybe."

"Okay, returning to the reason I'm here, how are we going to get Dean?"

"The circus is setting up tonight. We can figure out a plan and go to tomorrow night's show."

"All right." I stood up and nudged by Riley to get to the bathroom. "I'm tired. It's only seven for you, but ten for me and I've been traveling all day. I'm wiped out."

Riley reached to grab my hand. "I'm glad you came back."

I squeezed his palm. "I am too. Maybe you can get some sleep."

The next day we drove around Holbrook, scouted out the fairgrounds, and went to the grocery store. A girl cannot live on carrots alone and I convinced Riley that we needed something outside of the salad food group.

On the way back to the motel we stopped at a crossing to wait for a train and I looked up to my right at a huge green cement brontosaurus. A smaller baby brother brontosaurus and a brown triceratops were also hanging out in front of the rock shop.

I looked at Riley and raised my eyebrows.

He shrugged and raised his eyebrows in response. "I told you. I can't make this stuff up."

When we got back to the Motel 6 I pulled my deli sandwich out of the grocery bag and settled onto my bed next to Zelda. She put her muzzle on my thigh to indicate that she wanted to share. I tore off a piece of bread crust and handed it to her.

Riley sat on the other bed with a container of yogurt. He took a bite and said, "So we need a plan for tonight."

"I know. I haven't thought of anything yet. Our last attempt to snag Dean didn't go well, and I think setting a unicorn free is one of those things you can only do once before people get wise to what you're up to."

"The unicorn will be busy performing, so that's not an option. One problem I'm having is that Dean never remembers me, so I have to start over every time I talk to him."

"Maybe you're not memorable" I said.

"I think that's an insult, but I'll ignore it because it turns out I agree."

I gave another piece of crust to Zelda. "It wasn't an insult exactly. Blending in is good. But if you truly wanted to blend in, you'd need to get a different car. And maybe gain some weight and cut your hair."

Riley paused between bites of yogurt. "Let's not get off track here. I did have an idea, but I don't think you're going to like it."

"It wouldn't be the first one of your ideas that I didn't like."

"Did you bring that green shirt you wore to the bakery?"

"I did. I love it because it's super soft and comfortable."

Riley flashed a sly grin. "No doubt. It also shows off your, um, assets really well. Dean would have to be dead not to notice."

"You're saying my boobs are memorable?"

"In that green shirt they are."

I threw a pillow at Riley, which he warded off with a whack of his hand. Zelda jumped down off the bed to sniff at it and make sure it wasn't food, then leaped back up next to me.

Riley said, "You could pretend to be Dean's girlfriend, so he'll follow you."

"Girlfriend? Is this your euphemism for acting slutty and picking him up? I mean, are you seriously suggesting that I seduce him?"

"Not seduce. Just suggest that maybe he should go somewhere with you."

"I don't like this idea."

"I said you wouldn't. But you did say you thought Dean was hot, so that might help."

"I most certainly did not." Zelda was sniffing at me and I crossed my arms across my chest. Had I dropped a piece of sandwich down my cleavage? Because that would be extra-embarrassing right now.

"Yes, you did. At the bakery. You said some woman with purple hair thinks he's hot too, so it wasn't just you."

"Now you're being annoying."

"Do you have a better idea?"

"No." I scanned my mind, desperate for even the faintest glimmer of an idea, but given Riley's description of Dean's state of mind, or lack thereof, getting Dean's attention would require something drastic. I looked down at my chest. "All righty then, girls. It looks like we've got a hot date tonight."

Riley laughed, grabbed the pillow from the floor, and put it behind him as he flopped back on the bed. "Look out, Dean."

After lunch, Riley took Zelda out for their afternoon constitutional. I sat at the desk and looked at the chart he'd created listing my visions. One thing that I'd lost sight of was the question of why Dean was at the circus in the first place.

At first, we weren't sure if he was with them or if the guys in the blue van happened to be in the same place. Now it was obvious that he'd been traveling with the circus for a while. So that meant the guys in the blue van had dropped him there. But why? Was the circus a means to transport him somewhere without anyone noticing?

I picked up the circus flyer that Riley had left on the desk and read it over. While I had been in DC, Riley had followed the show through Utah with stops in Grantsville, Delta, and Cedar City. They had looped from California through Nevada and Utah and now were heading down through Arizona. After hitting the southern part of the state, they would turn west back to California.

Dean was green in my visions and Riley was blue. What did that mean? They had whacked-out senses in common with me. Could I see people who had screwed-up senses in my visions? Now there was a creepy thought. I couldn't see myself or tell myself to go look in a mirror during a vision.

What if there were more people out there who had sensory problems? That led to another question. Who else was in Dean's drunk-clown show? Was the circus hauling around a bunch of people who had problems like me and Riley? And if I had a vision, would I be able to tell who they were? If I could, that would be way more information than I wanted to know. It wasn't as bad as being a prophet, but still. Why me?

My mind was overrun with questions, so I ate a cookie to distract myself. Maybe I should start going on these walks with Riley and Zelda. I needed to retain my shapely figure to seduce drunk clowns.

I chewed slowly, enjoying the sweet goodness. There was no getting away from it. My life had become downright bizarre.

~

After Riley and Zelda returned, we went over the plan again and hammered out a few more details. Then I got all gussied up in my green top and my most expensive bra so the girls would be looking their best. Riley had now been to the circus so many times that he knew the agenda and the best time to sneak inside. Watching the same show repeatedly must have been incredibly tedious, but he'd seemed reasonably philosophical about it.

The show started at six thirty, but the drunk-clown phase of the show wasn't until an hour later, which had the advantage of being after sunset. It wasn't like we were going to buy a ticket, so we didn't have to sit through the whole thing.

Riley parked the Mustang outside the fairgrounds as he had the last time we'd been to the circus. Having such a conspicuous car did have some down sides, particularly because I was wearing high heels. I thought it would be a little incongruous to wear a beat-up pair of Addidas with my tight green top. If you're going to get all vamped up, you need to go all out.

We walked around the big top to the spot where Riley knew Dean would be sitting. I was impressed at the degree to which he'd scoped out the situation. Nothing like going to the circus a whole bunch of times to make you an expert.

Although it was dark, Riley had counted the lines holding up the tent and marked a spot on the canvas where we could sneak in unnoticed. He waved me closer and lifted up the canvas from the ground. I crawled under and once I was inside I realized we were hidden behind a set of wooden bleachers. Everyone was watching the action in the three rings, and thanks to all the noise and commotion, no one heard me grunt or the subsequent unladylike string of expletives when I tripped on a piece of wood on the ground and whacked my big toe. Wearing peep-toed shoes had been a bad idea and I was already regretting my decision to be a slave to fashion.

Riley grabbed my arm and put his fingers to his lips. He whispered "We're going over there."

I shook his hand away and crouched down to examine my foot and make sure my toe was still attached. I pinched at it and tried not to whimper. Ow.

Riley crouched next to me and gestured toward the ring. "That's Dean."

"Does he realize what he's doing?"

"I doubt it."

"Poor guy. That's humiliating."

We watched for a moment while Dean contorted in ways that would make Madonna, in her X-rated, leather-clad phase, blush like a little girl. The more time I spent at it, the more I realized Hector wasn't running the most wholesome family-oriented circus in the world.

Riley pulled me upright. "They're almost done. Once Dean sits down on the bench, go down there and sit next to him. I'll sit next to you."

"I know. I know." I needed a moment to mentally prepare myself to behave like Ms. Trashy Chick. It was not my style, but I'd had a part in *Grease* in high school, so I was going to channel Rizzo and hope for the best.

Dean finished stumbling through the drunk-clown routine and Billy the evil troll clown parked him on a bench afterward. Riley yanked on my arm to get me moving. Billy still creeped me out, but it was time for me to be brave. This was the moment of truth.

I slid onto the wooden bench next to Dean and tried not to squeak at the wood sliver that lodged in my thigh. Pantyhose weren't a good defense against old wood. I was going to need a tetanus shot if we survived this idiotic escapade.

Riley slid in next to me and shoved me closer to Dean. He hissed, "Snuggle up, Buttercup."

"Shut up!" If I got any closer I'd be in Dean's lap. I sidled up and put my hand on Dean's upper arm. I purred, "Oooh, it's a little chilly tonight, don't you think?"

Dean wobbled a bit, then turned his head to look at me. "Who are you?"

"Oh honey, you know who I am."

He shook his head and mumbled, "Rhonda?"

"Yes! Rhonda. Your girlfriend, remember?"

"No, Rhonda sister."

Oops. Bad guess. "No, you silly goose, I didn't say I was your sister. I'm your *girlfriend*." I shoved myself closer so he could get a good look at my boobs.

He looked down and his eyes widened. "Nice."

I turned my head to grimace at Riley before turning back to Dean. "How are you feeling, honey? I think we should get out of here. I missed you *so* much."

"Out? Out where? Who are you?"

I wanted to shake Dean, but I controlled myself and stroked his upper arm with my fingertip. "What's your girlfriend's name, honey?"

"Peggy."

"Then I'm Peggy. Remember?"

"Yeah, Peggy." He nodded. "Did you change your hair?"

I moved my hand to caress Dean's cheek and tried not to cringe at the slimy clown makeup. "I did, honey. It's so sweet of you to notice."

"Where have you been?"

"Waiting for you." I tugged gently on his arm. "We should go. I got us a place. I missed you and I know you missed me too."

He looked desperately sad for a moment and then reached out to grab my hand. "Where were you? I missed you so much."

"I'll tell you, but let's get out of here first." I turned, shoved Riley, and raised my eyebrows as I whispered, "Move it."

Riley got the hint, slid off the bench, and started up the aisle toward the back of the bleachers. The show was still going on and tigers were roaring. The animal trainers had the crowd enthralled with their performance, so our timing was perfect.

I squeezed Dean's hand. "All right, you keep holding my hand, honey. Promise me you won't let it go."

Dean shook his head. "I won't. Never again."

Riley was ahead of us and I crouched low, as if I were in a movie theater trying to discreetly sneak off to the restroom during the feature. Dean stumbled along clumsily behind me, which was a little worrisome. I looked back down the aisle, but the show was still progressing without incident. I didn't see Billy anywhere, and the lions and tigers were still doing their thing. All was right in the circus universe.

Riley held up the bottom of the canvas for us and I crawled under, pulling Dean after me. As it turns out, clown shoes get in the way when you're crawling, so it wasn't the most graceful exit I've ever seen. Riley followed us, tapped my shoulder, and indicated that we should head in the direction of the parking lot.

Dean stood up with a startled expression on his face. "Where are we?"

I pulled him closer. "Outside, honey. We took a shortcut. The car is that way. Follow me, okay?"

He blundered along after me, although I wasn't doing much better. We both had serious footwear issues. Riley waved emphatically and said sotto voce, "What is the problem? Can't you go a little faster?"

I motioned my hand toward a trailer and whispered. "We need to take off these stupid clown shoes. Dean can barely walk as it is and they're not helping."

Riley shook his head and gave me the classic charades hurry-up gesture. "We need to *move*. The animal act is almost over."

I dragged Dean behind a trailer, followed by Riley, who was getting increasingly agitated. I bent to remove Dean's big floppy shoes and stood up, holding a red shoe. "These are more complicated than I would have thought."

Riley pointed at something behind me, grabbed Dean's hand, and urgently whispered, "Run! Go that way."

I turned to look. Billy was stomping around the other side of the trailer. I dropped the clown shoe I was holding, ripped my peep-toed pumps off my feet, and took Riley's advice. I ran to the next trailer and tiptoed around to the other side as Billy walked the other way.

I placed my hand on my chest and watched as Billy strolled back toward the big top. My heart was thundering and I couldn't catch my breath. We were so screwed if Billy caught us with Dean. I turned my head to ask Riley if we should make a break for it, but he wasn't there. I turned around and placed my palms flat against the wood of the trailer.

Where were Riley and Dean?

~

I walked along the back of the trailer and didn't see Riley or Dean anywhere. It was dark and difficult to see much of anything except the lights from the big top. My shoes were gone and there was no way I was going back for them, since

Billy was over that way somewhere. They were cute shoes too.

A huge burst of thundering applause and cheering came from the tent. I had a bad feeling that it was an indication that the show was ending soon. When the show was over, there'd be people swarming everywhere. I wasn't sure what to do.

Billy wasn't visible, but I knew he had to still be nearby. I padded out into the open and walked down to the next trailer, toward the parking lot. The applause was still going strong. Did circuses do encores? More cheering ensued and it sounded like they were taking bows, reveling in the adoration. The logical thing to do would be to head for the Mustang, and that was undoubtedly where Riley must have gone with Dean.

I stepped on something and all the air left my lungs at the sudden jolt of pain. The brutal agony emanating from the arch of my foot left me gasping for breath and I slapped my hand over my mouth to keep from screaming. I crouched down and held my breath as I gingerly removed a piece of glass from the bottom of my foot as tears streamed down my cheeks.

I hobbled over into the shadow of a trailer and ripped the hem off the lining of my favorite black pencil skirt. I tied it around my foot, which helped dull the searing pain slightly. I took a deep breath and carefully stood up. This horrible circus was destroying my wardrobe, hurting me, and trying to do harm to people I knew. I was pissed.

Two large floodlights came on as people started to exit the big top, a wave of humanity wandering through the dim lights into the darkness. In the edge of my vision a white flash went by, then appeared by my side. I bent down. "Zelda! What are you doing here? You're supposed to stay with the car. Did Riley send you to find me?"

Zelda wagged and jumped backwards a few steps, which I took to be canine-speak for "Move it, lady."

I wasn't about to argue with the sentiment, so I hobbled along after her. The good thing about white dogs is that they're easier to see at night than a black dog like border collie or Labrador retrievers. My foot was throbbing, but I was trying not to be a baby about it. I could feel my mascara pooling on my cheeks though, which had to look horrifying. So much for impressing Dean with my feminine wiles.

We finally made it out of the parking lot and back to the big clump of bushes where Riley had parked the Mustang. No one was there. What was I going to do? I didn't have the car keys and even if I did, I didn't remember the code to start the car. Zelda jumped into the back and I climbed over the side to sit next to her and wait.

I unwrapped the cloth from my foot and took a look. My stomach clenched at the sight of all the blood. My blood. The cold air made the wound hurt more and I wrapped it back up. Zelda began rummaging around on the floor as if she were digging a hole. I leaned over to see what she was doing. I pulled on her collar. "Zee, Riley is going to kill you if you tear up this car."

Zelda looked up at me briefly and continued digging at the floor mats. I pushed her aside and kneeled down to get a closer look at whatever she was obsessing over. Zelda had moved the floor mats to reveal a small metal ring. I lifted it, yanked, and opened a tiny compartment in the floor. Inside, a set of car keys sat on a piece of paper. I lifted them up and unfolded the paper, which had the code to start the car.

Zelda had moved to the seat and was now sitting upright, looking pleased with herself. I got up off my knees and sat next to her. "So, where is Riley, Zelda? Do I need to go look for him? Should we wait?"

Zelda wagged her tail a few times. There was no way to know if she understood anything I was saying. And by the way, when had I started talking to dogs, anyway? My foot was throbbing and I wasn't sure what to do. If Riley hadn't come back to the car with Dean, maybe they were hiding somewhere. Should I go look? Maybe Zelda was so insistent on getting the keys because she knew something was wrong. Yes, she was smart, but was she *that* smart?

Cars were starting to exit the fairgrounds parking lot and our hiding spot didn't feel quite as secure as it had a few moments ago. I rested my palm on Zelda's neck. "I'm not sure what to do, Zee. Should we go look for Riley?"

Zelda jumped between the seats into the passenger seat, which I took for a yes. I said a silent plea to the automotive gods that I could drive the Mustang without destroying some vital piece of delicate machinery.

I got into the driver's seat and adjusted the seat and mirrors. When I started the car, it immediately stalled, apparently realizing who it was dealing with. This wasn't a promising launch to our journey to find Riley. The queasy feeling in my stomach got worse as I stalled the car a second time. Zelda slurped my cheek, perhaps as a show of moral support.

I stopped and closed my eyes for a second, then methodically put the car in neutral, pushed in the clutch, and turned the key. I ever-so slowly and carefully put the car into gear and let out the clutch. The Mustang moved without complaint and I pulled out of our shrub haven and onto the pavement.

I stayed in first gear for a while, driving slowly until an impatient circus-goer zoomed around me on the dark road. Going faster than fifteen miles an hour would be nice, but I wanted to keep an eye out for Riley and Dean, who were presumably still on foot. Or hiding. Or something.

Zelda and I drove around for what felt like hours on countless back roads in the Holbrook area. I ground the gears a few times and asked Zelda to promise not to tell Riley. My foot hurt from using the clutch, and I was starting to recognize various landmarks we'd driven by more than once. I couldn't think of anything else to do, except go back to the Motel 6. Zelda seemed equally despondent. It was dark and we were both tired. All I could think was that if Riley was holed up somewhere, I'd never be able to see him from the road anyway.

I opened the door to the motel room and closed it behind me. Everything was exactly where we'd left it, but the silence was deafening. Despair, combined with the fear that I'd never see Riley again, overwhelmed me and I burst into tears.

I flopped down on the bed so I could sob into a pillow. While I cried, I could hear Zelda pacing around the room. When I was too exhausted to shed any more tears, I rolled over onto my back. My foot hurt and I hadn't even bothered to wash it out. With my luck, it would get infected and gangrenous and fall off.

I went into the bathroom and ran some warm water into the bathtub. While I was soaking my foot, Zelda came in and sat in front of me expectantly. I reached out to pet the fur on her white muzzle. "What?"

Zelda wagged and stared at me intently. I shrugged my shoulders. "I don't know what you want, Zee. Riley fed you before we left."

Zelda wagged some more but wouldn't take her eyes off me. Maybe she wanted her evening walk. It had been a stressful night, which might have stirred up her digestive system. Heaven knows my insides felt strange from the anxiety and crying. I'd only been thinking about myself though. Good thing I'd never gotten a dog, since obviously I was a rotten dog mommy.

I dried off my foot and hopped out of the bathroom looking for Riley's first aid kit, which usually was stashed in one of the duffle bags we dragged in and out of motel rooms. I unearthed it and unzipped the little red nylon first aid bag to retrieve some antibiotic ointment and bandages. After patching myself up, I put on a sock and gingerly tucked my wounded appendage into one of my grungy old tennis shoes. There'd be no more big-girl footwear for me for a while.

After the TLC, the cut on my foot had settled into a dull ache, instead of throbbing pain, so I decided I could take Zelda out. She'd continued to pace around the room while I tended to my injury, so I grabbed the leash and hooked it onto her collar. "I'm sorry we're not going to be able to go on one of your marathon treks, but it's late, and I'm wounded."

Zelda wasn't convinced and launched toward the door, dragging me behind her. I yanked on her leash to pull her back so I could grab Riley's flashlight and close the motel room door. "Get a grip, Zee! Would you please slow down?"

I followed her across a field to a path that led away from the motel. Maybe this was where she and Riley liked to walk. I felt bad that her master was missing. What if he was missing for good? Did Riley have provisions for his dog? If so, how would I know? You never think to talk to people about these things until it's too late.

My thoughts spiraled downhill and I limped along behind Zelda, who was still quite sure she wanted to go a particular direction. I didn't care one way or another and in some ways it was a relief to be out of the motel room and in the fresh night air again. It was clear and the huge night sky was filled with stars twinkling everywhere. The Milky Way sprawled across the sky and the moonlight gave the desert an otherworldly silvery cast.

As we walked, Zelda continued her beeline to somewhere. A small rustle in a bush caused my thoughts to drift to whatever wildlife might be out here with us. Maybe squirrels and rabbits. But what about snakes? Did snakes hibernate? Was it warm enough for them to be awake? Mountain lions didn't hibernate. I looked down at Zelda, who continued her march, one paw after the other. At least one of us wasn't worried.

My foot was starting to hurt again and I stopped. "Come on Zelda, we need to go back. You've already done what we came out here to do."

Zelda sniffed the air, looked at me, and yanked hard on the leash, which with my bum foot almost toppled me over. I sighed. "All right fine. I suppose we can go a little farther."

We started walking again, and Zelda's nose was still pointed straight ahead along the trail. Did she smell something? Did she smell Riley? Was that possible? I tried to hobble a bit faster. If Zelda knew where Riley was, I was on board with the idea.

A sound came from ahead of us on the trail and Zelda hurled herself forward. I stumbled to keep up, squeaking at every step as I broke into a tortuous jog. Ow, ow, ow, ow! We crested a small rise and a silhouette of a man came into view in the moonlight. An *extremely* skinny man. I let go of the leash and shouted, "Riley!" as Zelda hurtled off down the trail. Zelda leaped up, pirouetting in circles around Riley, who crouched down to pet her.

I finally caught up and a huge grin spread across my face as I tilted my head to look at him. "I've never been so happy to see anyone. Are you okay?"

He shot me a tired half-smile. "My feet hurt and I'm pissed off because I lost Dean."

"What do you mean *lost*? Where is he?"

Riley gestured in the direction from which Zelda and I had come. "It's a long story. I'll tell you on the way back. Why are you limping?"

"I cut my foot. You aren't the only one whose feet hurt. It's been a rough night."

"No kidding."

~

As we slowly walked back along the trail to the motel, Riley and I shared our versions of the evening. While I'd been driving all over Holbrook, he'd been hiding out with Dean in a barn near the fairgrounds.

Riley asked, "Did you kill Shelby?"

"No, I did not, although I'm sure you'll need to check. Your car is fine, but how on earth does your dog know about the spare key?" I looked down at Zelda. "I mean, it's not like she knows how to drive."

"At one point when I was really sick, I showed her where the key was in case something happened and someone else had to drive Shelby."

"You think she remembered that?"

"I told you she is smart. What happened to your face? Are you all right? I hope that's makeup and not bruises. You didn't fall or get hit, did you?"

I reached up and touched my cheek. I'd forgotten about the layers of mascara I'd applied earlier. "It's raccoon eyes taken to an unattractive extreme. Waterproof mascara is a dirty lie that has been perpetuated by cosmetics companies for years."

Riley chuckled. "Well, you do remind me a little of a raccoon. You eat a lot of junk, stay up all night, get into places you shouldn't, and occasionally act like you might be rabid."

"Aww, you missed me, didn't you? Raccoons are cute!"

"True." He pointed at my foot. "Are you sure you're all right?"

"I might need a tetanus shot, I guess. At the circus, I turned around and you'd disappeared. Where did you and Dean go? And how did you manage to lose him?"

"We hid in a barn that is about a twenty-minute walk from the fairgrounds, kind of back behind it in a field. I thought Billy might have spotted us and Dean was falling all over the place. There was no way we could outrun that troll, so I found a place to hide out instead."

"Where's Dean?"

"I have no idea. We talked for a long time, then he said he had to go take a leak and he never came back."

"Wow, you weren't kidding. You actually lost him."

Riley turned to look at me. "Hey, you lost *both* of us. I think you win the prize for losing people this evening."

I sighed. "We really stink at this rescuing thing."

"I know. It's pathetic, and I'm so tired I can barely think straight. That barn behind the fairgrounds is about as far away from the motel as you can get and still be in Holbrook."

"So what did you and Dean talk about?"

Riley perked up a little. "That part was interesting. We were there in that barn long enough that his drugs wore off somewhat. He was still slurring his words, but he kept saying he had to get back home. Back to Alpine Grove and Gleasonville."

"California?"

"Yes, and I think your imitation of his girlfriend might have been a little too good. He told me that she disappeared too, and he thought she'd dumped him, but then after he was abducted he realized that she may have been kidnapped too."

"Uh, does she have some weird sensory problem like we do?"

Riley stopped to wait for Zelda to sniff at a particularly interesting sagebrush bush. "You guessed it. They first met at that cafe at the Enchanted Moose in Alpine Grove. She was on vacation and they started up a thing."

"A thing?"

"A fling, dating, hot sex, whatever you want to call it. But he was smitten."

I laughed, "Smitten? Who says smitten?"

Riley waved his hand to brush off the comment. "You're missing the point. About six months ago, Peggy became obsessed with food because her taste buds went haywire. That's why she was at the cafe eating pie when they met. She could figure out recipes by tasting them, and was working out the ingredients for those disgusting pies. Ugh."

"No editorializing."

"Sorry. Anyway, they had this fling in Alpine Grove and then Peggy disappeared."

"Gee, this sounds familiar."

"I know. Dean thinks she was kidnapped like he was, but our parents weren't kidnapped."

"You're sure about that? What else did you learn about our parents?"

"Apparently they went to a retreat, where they're doing research on whatever our problem is."

"What *is* our problem?"

"We didn't get to that. Dean calls us specialists. It sounds like my Dad made up the term. Anyway, Dean didn't say where our parents are."

I shoved at Riley's arm, knocking him off balance. "I swear, you are the worst interrogator ever! You already told me that."

"I wasn't interrogating. We were talking and I mentioned some of the stuff we'd talked about before to see if he remembered. I would have been a little more persistent if I'd known he was going to ditch me." Riley kicked a rock off the trail more forcefully than necessary. "I mean, I thought he'd be *happy* we got him out of that horrible circus! Maybe even a little grateful. A 'thank you' might be nice."

I scowled. "I know. This is so annoying. No one ever says thank you. And come on. We're *specialists*? Give me a break. My foot hurts, and I'm not feeling the least bit special at all."

Riley put out his arm and I clasped it, happy to lean on him and take some of the weight off my injured foot. He said, "Maybe I should take a look at that cut when we get back. I doubt going for a moonlight hike did it much good."

"It's fine. I'm glad Zelda dragged me outside. Give your dog an extra treat tonight, okay?"

He reached across to place his hand on mine. "I will."

After we got back to the motel, I soaked my foot again and Riley and I examined it. The cut didn't seem deep and we agreed I didn't need stitches, but Riley thought I should visit a doctor, just in case. I wasn't excited about the idea, but I was too tired to argue.

Riley went to take a shower and I curled up on my bed with Zelda next to me. I made sure to tell her she was the greatest dog in the whole world before I passed out.

When I opened my eyes, Riley was sitting on his bed reading and eating a yogurt while Zelda supervised.

I sat up and rubbed my eyes. "What are you reading?"

Riley flipped the cover closed and held up the book. "*Design Patterns: Elements of Reusable Object-Oriented Software.*"

I curled back down on the bed and threw my arm over my eyes. "Ugh. Who *are* you?"

"It's interesting. I only dabble in programming, but one of my employees said I should read it, and I'm finally getting around to it."

I got up and began rummaging for food. I chomped on a piece of dry bread. "I think this is getting stale."

Riley pointed his spoon at the micro-fridge. "There's more yogurt."

"Yuck."

"It's good for you. With friendly bacteria that improves your intestinal flora and all that."

"Eww." I finished my stale bread and sat on the bed. "Now what? Dean is gone again. What do we do?"

"I've been thinking about that this morning," Riley said. "I think we should go back to California. I'm not sure how Dean will get there, but he was incredibly determined and the drugs should have worn off by now."

"Does he have money? What's he going to do?"

"I don't know. Hitchhike? We're right off the interstate, so he could hitch a ride with someone. It's a pretty straight shot to California and I have a feeling he's headed that way."

"Is this another one of your sniffing feelings?"

"Maybe a little."

I leaned forward, rested my elbows on my knees, and looked at Riley. "So last night before Zelda made me go for a walk, I was here by myself and, well, I was kind of upset."

Riley regarded me with an unmistakable twinkle in his dark eyes. "Aww, you missed me, didn't you?"

"Okay, maybe I did. But it also made me think about some stuff, and I need to ask you something, sort of…well… uncomfortable."

"You don't seem to have much of a problem with that."

"You have gazillions of dollars and you've talked about dying a lot. Do you have, um, provisions for Zelda and, well, everything? Like a will? That kind of thing? It's, um, I mean I was here all by myself and I realized I didn't know."

Riley sat up straighter. "I do. It's all set up, and an animal sanctuary in Utah scores some big bucks if I cork off."

"Don't say that. What about Zelda?"

"Well, the way I have it set up right now, she'd stay with Dad, along with a substantial amount of money for her care and feeding. Now that I don't know where Dad is, I don't know. She likes you though. Would you take care of her?"

"Of course."

"I guess I should call my lawyer. I have to talk to him anyway."

"Sorry to bring this up, but I was a little freaked out."

"Do you have anything set up?"

"Mom gets everything, such as it is. An old sofa and all the junk in my apartment."

Riley leaned back on the pillows. "You know, we never figured out why your mom's house in Alpine Grove was empty."

"I know. At the same time, your dad went to Alpine Grove to be with my mom. Where was he living before that?"

"The same place I grew up. It's in Ventura County. The Thousand Oaks, Newbury Park area, which is near where he worked."

"You mentioned you used to play with the wave-measuring thingie. What happened to all his stuff?"

"You mean an oscilloscope. But yes, there was a bunch of equipment. I was on my road trip and didn't talk to him for a while, but maybe Bubba knows if Dad sold the house. Or he could have rented it, I guess. The place is worth a fortune now. It's odd to me, since it's the boring old tract home I grew up in, but real estate prices went through the roof."

"We're going to California anyway. Should we stop by and take a look?"

"I guess we should." Riley groaned. "But yuck, if we go back there, I'm going to feel bad again."

"I know. I'll probably freak out and have another screaming hallucination."

"Yeah, this oughta be fun."

Chapter 13

Connections

After a stop at the local urgent-care clinic to get someone to look at my foot and give me a tetanus shot, Riley and I took off from Holbrook and hit Interstate 40 at typically high speed. I think both of us were feeling a little depressed that after so much running around we still were no closer to finding our parents, so when Riley turned on the stereo I didn't object. Sometimes listening to extremely loud music is good for the soul.

I did take some small consolation from the fact that according to Dean, our parents were fine and happily researching away. Mom adored research and could be experiencing fact-finding nirvana, for all I knew. From the sounds of it, Riley's father was as much of a study freak as my mother. They were probably happy campers and would scold us for making such a fuss. Well, assuming we ever found them, that is.

As we drove, I went over everything that had happened. I had certainly taken more than a few wrong turns, and a couple of things had been overlooked. Case in point: despite my best efforts, I never had talked to Hector. And that was assuming Hector was the owner of the traveling circus. If the circus was kidnapping and transporting people, it must be for a reason. And who owned a circus in this day and age, anyway? I mean, these guys weren't exactly Ringling

Brothers, which had been around for a hundred years. Where did Hector's little troupe of weirdos come from?

The other thing I hadn't done was check in with the Alpine Grove cops to see if mom's furniture had ever reappeared. Okay, it was a huge long shot, but you never know. I turned down the radio and Riley glanced at me.

I gestured toward the signs for Flagstaff. "The sign says Northern Arizona University is located here. Can we stop and visit the library?"

"What?"

"I need a library. And food."

Riley shrugged and flipped on the turn signal to change lanes. "All right. I could use a break from driving anyway."

We drove around and found the NAU library. Riley stayed in the car with Zelda and I hustled inside. Most universities had access to databases of business listings.

I ingratiated myself with a reference librarian by telling her I was working on a story about traveling circuses. Like most librarians, she was thrilled someone was interested in books and learning anything, so she immediately started digging into a few online databases while I riffled through a pile of gigantic tomes she handed me.

As a reporter, librarians are some of my favorite people. Whenever I had a particularly thorny question on a story, I'd head for the closest library. After about fifteen minutes the librarian, who I now knew was named Jane, had printed out a couple of corporate listings. She handed them to me and I thanked her.

As I scanned the pages, my jaw dropped. I held the printout to Jane and pointed my index finger at an entry.

"Does this mean Hector's circus is a subsidiary of this company?"

"Yes, exactly! All of these companies fall under this umbrella." She pulled out another page. "And I did a quick search on a couple of business news sites. I guess the company is about to become quite a bit larger."

I wanted to hug her, but clutched the papers to my chest instead. "Thank you so much! You have no idea how incredibly helpful this is."

She beamed at me. "You're welcome. Good luck with your story."

I left the library and returned to the Mustang, where Riley and Zelda appeared to be taking a nap. I pulled my sweater off Riley's head and he sat up straight, his eyes wide. "What?"

I threw the papers onto his lap and ran around to the other side of the car. "Check this out. You aren't going to believe it!"

Riley threw my sweater at me and collected the papers. "What am I looking at?"

I rearranged the sheets and pointed out the key information. "Hector's traveling circus is one of the many companies owned by Online Systems United, which we know is merging with Archetypal Media."

Riley looked at me quickly. "That can't be a coincidence."

"I know! The cable guys are related to the circus guys who are related to the media guys. It's all connected. All of it!"

"This is good information, but I'm not sure what it means."

"I think it means that whatever our parents are researching is something that these companies are interested in."

"Right. But why?"

"Why is any business interested in anything? Money. We need to follow the money."

Riley started the car. "Where? Are you saying we shouldn't go to California after all?"

"I still think we should go back to Alpine Grove. I never checked to see what happened with Mom's house or talked to anyone there."

"If Dad is sitting there with her playing canasta, I'm going to be so irritated."

I shook my head. "I know they're not. I keep calling. The phone is disconnected. But the empty house is another loose end. Maybe the neighbors saw a moving van. We never looked into it."

"True." He shifted gears as we accelerated onto the freeway. "And I still think Dean is going to turn up there. To hear him tell it, Peggy is the love of his life."

"Aww, that's sweet."

Riley's mouth twitched in amusement. "Are you having a girly romantic moment over there?"

"Nope. I'm the hard-nosed reporter uncovering facts. You're the one with the girlfriend that I'm assuming you're *smitten* with." I leaned over and made a few smoochy noises for emphasis.

He lifted a hand off the steering wheel to shove me back to the passenger side. "I liked Alpine Grove. What if we skip the whole LA part and go there?"

"I think we should check on your Dad's place."

"I suppose."

"And maybe you can visit your *girlfriend*."

"Jeez, would you let it go, Meg?"

"But I'm having too much fun." I raised my hands straight above me and spread my fingers so I could feel the wind rushing by. "Score one for journalistic research. I love the library!"

~

After a lot of driving on Interstate 40, we stopped at a Motel 6 in Barstow, California. The only thing I knew about Barstow is that Hunter S. Thompson mentioned it at the beginning of his book *Fear and Loathing in Las Vegas*. According to Hunter, Barstow was where the drugs began to "take hold" and they saw giant bats swooping around in front of the car. The book details lots of bizarre drug-induced hallucinogenic experiences. Although I had hallucinations without the aid of drugs, they hadn't given me any insight into gonzo journalism. I had learned I never wanted to see Las Vegas again though.

By the time we arrived at the motel it was dark, so we couldn't see much of Barstow. After I tended to the bandages on my foot, we crashed hard. It had been a long day of serious road time and even Zelda was wiped out. The next morning we got ready to roll south toward the Los Angeles area. As we packed up our stuff before heading out, I glanced at a booklet on the desk. It was a directory of all the Motel 6s in the United States, and almost every motel room we'd stayed in had one. Riley even had a directory stashed in the Mustang's glove compartment.

I held up the booklet and flapped it at Riley. "I don't like to quibble, but why do we keep staying at Motel 6s? You're loaded, and we could stay somewhere nicer. I wouldn't mind a chocolate on my pillow, not to mention towels larger than dinner napkins."

Riley looked up from his packing. "How about if I throw a package of M&Ms on your bed. Would that work?"

"I'm serious. I know you're not a cheapskate, because you paid off my student loans."

Riley gestured toward Zelda. "If you can find another place that takes dogs, feel free to suggest it. When there's nothing available that takes dogs, sometimes I have been able to haggle with the owner of an independently owned place like that dump we stayed at outside of Vegas. Motel 6 always accepts pets, so I don't have to deal with a big argument about it."

I bent to pet Zelda. "So we can blame you for these fine accommodations, huh?" Zelda wagged her tail, looking proud of her accomplishment.

Riley added, "When we were on our road trip, Zelda and I camped out more. I figured you wouldn't be up for that, so I haven't suggested it. I do have a little tent, but I can't imagine you willingly sleeping in it."

"You got that right. Mom isn't the only one who hates camping."

"Good thing Thousand Oaks has a Motel 6."

"Yippee."

Riley checked us out, we got onto Interstate 15, and two hours later we were sitting in traffic outside San Bernardino. There had been an accident, and we were creeping along so slowly that it would have been faster to walk.

Riley had his hand draped over the steering wheel and looked at me as he moved his hand down to the gearshift. "I hate it here. After my road trip, when I was packing up my apartment, I kept asking myself why I lived here for so long."

I rubbed at my temple, wanting to pretend that the twinge wasn't there again. "Well, you grew up in the area. Family. Friends. It's familiar. People tend to stay in one place unless they have a compelling reason to leave."

Riley scowled, but didn't say anything. We made our way onto another freeway and cruised though Pasadena and Glendale until we were on the 101 heading west toward Thousand Oaks. I was glad Riley knew where he was going, because I found the traffic and freeways incredibly confusing. At least in Washington, D.C., the Beltway goes in a circle. Here, freeways merged and diverged all over the place, crammed full of people driving extremely fast and changing lanes every which way.

The Motel 6 was right off Route 101, so after Riley checked in and we unloaded, we drove to a shopping center that was near a deli with outdoor seating where we could get lunch. I'd pointed out to Riley that given the state of my head, it might be a good idea to stuff me full of food.

Riley attached Zelda's leash to her collar and we walked slowly through the parking lot to the street, passing a drug store on the way. My foot was feeling better, but I still wasn't moving particularly quickly.

Riley pointed at the sign. "Burt's Pharmacy had the best candy when I was growing up. Jolly Ranchers, Lemonheads, and every possible type of chocolate."

"It's encouraging to learn that you have a memory of enjoying candy, since you're such a health nut."

"I'm not a health nut, but I do have a better idea of what goes into food now."

"How far are we from your dad's house?"

"A few miles. I used to ride my bike all over this area. It was nowhere near this congested back then though." He waved a hand toward the road behind us. "We're dangerously close to my high school."

"From your tone, I get the impression that you didn't like high school."

"I was a brainy geek. What do you think? Let me guess. You were a cheerleader, right?"

"Nope. Not my style. I was on the school newspaper staff all four years. Sadly, writing about your fellow students doesn't make you popular, particularly when you say unflattering things."

Riley chuckled. "This must be good. What did you do?"

"Let's just say the homecoming-queen exposé I wrote in my freshman year didn't make me any friends. The title was, 'Stuffed ballot boxes and stuffed bras.' My capacity for rabble-rousing only increased, so by my senior year I had a college scholarship, but no date for the prom."

"You win some, you lose some."

"Hey, I wasn't the one who rigged the homecoming election. I stand by my First Amendment rights." I raised my fist. "Freedom of the press! People need facts to make informed decisions."

"You're kind of hard-core on this topic, aren't you?"

"The media has the ability to expose corruption and wrongdoing and reveal the truth. The power of the pen is awe inspiring."

He glanced at me with a smile. "Truth, justice, and the American way, huh?"

After powering down an enormous lunch, I felt substantially better. The Thousand Oaks area was a pleasant suburban community surrounded by mountains and filled with lots of soccer moms driving minivans. It was close enough to Los Angeles that I was likely to have problems, but it did have zillions of oak trees, as the name suggested, and reminded me a little of the area where I grew up. Knowing that families continued to raise their kids in the same peaceful community where Riley grew up was somehow comforting.

Riley was quiet during lunch, silently picking at his pale food. Maybe he was reliving old high school horrors. I knew how going back to where you were a kid could dredge up some unpleasantness. A couple of years ago, I'd seen my junior high school nemesis Ellen Palmer at a mall in Silver Spring. Although she no longer had the Farrah Fawcett hairdo, I knew it was her. I was so horrified, I turned around and fled to the nearest ladies room. It was not perhaps one of my most courageous moments, but in junior high school, she'd represented evil incarnate. She was mean in the way only fourteen-year-old girls can be, teasing me mercilessly about my braces and lack of social standing.

I put my napkin on the table. "Are you going to eat that or stare at it?"

"Working on it." He jabbed at the baked potato with his fork.

"If you don't want it, I think Zelda would like to share."

At the sound of her name, Zelda stood up and snuggled closer to Riley's leg. He handed her a piece of potato skin, which she gobbled down hurriedly before he could change his mind.

Zelda ended up eating a lot of Riley's lunch and afterward we walked back to the Mustang. Or more accurately, I waddled. Although I might have overdone it on the eating program, I was increasingly worried about having a screaming episode right here in the middle of Riley's hometown.

We drove through a bunch of residential streets and ended up on a cul-de-sac that looked like the set of the Brady Bunch, with a string of ranch homes that appeared to have been built in the sixties or seventies.

Riley parked in front of a single-story ranch with a large garage. "That's it."

The house was a typical tract home, like Riley had said, with light tan siding and white trim. I touched Riley's arm. "Look! Someone mowed the little patch of lawn."

"Then either Dad is selling or has already sold it. That patch of grass was typically filled with ten-foot-tall weeds."

"There's no real estate sign."

Riley got out and motioned toward the house on the right. "That's Mrs. Washburn's house. Mrs. McDowell lives over there and the Browns are down there. One of them will know if the house is for sale."

"Your dad has nosy neighbors?"

"Very. After she and her husband divorced, Mrs. Washburn set her sights on Dad. She had a crush on him for years. We can start there."

We walked up Mrs. Washburn's short concrete driveway and Riley knocked on the door. An older woman opened the door a crack and peeked out from behind a security chain.

"Who are you? If you're selling something I don't want it and I'm happy with my religion, thank you very much."

Riley said, "Hi, Mrs. Washburn, it's me, Riley O'Shea, from next door. This is my friend Meg. We were wondering if you'd talked to my father lately."

Mrs. Washburn removed the chain and opened the door the rest of the way. She looked Riley up and down. "Good lord in heaven, what happened to you?"

I could hear Riley let out a deep breath . He had to be tired of that question. I asked, "Did the O'Shea's house sell recently?"

Riley added, "The yard looks better than usual."

Mrs. Washburn ignored me and kept staring at Riley. "Oh dear heart, did you get the AIDS? I always thought you might be, well, you know. Did you come out? Does your father know? Are you dying?"

"I hope not," Riley said. "When was the last time you saw my father?"

"Oh it must be a few weeks ago now."

"Did he move?" I asked again.

Mrs. Washburn turned her head, finally acknowledging me. "Yes, a lovely young couple will be moving in next door in a few weeks."

"Did Dad sell the house?" Riley asked.

Mrs. Washburn smiled and clapped her hands together. "Oh yes dear, it sold lickety-split in only two days and he made a mint! This is such good news for our property values."

Mrs. Washburn regaled us with the story of the incredibly speedy sale of the O'Shea property, real estate appreciation, and a lot of neighborhood gossip that was meaningless to me.

Finally Riley said, "Well, Meg and I should be going. Do you think anyone would mind if I walk around the house for a few minutes?"

"You want to say good-bye, don't you?" Mrs. Washburn frowned. "I'm so sorry, Riley. I hope some of the new cocktail therapies I read about will help you."

Riley shook his head. "I don't have AIDS and I'm not gay. I simply want to look around the house I grew up in one last time before the new people arrive."

I took Riley's arm and patted it as I sidled up to him. "I'm sure he's fine. Promise."

Mrs. Washburn looked relieved and we all said our good-byes. As we walked back to the car, Riley said, "Thanks for supporting the fact that I don't have AIDS. Mrs. Washburn is the biggest gossip in Thousand Oaks. If that got back to Erin…well…I don't want to have that conversation."

"Does Erin live here?"

"No, but some of her family does. She's got a huge family and they're scattered all over Southern California."

Riley got Zelda out of the car and we walked around the former O'Shea residence, peeking in a few of the windows. Like my mother's house, it was empty.

We opened the gate and went into the small backyard. A single flowerpot sat on the patio. Zelda sniffed at it and Riley picked it up. A note was taped to the bottom. He peeled it off and opened up the paper.

I said, "Well, what does it say?"

Riley crumpled the note into a ball in his fist and stuffed it in the front pocket of his jeans. "Call me. If you can't reach me, talk to Dean Wolfe. He's in Alpine Grove."

"Gee, where have I heard that before?" I rubbed my temple. "If it's okay, I'd like to go back to the motel."

Zelda made a low *rrr* in her throat and Riley said, "Are you having a problem?"

I grabbed his hand and pulled him toward the gate. "Let's just go, okay?"

~

We were only about ten minutes away from the motel, and I was relieved to have not caused a disturbing incident out in the middle of a suburban cul-de-sac. Back in the room, I curled up on the bed and Zelda hopped up next to me. How is it that dogs always seem to know when you feel rotten?

Riley sat on the other bed and looked at me. "Are you all right?"

"Yeah. I started feeling funny, and when that happens, the main thing I want to do is get away from people."

"Should I leave? Zee and I could go for a walk."

"No, don't go! I didn't mean you. *Other* people."

He looked taken aback at my outburst, then turned to reach for his book. "Right. I'll hang out and read then. We've seen what we need to see here, so we can relax tonight and take off for Alpine Grove in the morning."

I nodded in agreement and closed my eyes, hoping a little nap might make me feel better. I started awake when Zelda jumped off the bed. I sat up and rubbed my eyes. Riley was rummaging around in the food bags and held out a box of crackers to me. "Want some?"

"No thanks." I got up and maneuvered around Riley to get to the bathroom. My face felt all sweaty and sticky from my nap . A breeze fluttered against the curtains and shadows from the eucalyptus trees outside danced with the light coming in through the window.

Zelda made another *rrr-ing* noise and I glanced back at Riley. He was blue and I said, "Oh crap" as I turned around and reached for his hand. I missed and ended up flailing at empty air. As if from far away, I could hear him say, "Meg?"

The teal blue washed into green as if it were an animated watercolor painting. Dean was walking along a highway somewhere and I tried to wave to him, but he didn't seem to see me. Then Matt was standing next to me. He sneered, "So is that guy wandering on the road your new man? What is he, a hobo or something? Kind of a step down after me. You're scraping the bottom of the barrel with this one, aren't you?"

I tried to slap him, but he was gone. I yelled at Dean, trying to get his attention, but he still couldn't see me. I turned at a sound behind me and Mom was standing next to a tent saying, "This is where I am. What happened?" I screamed for her and then Leo walked toward me and said, "You know how it is, Meg. Just the same ole nuthouse."

I felt something move next to me and I opened my eyes. I twisted around to look up at Riley's face. He was cradling me in his lap on the floor and Zelda was staring at me panting, her big pink tongue about three inches from me. She moved forward and gave my cheek a big slurp. "Eww, Zee. Yuck!"

As I sat up, Riley crab-walked backward, out from under me. I turned to grab his foot before he scuttled away. "I'm guessing you kept me from crashing onto the floor."

"You gave me a little warning this time, so I had my eye on you."

"Thanks."

Riley stood up and sat at the desk. "So what happened? Did you learn anything useful?"

"Who knows?" I got up off the floor, sat on the end of my bed, and went over what I could remember of the hallucination. When I was done reciting my colorful tale of weird, I shrugged. "I don't know what any of it means."

"I think we're on the right track. Dean is on the move going somewhere, which is what he said. If he's going to Alpine Grove to find his girlfriend, we'll find him."

I went to the bathroom, washed my face successfully this time, and returned to my bed. I moved up to lean back against the pillows. "When did you and your dad move to Thousand Oaks?"

"Dad bought the place in 1971 for twenty-eight-thousand dollars, which means if Mrs. Washburn is right about the sales price, he made a cool four-hundred grand and change. Go Dad."

I laughed. "Maybe Mom is after his vast fortune. Little does she know that you're the one with the real bucks."

"I guess you're feeling better." He went to his bed and picked up his book. "If your ex-boyfriend is as big of a tool in real life as he is in your hallucinations, I think you need to re-think your dating selection process."

"The fact that I'm spending all my time in motel rooms with you isn't exactly helping my social life."

Riley looked up and we were silent as the truth of the comment sank in for both of us. I suspected that the mysterious Erin didn't know I was spending so much time with her boyfriend or ex-boyfriend or whatever he was, either. It was way past time to find our parents, end this bizarre trip, and return to our normal lives.

The next morning we checked out and got away from the Los Angeles area as quickly as possible. I suspected I wasn't the only one who was looking forward to feeling better again. Riley hadn't eaten much, which probably meant he was feeling crappy too. He had enough money to move to an ashram or travel to remote locations forever, but if I could no longer live in a city, earning a living was going to become problematic. It wasn't like I had farming experience or something. What did people do in these tiny towns?

On the drive I had plenty of time to think, since Riley was in another of his silent moods. At this point, thanks to so many strange shared experiences, there was no way we could say we weren't friends. But the way he sometimes retreated into enigmatic silence still mystified me. What was he thinking about? After spending so much time on the road with him, I'd learned better than to ask, since the answer was invariably "nothing," which in reality meant "nothing I'm going to tell you."

As we drove up into the mountains the vegetation began to change dramatically. After so much time in the desert, I was pleased to see trees again and feel the fresh pine-scented breeze wash through the Mustang. The plan was to visit Mom's house and then more or less retrace our steps starting with the diner at the Enchanted Moose in Alpine Grove, since that's where Dean and his girlfriend had met.

From what Riley remembered, most of the time Dean and Peggy were together they had stayed in Alpine Grove at her place. My job, as Riley put it, was to "talk to everyone," so first I needed to find out Peggy's last name and then I'd go from there. In a town the size of Alpine Grove, even if I talked to "everyone," it wouldn't take long.

If my interrogation didn't result in any useful information, we'd head south to Gleasonville again and see if Dean had turned up at the bar or the pie factory. Given how long he'd been gone, Dean must have been fired quite a while ago, but maybe we could find out where he lived if no one in Alpine Grove could tell me.

Questions continued to swirl through my mind, but at least I was no longer worried about having screaming hallucinations. Returning to small-town America did have a few advantages.

~

We drove slowly down the main street of Alpine Grove, passing by a bunch of little shops and offices. I hadn't noticed the bookstore or gift store on my last visit. People were sitting on the benches in front of the shops, chatting and enjoying the sunny spring day. A man standing in front of a law office waved at us when we stopped at the single traffic light. Ahead of us, a guy who must have been a male model was walking along the sidewalk with a white dog that looked a lot like Zelda. I nudged Riley's arm, "Hey, check out that dog."

"Looks like a Samoyed."

I turned to look at Zelda, who was curled up on the backseat. "Look Zee, you have a twin!"

Zelda thumped her tail a couple of times, but didn't seem impressed. I could relate. It was hard to muster up much excitement after logging so many hours in the car over the last couple of days. I noticed the H12 motel that Riley had mentioned because it didn't allow pets. That conversation felt like a lifetime ago.

North of town we turned into the Enchanted Moose motel, RV park, and conference center. Riley pulled up near the office and went to check in. I got out of the car to stretch my legs and unhooked Zelda's seat belt so she could stretch too. Since we'd been here last, the construction had resumed. With any luck, Riley would get us a room away from all the hammering.

After getting installed in our room, we had lunch at the cafe, which looked exactly the same. I slid into the red vinyl seat at a booth and as soon as a waitress appeared, I started peppering her with questions. It was the same waitress we'd had before who had accused us of trying to stiff the restaurant, but either she'd forgotten about the whole thing or had forgiven us after Riley coughed up the money in the end.

When I asked her about Dean, she said he'd stopped by for some pie the day before and was asking after Peggy.

"What's Peggy's last name?" I asked.

She held up her pencil. "I'm not sure. Dean mentioned it, but I don't remember. She was a tourist I think. Are you ready to order yet?"

"Did she buy anything here? Could you look up the receipt?"

She said she'd try if she had time, which was likely to be waitress code for "not gonna happen in this lifetime." I asked if she'd ever heard of our parents, which got a negative response and she made it obvious she was getting antsy about returning to her other customers. I gave up on my interrogation and ordered some restorative diner chow. Riley ordered a typically odd collection of bland but healthy rabbit food.

I doodled on the placemat with a crayon and sketched a truly gruesome picture of Dean as I remembered him. I wasn't much of an artist and using red crayon as my drawing implement didn't improve my skills.

Riley speared a lettuce leaf from his salad bowl. "That was a good start to your interviews. You've already found out that Dean is here somewhere. That's progress."

I was less pleased with my findings. "Where's our food? I'm hungry."

"They might be waiting for me to finish my salad. You could have had a salad too."

I'd had far too many vegetables and was looking forward to some fries. Riley was going to have to deal with the odor of stinky rancid oil. Too bad. I doodled some clown shoes and suddenly remembered something. "When we were here before and you saw Dean, you said he looked familiar. Why?"

"I don't know. Maybe I'd met him before."

"Where?"

"I don't know."

I put my elbow on the table and thumped my chin into my palm in disgust, watching Riley consume more sticks and leaves. I lifted my head. "What do people do in small towns?"

"I don't know. Why are you asking me? I lived in LA and grew up in Thousand Oaks."

"Hey, you've traveled all over the place. What do all these people out here in the middle of nowhere do for a living?"

"The same things they do anywhere." He gestured toward the counter. "Work in restaurants or retail stores, open a business, offer services like accounting? I don't know. Dean delivered pies and worked as a bartender. Why are you asking?"

"If I'm going to have to live the rest of my life in some fresh-air place like this, I need to find some type of work to do."

"There might be a newspaper here. Or maybe a magazine. Who knows? Or assuming we ever find them, our parents might know how to fix whatever is wrong with us. Then you can be a reporter again."

I leaned back and crossed my arms. "I doubt it."

Riley chewed more slowly and swallowed. "You might be right. The first step would be to isolate what's going on. Something about cities causes our problem or makes it worse. If you don't know the cause, it's hard to find a solution."

"Do you think that's what they're researching? The cause?"

"Maybe."

"Your dad's research revolves around radios and my mom's revolves around child development. This comes back to the question of what on earth those two see in each other. What do they have in common?"

"Well…" Riley paused and looked thoughtful, holding his fork in the air.

"Well, what?" I turned to look at a man at the counter who was complaining loudly about something to do with a phone call while he paid his bill. What a crank. It wasn't like the waitress could do anything.

Riley put down his fork and it clattered on the plate. "What happens when you combine everything? The circus, the cable guys, the media guys, the Internet, phones?"

"I don't know. We already had this conversation and decided it was a random collection of words à la Sesame Street."

"But it's not. A lot of it involves connections and transmission. Television, cable, the Internet, phones—some of it's wired, but a lot of it is wireless now. Cellular phones, for example. That guy at the counter was whining about how he can't get a signal here."

"What are you talking about?"

"Electromagnetic radiation. Cell phones emit an electromagnetic field, and there are more people using cell phones in LA than there are here or someplace like Ely, Nevada. And more cell towers." He pointed the fork at me. "What if our problem isn't from pollution? What if it's from radiation? That's where our parents' research intersects. Software design, user interfaces, wireless. They probably talked about all of that at the SIGGRAPH conference."

"So I can look forward to dying from radiation exposure? This is not an uplifting thought."

Riley made a wry face. "No, it's not. But it explains why I felt the worst in LA. They started setting up new cell towers everywhere, including one on the roof of my apartment building. It's a good thing I hit the road and ditched that place when I did."

"You really think that's it?" I shook my head. "But wait, I had a vision on the way south to Gleasonville in that thunderstorm. Gleasonville isn't exactly LA. I thought it was the flashing lights that set it off."

"I pulled over next to a radio transmission tower of some sort. I didn't think about it because I was freaked out by your screaming. But I looked up and saw the steel girders when they were lit up in the flashes from the lightning."

"You did?"

"We were *right* next to it."

I flapped my hands in a settle-down motion to get him to be quiet. "Okay, waitaminute. Let's think here. This is starting to sound as off the wall as my subliminal images idea. And we all know how well that worked out."

"Maybe the recruiting video *was* simply that. The more people you get signed up for phone and Internet, the more money you make. Like you said, follow the money. I read that the number of people with a cellular phone doubled in the last couple of years."

"Even I had one."

"I know. And what if *everyone* had one? Somebody stands to make a fortune. When did your hallucinations start getting bad?"

I thought back. Leo had given me the phone as a bonus after I'd broken a story and complained about how hard it had been to call it in. "Oh wow."

Riley raised his eyebrows. "What?"

"The little headache started right after Leo gave the cell phone to me. Then, well, you know what happened. Things got a lot worse. I don't feel so bad about having to give it back now."

"As I recall, you complained about not being able to order pizza from anywhere anymore."

"I've learned to live with that." I looked up at the waitress, who set a plate in front of me, then back at Riley. "I hope you're wrong about this."

"I don't think I am. The more I think back over what happened to me when and where, the more it make sense."

"What are we supposed to do?"

"It would be easy enough to test by driving down to that cell tower again and see how we feel."

"Do we have to?"

"Not right now. Let's forget about all of this for the moment and find Dean."

I nodded. "You're right. First things first. Find Dean. Get him to tell us where Mom and your dad are. Then yell at them for getting us involved in this."

Riley laughed. "Yeah, no kidding. What were you thinking, Dad?"

Chapter 14

Questions and Customizations

Our next stop was Mom's house, which was still empty. Like the diner, nothing at all had changed. It was as if time had stood still in Alpine Grove while we'd been gone. Then we stopped by the police station to ask if anything had happened on the abduction case. On a couple of my phone marathons I'd called to check in, but nobody knew anything. It was time for me to get in their face and extract answers.

The cop at the desk was decidedly relaxed, leaning back in his chair reading a magazine. I walked up to the desk and glanced at the nameplate. "Officer Reynolds, I presume?"

He dropped the magazine on the desk and shoved an errant lock of black hair off his forehead. "That's me."

It was the same baby-faced police officer we'd talked to about Dean. I put my palms on the desk and leaned forward toward him. "I'm Margaret Jennings and you took my statement about an abduction on March twenty-sixth. I've called a couple of times since then and talked to a person who claimed to know nothing. I'm guessing that was you. Has anything changed?"

Officer Reynolds scooted his chair back away from me. "No ma'am, not that I know of right at the moment."

"Are you pursuing any line of investigation at all?"

"Um, not like what you might call extensively. We don't have a big staff, but I asked around a little. Nobody's seen that guy anywhere in town lately."

"When we were here last time I also told you my mother was missing, along with another man. Ellen Jennings and Tim O'Shea. They were last seen in Alpine Grove. They're still not here as far as I can tell. That means three people are missing from this little tiny town. Don't you think that's a serious problem?"

He pulled open a desk drawer and shuffled through some papers. "I filed the report. It's here if you want to see it."

I tried not to sigh. "Yes, I would."

I sat in the chair and read over the report, which seemed accurate. Baby Face might not be a crack investigative detective, but he did write down the facts I'd given him. I handed it back to him. "I'll be here for a few more days, I think. We're staying at the Enchanted Moose."

"Okay, ma'am. If you find them, let us know."

I went back out to the Mustang and shared my lack of progress with Riley, who wasn't exactly shocked that nothing had happened with the authorities.

I said, "I guess now we have to systematically go through this town and ask everyone and anyone we can find if they've seen our parents or Dean."

"This would be a lot easier if we had photos of our parents or Dean."

"I know. And I'm still gimpy. Pounding the pavement isn't going to be any fun for my wounded foot."

We agreed that Riley and Zelda would go down one side of the street, which had an advertising agency, a couple of bars, a bookstore, and some real estate offices. Meanwhile,

I'd take the other side, which consisted of the gift store, an Italian restaurant, a law office, the H12 motel, a one-hour photo place, and a couple of other little retail businesses.

I went into the Italian restaurant and talked to a very young, very blonde hostess who was rolling silverware into napkins and placing them into a basket. She revealed nothing beyond the fact that her boss was a creep and she hated her job.

At the gift store, I talked to a pleasant older woman who had apparently lived in Alpine Grove for a long time and knew lots of people, but hadn't seen Dean lately. My mother and Riley's father seemed to be the only people she *didn't* know in the area. It figured.

Moving on, the law office sported a weasel-faced guy who made a feeble attempt to hit on me, but knew nothing about the whereabouts of anybody. The photo place and other shops were equally unsatisfying. The motel had a basket full of condoms, but no information about my missing persons. After two hours of walking and talking, the only thing I'd learned was that Alpine Grove was supporting safe sex.

I trudged back to the Mustang, which was parked on one of the residential side streets, where I'd agreed to meet Riley. He and Zelda were dozing in the sun again and they both sat up and yawned when I got into the car.

He handed me my sweater, which I set in my lap. "Did you learn anything?"

Riley yawned again and shook his head. "The bars are skeevy, even in broad daylight. At the advertising agency, a woman at the front desk with small clothes and big hair is convinced I'm a vampire."

I stifled a laugh. At least I'd never said that about Riley out loud. "I struck out too."

"Zelda got to meet the other Samoyed though, so that was cool. Now what?" He gestured toward the pretty tree-lined street. "Do you want to go find that cell tower and see if we melt into radioactive goo?"

"Uh, no thanks." I glanced to my right and a flash of red caught my eye. There was movement in a hedge, and Zelda suddenly sat up, which made me think she saw it too. I turned back to Riley. "What was that?"

"A squirrel? Zee, settle down. The squirrels live here. You need to accept that."

Zelda made a growly noise and stood up. A dark blue van cruised by and I whipped my head around to follow its path. "What the? Is that...?"

Riley started the car and I pointed at someone in red running across a front yard. Riley opened the driver's side door and leaped out as he said, "Meg, you drive. Follow the van."

Zelda jumped out of the car and she and Riley ran after the guy in the red sweatshirt. I maneuvered myself into the driver's seat of the Mustang, trying not to take my eyes off the van, which was rapidly disappearing from view. I closed the car door, adjusted the seat and mirrors, and fastened my seat belt as quickly as I could. I let off the parking brake, put the car in gear, and immediately stalled it. I yelled a stream of vulgar and disgusting expletives about the Mustang's heritage and mechanical limitations while I tried to get it started again.

Finally, I put in the right code, got the stupid thing in neutral, and the engine roared back to life. I drove down the street and turned where I'd seen the van disappear. Riley was following Zelda across lawns and backyards, trespassing with reckless abandon. Hopefully, the town wasn't filled with a bunch of gun-toting privacy zealots.

Zelda gracefully launched over a white picket fence, followed by Riley, who was significantly less graceful, but largely thanks to his height managed to not get racked on the way over. Good thing too, because pickets would really hurt.

As they disappeared into a backyard, I turned another corner. The van had slowed down and I ended up right behind it again. It stopped so suddenly the whole vehicle shook and I had to slam on the brakes. The Mustang stalled and I belatedly realized that putting in the clutch would have been a good idea. A passenger door on the van opened and a man in a dark gray suit ran out across a perfectly manicured green lawn to a gate that led into a backyard.

Ferocious barking erupted and the man returned through the gate back to the van, followed by Zelda at high speed, biting at his legs and feet. He heaved himself into the van and slammed the door as Zelda leaped and snarled. For a moment, she had her paws up on the door growling, and then the van took off down the street.

Zelda turned around, galloped across the lawn, and disappeared into the backyard again.

I fiddled with the Mustang and finally got it to start. I took a deep breath and methodically tried to let out the clutch extremely gently this time. A high-pitched screech pierced the quiet as I ground the gears, but I successfully got the car in motion. With any luck Riley hadn't heard the noise. He was going to have a heart attack if I killed the transmission. I swiveled my head, scanning the pretty landscaped yards and seeing nothing.

Crap. Where'd everybody go?

~

I drove around the block slowly. The van had disappeared, along with Riley and the guy in red, who I assumed must be Dean. I continued to slowly circle the neighborhood, expanding my search. On one of my passes, I discovered the van parked in front of a house that didn't seem particularly special in any way other than the fact that the garage door was open. I tried to look nonchalant as I drove by, but it didn't make any difference, because no one was in the van.

Where had everyone gone? Had I lost everyone *again*? This was starting to be a disturbing trend. Now I'd managed to lose Riley, Dean, and even Zelda. This time I'd even lost the *dog*. What was wrong with me? I stunk at this!

I tried to rein in my panic and kept driving. If nothing else, I was getting quite a tour of the Alpine Grove residential areas. If I had to move here, I'd know all the neighborhoods well.

I went down the street where I'd seen the van and passed it again, but this time the bad guys were there. I gulped and did my best to look unobtrusive in this unbelievably conspicuous car. My efforts were meaningless, because the two men were too busy peering into the engine compartment of the van to notice me. The small hood was up and they were enthralled by whatever was in there. Men and their automobiles. Sheesh.

I turned left on the next block and slowed to a stop at a stop sign. If it hadn't been for my seat belt, I would have jumped about twenty-five feet when Riley yanked open the door of the Mustang. I turned to look as Zelda and Dean got into the backseat of the car.

Riley pointed his thumb away from the car. "Get out before you do any more damage to Shelby."

I unhooked my seat belt and wrapped my arms around his neck, "Thank God you're okay."

He disentangled himself from me and said, "I'm fine, but we should leave."

I ran around the car, giving Zelda a pat on my way, and got in the passenger side. I turned in my seat, "Hi Dean."

He lifted his hand in greeting. "Nice to see you again."

Riley said, "Put on your seat belt, Meg."

"Where are we going?" I asked.

"To pick up our stuff and get out of town before the guys in the van figure out what I did to it."

"Did you customize it?"

He grinned. "Maybe a little."

Dean added, "Even in a small town, you should think about locking your garage if it's filled with expensive automotive tools."

We hurriedly packed up and checked out of the Moose. Once we hit the highway, Dean directed us to a remote location out in the woods north of Alpine Grove. We went down a long rural paved road, turned onto a few fairly wide dirt roads, then a few narrow dirt roads, then another road that was in such poor shape that it was barely a road at all.

By the time we turned into a grassy driveway, I had absolutely no idea where we were. Riley drove slowly, dodging the giant potholes hidden in the weeds, to a single-story structure. It looked like a pile of rotting logs that had been stacked on each other with some metal roofing thrown on top. Rustic was one thing, but this place made a tent look opulent.

We all got out and Riley crouched down and peered under the car. "Sorry, Shelby."

I wandered toward the shack. Were we really staying here? Zelda ran around in circles in front of me, sniffing trees and cavorting like a lunatic. I laughed at her antics. "I think we have found canine nirvana. Trees everywhere. It's the biggest doggie toilet, ever."

Dean led us inside the structure and lit a kerosene lantern. "Sorry, but the cabin doesn't have electricity."

I pursed my lips. "Please tell me there's indoor plumbing."

"It depends on what you mean." He pointed at a rusty hand pump at the metal sink, which was set into a counter made from a long plywood plank. "There's water from the well over there at the sink, which is inside. The outhouse is, well, outside."

I glanced at Riley. "Did you forget our conversation about camping?"

"It's one night, Meg." Riley said quietly.

"I'm guessing no phone either," I said as I sat down on a brown plaid sofa that looked to be older than I was. Zelda leaped up next to me with a thump. A cloud of dust wafted around us and Zelda sneezed in my face. Eww. The only thing nastier than dog snot is dusty dog snot.

Dean said, "A friend of mine owns this place. It was an old logging shed, and he converted it into a hunting cabin."

"Nice upgrades." I reached over to sweep some of the dust off Zelda's back. The shack was a single room with the kitchen sink and a couple of cabinets on one wall and a cot on another wall. The plaid sofa sat in the middle of the room across from a hideous forest-green wingback chair. An extremely stained, ancient bluish-gray rag rug lay between the two pieces of furniture, with a rickety, scratched wooden table sitting on it. "I'm guessing this person doesn't stay here often."

"He lives in LA and comes up here to go hunting a couple times a year. He said I could stay while I look for Peggy." Dean said.

"Why didn't you go home?" I asked.

"Those guys in the van know where I live," Dean said as he sat down in the green chair, which wobbled precariously.

"Who *are* the guys in the van?" I stretched my arms wide. "And more importantly, what do they want?"

"I'm not sure," Dean replied.

I stood up, unable to believe what I was hearing. "You're saying we tracked you and those horrible clowns all over the western United States and you don't know *why* they took you? Are you kidding me? Do you even know our parents? And, oh yeah, where *are* they? Do you have any clue what's going on at all?"

Riley took my hand and sat down on the sofa. I looked down at him. "Did we go though all this for *nothing*?"

Dean frowned, "It's a long story."

"I'm listening." I sat down again and yanked my hand away from Riley so I could cross my arms across my chest. The couch had no springs, which made for an uncomfortable pout.

Dean said, "Your parents are doing research at a retreat."

I uncrossed my arms and waved my hands in a hurry-up motion. "I know this part. How about we get to the part where you tell me where they are, like geographically speaking. A map would be nice."

"The location is a secret because the research is somewhat controversial." Dean looked uncomfortable. "Your parents stumbled onto something unexpected."

"What? And how?" I asked.

"As you know, your mother was doing research on children and computers. She did quite a bit of work on addiction. One of the kids she was working with was hooked on a game called Twisted Warriors. He played it all day, every day. Needless to say, his parents were worried."

"I know she was studying game addiction." I shrugged. "So what?"

"This child started having episodes where he was in the game acting it out. He was hallucinating," Dean said.

Riley said, "Sound familiar?"

I glared at him and gestured at Dean to continue. "So what happened?"

"She studied the child's environment and also did research into how games are designed to promote addiction. Nothing explained his hallucinations, however." Dean turned to Riley. "But then she met your father, who had experience related to communications."

Riley said, "Let me guess. The kid lived near some type of transmission tower."

Dean looked startled. "Yes that's right! Did you talk to Tim?"

"Meg and I figured it out, thanks to quite a bit of empirical evidence," Riley said.

"It was Riley mostly. My idea was a little more out there." I added. "I came up with more of a conspiracy theory."

Riley turned to me. "I still think you're right about that part."

"Maybe. It does fit," I said.

Dean looked from me to Riley and continued, "Your parents met a cousin of mine at a conference who told them about Alpine Grove. They wanted to get out of the city, so they decided to take an extended vacation here with the idea of maybe moving here permanently. My cousin gave them my number and I ended up helping them find the house. I was here a lot because of Peggy, so I knew it was available. Finding rentals around here can be difficult."

"When did they go to this retreat?" I asked.

"They had been in town a couple of weeks, then they were contacted by an environmental group that heard about their research. These guys think that the rapid increase in radio towers is affecting habitat and animal life. And that maybe the radiation could be causing an increase in cancer in animals and humans."

"Are they sure about that? Who is this group?" I asked. Hallucinations were one thing, but cancer? Yikes.

Dean said, "The group is called Enviro Freedom and from what your mother said, they don't have any proof of a link to cancer. But because of the child with the hallucinations and talking to me and Peggy, your parents think some people are having bad reactions to electromagnetic radiation."

"Like whacked-out senses, for example." Riley said, "And we're part of that population."

"You, me, Meg, and Peggy so far. They don't know how widespread the problem is. Ellen called us people who have 'special gifts,' which Tim shortened to 'specialists.'" Dean said.

"Typical Dad. I'm surprised he didn't use an acronym. I guess SGs didn't have the right ring to it." Riley said.

I waved off Riley's grumpy comment. "You said they went to a retreat. But why?"

"They wanted to help." Dean said. "According to Tim, the place supposedly had a great lab and resources, I guess."

"But where did all my mom's stuff go?" I asked.

Dean took a deep breath. "That's where things get a little confusing. They wanted me to come to the retreat with them, but I didn't think the idea of being a guinea pig sounded particularly appealing."

"But where did they *go*?" I demanded. "Where is this place?"

"I don't know, but the last time I saw Tim, he said something had happened, so they needed to leave sooner than expected. The EF people were taking them away in secret, along with everything in the house. That's when he asked me to talk to you." Dean paused. "I thought it was strange, but not too long after that, Peggy disappeared. I thought she'd dumped me, but after the guys in the van took me, well, now I think she was taken too."

"Wait! That means our parents could have been abducted too." I stood up again. "Oh my God, did the van guys dump them with Hector's horrible circus like they did with you?"

Riley took my hand and pulled me back down. "I don't think so."

"Why not?"

"Zelda and I spent a lot of time snooping around that circus. Zee knows Dad and I know she would have been able to tell if he was there. I might have been able to tell too, but I didn't. Also, the guys in the van took people, not stuff. It feels different."

"But where is Peggy? Is she still at the circus?" I asked.

"I heard her voice. It was like a dream." Dean said.

"Dean, that wasn't a dream. That was me in the green shirt, not Peggy." I looked down at my chest. "I was wearing a better bra."

Dean shook his head. "I never heard her at the circus. It was before that, when they were dragging me to the van before we left Alpine Grove."

"Was she in the van with you?" I said.

"No, it was my—whatever you want to call it—*special* hearing. That's why I thought she must be back here somewhere. The last time I heard her was right before I got in that van," Dean said. "I don't know why they didn't take her to the circus, but they didn't."

"How can we find out where this retreat is?" I asked. "I want to know more about what's going on with Mom."

"Like I said, I don't know where it is," Dean said, "I want to hear about your conspiracy theory."

I explained that Hector's traveling circus was owned by Online Systems United, which was merging with Archetypal Media. They were recruiting people to install cable and trying to sign up everybody in the known universe for Internet and cell phones.

After my complicated recitation of the facts, Dean looked a little shell-shocked. "You two figured all this out?"

"Yeah. Between Riley's olfactory feelings and my hallucinations and endless investigation and interrogation, we pieced it together." I said.

"Along with lots and lots of driving. Oh, and Zelda chasing people," Riley added as he patted her head.

I laughed, "Yeah, Zee bit one of those van guys in the butt. It was great."

"You two are amazing. It's like you're on the same wavelength." Dean said.

Riley and I both groaned and Dean looked confused for a moment. He continued, "Oh yeah, wavelength. Ha, that's kinda funny! Your parents are like that too. They're in sync with each other. How long have they been married?"

"So you're saying they *are* married?" I asked.

Dean shrugged slightly. "Aren't they? I mean I kinda assumed they were. I know you guys aren't blood relatives, so I thought you were together. You kinda act like it, so I just figured."

I stole a glance at Riley, who had a horrified expression on his face and blurted out, "No, we're not. *Absolutely* not."

"Riley has a girlfriend, um, somewhere," I said.

"Oh, I didn't know that." Dean leaned forward in the chair. "Anyway, you *have* to help me find Peggy. I think you're right and something bad is going on."

Riley and I glanced at each other and I piped up, "Only if you help us find our parents at this mysterious retreat. I know you think they're fine and maybe Mom will yell at me for interrupting her research, but I want to talk to her and give her a piece of my mind."

Riley said darkly, "And if they're not fine, I want to get them out of there."

Chapter 15

Deep Insight

After an uncomfortable night on the dust-infused sofa with no springs, I was ready to leave Casa de Filth. Riley had slept on the floor in his sleeping bag and Dean scored the cot.

There was no hot water or shower, so I washed my face in the frigid water from the hand pump and was subsequently extremely awake. I sat down on the couch and kicked the lump of sleeping bag that contained Riley.

He sat up and rubbed his eyes. "Good morning to you, too."

"Can we leave now? I want to take a shower somewhere. Anywhere with warm water would work."

"Where do you suggest we go? I'm guessing the people in the van are pretty cranky about losing Dean, so we probably can't go into town."

"Oh come on, there has to be some place better than this. The outhouse is scary. There are spiders in there." I put out my hands. "*Big* spiders."

Riley ran his fingers through his hair, probably checking for spiders. All of the creepy crawlies might not be outside. It was warmer inside and some intrepid arachnids might have scampered in across the floor. I lifted my feet up onto the couch and wrapped my arms around my knees.

Dean sat up on the cot, which lurched and tipped over, heaving him onto the floor with a thud. I was feeling better about the dirty couch now. Zelda strolled over to see if Dean was alive and if he might have brought food onto the floor with him. He sat up, pushed her nose away, and rubbed his elbow.

I waved over the back of the couch. "Good morning. Riley and I were just discussing leaving. Do you have thoughts on alternative accommodations?"

Dean turned his arm around to peer at his elbow. "I don't know. I also need to get my car. It's parked in a lot in Alpine Grove."

I pointed at Riley on the floor. "What you may not know is that our friend Riley here is rich beyond the dreams of avarice. There must be places we can stay that have indoor plumbing."

Riley said, "Riley also doesn't want to hear Meg complain anymore."

"And he likes to talk about himself in the third person." I added.

Riley stood up and went to the sink to wash his face. He put out a hand and pulled Dean upright. "I'm not kidding about Meg. She's a whiner. Do you know of a place we can stay that's out of the way? We need a little time to regroup and come up with a plan to find all these missing people."

"I heard that, and I am *not* a whiner." I said. "I don't think there's anything wrong with wanting to keep the great outdoors outside."

Dean rubbed at the stubble on his chin. "A lot of seasonal places on the lake aren't rented until at least the Fourth of July. We could talk to the vacation rental place in town."

"Sounds great! I'm in." I said.

We gathered our stuff together and rumbled our way out of the woods, leaving the horrible cabin behind to decompose on its own. I mentally vowed, once again, never to go camping. After we were out on the highway, Riley stopped at a pay phone next to a Kmart north of Alpine Grove.

When he returned to the car, he said, "I called my lawyer, who talked to the rental company here and found a house that's available on the lake. The keys will be in the mailbox at ten. I have the address."

We dropped Dean off at his car in the lot and agreed to meet out at the lake house. Dean warned us to keep a low profile. Riley and I had talked to half the town the day before, so half the town knew who we were and by now had undoubtedly told the other half about the redhead and the skinny guy with the white dog asking questions.

Riley drove south toward the lake. I was starving, so he suggested a picnic overlooking the water. I was glad Dean was gone, because I wanted to talk to Riley alone. Partnering up with Dean sort of happened out of nowhere, but what did we know about him other than that he'd met our parents? I wanted to help him find Peggy, but who was she? We didn't know anything about her either. Could we trust Dean? My mind was filled with a whole lot of questions and no answers.

We cruised down a long road that ran along a hillside high above the lake. The view of the brilliant blue water was stunning. Some areas in the water below were almost the same teal blue as Riley's aura in my hallucinations. That was another thing. I'd never seen Peggy in my hallucinations. Should I have? Could we trust Peggy?

Riley pulled off the road at an empty lot that had a driveway, but no house. Somebody was going to end up with an amazing vista out their living room window once the house was built.

I made myself a sandwich and leaned on the back of the Mustang next to Riley. Zelda sat in front of us looking up expectantly, and I tossed her a piece of crust. Something else was bothering me. I turned to Riley. "I hate to say this, but my time is almost up."

"What do you mean? Are you about to turn into a pumpkin or something?"

"I have to go back to work. I got a job, remember?"

Riley scratched at his ever-more scruffy chin. "Yeah, about that…maybe you should turn it down."

"I can't do that. Not all of us are made of money like you are."

"I know, but you can't leave now."

"It's not like I can drop everything. I have to earn a living. This job fell in my lap. There's no way I *can't* take it."

"I can pay for stuff. I already have. It's not a big deal and you know I don't mind."

"But I mind. I'm not going to live off you, Riley. Paying off my debt was kind and brotherly and generous. I appreciate it, I really do. But I need to earn a living."

Riley picked up a rock and whipped it out over the cliff. "You're not even excited about the job. You haven't mentioned it since you came back, and when you told me about it, you said it would be boring. Research like that isn't the same as real journalism."

"I know, but it's not like I have a choice."

"What about finding your mom?"

"Maybe you and Dean can do it." I looked up into his face. I knew that wasn't true. Dean wasn't wrong about me and Riley. For whatever odd reason, we worked well together. We drove each other nuts sometimes, but our respective "specialties" complemented one another.

"I don't think that will work. We need you, Meg."

I pulled a corn chip from the bag and flipped it to Zelda. "You don't know Dean yet. Once you spend some more time with him, you guys will figure it out."

"I know him well enough. He's a nice guy, but he doesn't have visions. And he doesn't have anywhere near your investigative skills."

"I'm flattered, but the fact remains that I need to work."

Riley chewed on a carrot stick and stared out at the lake for a few moments before speaking. "What if you had a job? Then you could stay, right?"

"I don't think Centerline is going to let me do research from here. Or anywhere else, except their offices. That wasn't the deal. You should see their offices. Totally swanky."

"What if I offer you a job?"

"You don't have a company anymore, remember?"

"One call to my lawyer can fix that. I think I want to start a publishing venture."

I chuckled, "Oh, come on. Give me a break."

"I'm serious. If what our parents accidentally discovered is as big as we think it is, it's the story of a lifetime."

I tossed another chip to Zelda. "What do you mean *story*?"

"An exposé about the health and environmental risks of increasing amounts of electromagnetic radiation. We can reveal what we know online as we find out more."

"I thought we were hiding."

"We can do it anonymously. Get a server under my new untraceable corporation and start posting articles. Get a cloaked email address and alert the media. I mean, what if people knew what was going on? What if Archetypal Online Systems is involved somehow and they know that people are being harmed? What if all your conspiracy theories tie in somehow? People are being abducted and Hector is carting people off with his circus full of creeps. And that cable guy fixing Bubba's TV really is a spy. Then what if the *New York Times* or *Washington Post* picked up on it. You could become a secret informant."

"You're saying I should become the next Deep Throat? Seriously?"

"You *were* the one who said 'follow the money,' after all." Riley grabbed another carrot. "You can be Deep Insight."

"You're hilarious."

"I'm being totally serious here. My new corporation pays you a salary and you do what you're good at. Maybe you could pay for lunch every once in a while, too."

I ate another chip. "It would be an amazing story, wouldn't it? Giant conglomerate hooks people on technology and abducts 'specialists' like us to keep them from spilling the beans that the radiation oozing from cell towers is affecting us, even as we become more addicted to technology every single day."

Riley crunched his carrot stick. "I told you. It's huge."

"Are you sure you want to do this?"

"I've got to find my father, Meg."

"I know. I feel the same way about Mom. I just…I don't know." I looked down at Zelda. "What do you think, Zee?"

Riley bent to pet the fur on the dog's head. "Zelda is like you. She's all for truth, justice, and the American way."

I leaned over so my head was resting on Riley's upper arm and stared out at the lake. He moved to put his arm around me and I closed my eyes. The sun was warm on my face and for an instant, I was utterly relaxed. I wished I could stay in that moment forever and forget about our missing parents, fire, radiation, and scary clowns. Was I really going to go off and hunt down people with someone I barely knew and then write about it?

To be fair, by now I *did* know Riley and I *had* been thinking about doing something different. But this was beyond different. It meant trusting Riley and my own ideas and visions. Was I really up for that?

Riley moved his arm and I opened my eyes. I stood up straight and turned to face him. "Okay, I'm in. Let's find our parents, find Peggy, and take down those losers."

Zelda *rrr*-ed happily and I bent to pet her. "Yup, that includes you too, Zee."

Thanks for Reading

Thank you for dedicating some of your reading time to *Sensing Trouble*. I hope you enjoyed Meg, Riley, and Zelda's adventures. The next novel in the Jennings and O'Shea series, *Sensing Secrets*, is available now.

If you would like to be notified by e-mail when I release a new book, you can sign up for my New Releases e-mail list at SusanDaffron.com.

I know that not everyone likes to write book reviews, but if you are willing write a sentence or two about what you thought of *Sensing Trouble*, I encourage you to post a review at your favorite book vendor site or share a message with your social networking friends.

If you would like to share your thoughts about the book with me privately, you can reach me through the contact page on the SusanDaffron.com web site.

I look forward to hearing from you!

~ Susan C. Daffron

Acknowledgements

Writing a novel is never easy and I'd like to thank my husband James Byrd for his support and encouragement throughout the publishing process.

I'd also like to thank my alpha and beta readers for their eagle-eyed reading and great feedback. I couldn't do it without you!

About the Author

Susan Daffron is the author of the Jennings and O'Shea novels and the Alpine Grove Romantic Comedies, a series of novels that feature residents of the small town of Alpine Grove and their various quirky dogs and cats. She is also an award-winning author of many nonfiction books, including several about pets and animal rescue. She lives in a small town in northern Idaho and shares her life with her husband and three really cute dogs.